A DCI FINNEGAN
YORKSHIRE CRIME THRILLER BOOK 12

# WHALE CEMETERY

## MURDER ON A SMUGGLER'S TIDE

# ELY NORTH

RED HANDED PRINT

Website: https://elynorthcrimefiction.com
To contact ely@elynorthcrimefiction.com
https://www.facebook.com/elynorthcrimefictionUK

Cover design by Cherie Chapman / CCBOOKDESIGN
Cover images © Adobe Stock / dvoevnore (ship) / oporkka (ocean) /
BESTIMAGE (sky) / Rabia (ocean) / LeticiaLara (ocean wave)



Published by Red Handed Print
First Edition
Kindle e-book ISBN-13: 978-1-7638413-9-0
Paperback ISBN-13: 978-1-923588-00-4

# Contact Ely North

ely@elynorthcrimefiction.com
Website: https://elynorthcrimefiction.com
Facebook https://facebook.com/elynorthcrimefictionUK
Free book – sign up to my newsletter.
QR below

# Also By Ely North

## DCI Finnegan Series – Crime Fiction

Book 1: Black Nab

Book 2: Jawbone Walk

Book 3: Vertigo Alley

Book 4: Whitby Toll

Book 5: House Arrest

Book 6: Gothic Fog

Book 7: Happy Camp

Book 8: Harbour Secrets

Book 9: Murder Mystery

Book 10: Wicker Girl

Book 11: Crucifix Knot

Book 12: Whale Cemetery

Book 13: Lock Keeper

Prequel: Aqua Phobia (available free by joining Ely North Newsletter)

All books are available on Amazon in ebook, paperback, and some in audio. Paperbacks can be ordered from all good bookshops, distributed by IngramSpark.

# 1

## Wednesday 7th August 8:05 am

Tucked away on a Whitby backstreet, Miserly Joe's Cafe is particularly busy this morning, the door banging open and shut as fresh customers push in and others leave clutching takeaway coffees and bacon butties.

Inside, the clamour of conversation and shouted orders reverberates off hard walls, and the grimy tiled floor.

Council workers in hi-vis vests nurse mugs of tea as if it were their firstborn. Tradesmen—bricklayers, joiners, sparkies, plumbers—attack their full English breakfasts as if they've never eaten before. Old hands with knuckles like rope sit shoulder-to-shoulder with fresh-faced apprentices still soft and pink around the gills.

No subject is off-limits: politics, religion, immigration, the rising cost of materials, family. But mostly it comes back to sport—football or rugby—argued with the same certainty and blind intensity as faith.

The menu board doesn't offer smashed avocado on toast or saffron-infused scrambled eggs dressed with slivers of smoked salmon. No artisan sourdough. Not a caper, pine nut, or drizzle of basil reduction in sight. No espresso. No soy latte, or almond milk cappuccinos.

Behind the glass of the bain-marie, silver trays steam under strip lights: baked beans thick and glossy, bacon curled and blistered, black pudding dark and crumbly, sausages split at the seams, fried eggs set hard at the edges, fried bread soaking with fat, mushrooms slumped, and tinned tomatoes collapsing into themselves.

It's scooped out by women young and old—some gnarled by heat and toil, faces scarred by life's disappointments; others fresh-faced and efficient, their futures already mapped out in shifts, minimum wage, and the endless grind, even if they don't know it yet.

This is old-school, solid fare that has survived generations—doled out on a chipped plate or shoved between bread without flourish or grace. Simple food for hard-working men and women, washed down with tea from the bag or coffee from granules.

And it's cheap.

Cheap enough to matter when wages haven't shifted in a decade and the country has lurched from one set of austerity measures to the next. Austerity always seems to be served to the same people on the same cracked platter.

And yet, the cafe is a broad church.

In the corner sit two men in quiet conversation. One is a regular—DCI Frank Finnegan, almost part of the furniture. No one gives him a second glance.

The man sitting opposite, however, is slightly incongruous in the setting. Smartly dressed in shirt, tie, and jacket, slacks neatly pressed, shoes polished to a dull shine. A clipped, educated voice. Not Cambridge or Oxford, but a different pedigree to the rest of the clientele—including Frank.

Jenny, the owner, places a full English breakfast on the table.

'Here yer go, Frank.'

He stares disdainfully at an American imposter on his plate. 'I've told you before, Jenny—hash browns don't belong on a full English breakfast.'

She hisses softly with a shake of the head, having heard his complaint many times over the years.

'Frank, customers like them. Build a bridge and get over it.' Her hand darts out to grab the offending article. 'Tell you what, I'll take it off your plate and put it in the bin. I'll refund you thirty pence.'

Frank fends the hand away. 'Nay, lass. No need for waste. Dare say I can force it down.'

She pulls a mock pout, masking a smile, and turns to the man opposite.

'Sure I can't get you anything, love?' It's said in a caring voice.

The man smiles weakly and clutches his pot of tea. 'No, thanks. I've already eaten.'

She turns and heads back to the counter as Frank attacks his breakfast—hash brown the first thing to be devoured.

The man gazes nervously around the cafe. 'Well, it certainly has character,' he muses. He was hoping for somewhere slightly more clandestine for the meeting; a park bench or a stroll along the beach, perhaps.

Frank detects his reticence to talk. He hasn't seen his old colleague, DCI Hedley Keegan, since they worked together on Operation Dragnet a few years ago.

'Don't worry. There are no spies or fifth columnists in our midst. I know every face in here. You're safe.'

Hedley relaxes and begins his tale as Frank focuses on his plate.

'This operation's been running for twelve months,' he says quietly.

Frank nods, mouth full. Reaches for his tea.

'In the next month or so, we think they'll make their move. Product shifting. Routes opening up. Organising their distribution network.'

Frank slurps. Winces at the heat. Squirts HP sauce onto the edge of his plate.

'We're allowing them free rein. It's risky, but we have everything in place. When it comes, it'll come hard and fast. International. Coordinated.'

Frank cuts his bacon into neat strips. Says nothing. Simply listens.

'Simultaneous strikes. Different countries. Different agencies. One moment they're untouchable—the next, it all collapses.'

Frank scrapes beans across the plate. 'Ambitious.'

'Necessary,' Hedley replies. A pause. 'From the king to the lowliest pawn. We capture them all in one fell swoop. We have operatives in the field, deep undercover, so deep even I don't know *who* or where they are.'

Frank chews, swallows, and lets the man articulate for another five minutes.

There are no specifics—no names, no dates. It's the big picture, the overview, and for good reason.

Hedley leans forward, glances briefly around the cafe.

'I'm head of intelligence,' he says. 'Everything comes through me. Every report, every intercept, every whisper.' He lowers his voice. 'After enough years of doing this, you notice when gaps start appearing. Things you expect to see that never materialise. Intel that arrives and doesn't add up, and...' he hesitates as if what follows carries the real weight. '...pertinent information that isn't acted upon.'

Frank is no slouch at deciphering guarded language.

'Sounds like you have a leaky boat. You suspect a mole?'

Hedley tilts his head nonchalantly. 'Suspect—yes. Certain? No. It could be my hypervigilance or—'

'Your instinct ringing the alarm bell?'

'Precisely.'

'So, this suspected leak—inside or outside?'

'Definitely on the inside.'

'Mid-level or higher up?'

He hesitates, then speaks carefully. 'It would have to be someone senior. Someone with the authority to disregard warnings and deprioritise critical intelligence.' A pause. 'A person who, on paper, is beyond reproach. For example, just last week…'

He breaks off suddenly self-conscious. 'I'm sorry. I can't be more specific. It could compromise us both.'

Frank licks the end of his knife. 'I understand. And where do I come in?'

'I want you on the periphery. Another set of eyes and ears. You report directly to me. No one else.'

Frank takes a slice of white bread thick with butter, mops up egg yolk, brown sauce, and bacon fat, and drops it into his mouth. He washes it down with a slurp of sugary tea, leans back in his chair, undoes a notch on his belt.

'There's one huge obstacle I can see right from the outset, Hedley.'

'Which is?'

'I can't simply join the game. It'd be a massive red flag—raising suspicions immediately.'

Hedley nods. 'I've already considered that. You don't *join* the operation.' A faint smile. 'You stumble into it.'

'How?'

'You receive a legitimate tip-off. Routine. Nothing that raises eyebrows. But enough to give you cause to act.' He hesitates. 'That's where I need your help.'

'Go on.'

'The name of a local informant. Someone solid. Someone you've used before.'

'Not a lowlife,' Frank says.

'Exactly,' Hedley replies. 'I'll arrange for him to overhear something of interest. He won't know it matters—and he won't know where it came from. He feeds it to you or Zac, and you act on it. Normal policing.'

'What sort of information?'

'Banal. Run-of-the-mill. But actionable.' He shrugs. 'After that, everything you do is legitimate. Day-to-day police business. No suspicion.'

Frank thinks for a moment. 'There is one bloke Zac uses. Straight. Dependable.'

'He'll do.' Hedley nods. 'I'll need a name, a description, and where he tends to hang out.'

Frank pushes his plate aside. 'I'll need twenty-four hours to think about it. There are implications—not least the welfare of my officers.'

'Fully understood.'

Hedley rises, pushes his chair neatly under the table, then leans forward once more.

'And one more thing. Absolutely no one else is to know about this. Not your juniors—and *especially* not your seniors. Are we clear?'

'Aye,' Frank says. 'One last question.'

'Yes?'

'Why me?'

Hedley doesn't hesitate.

'Because I need a man I can trust.'

# 2

## Six Weeks Later – Thursday September 18th

Slithering fog stalks the dark streets of Whitby, curling over glistening cobblestones, slinking along dank alleys, snaking up slick brick walls, encircling cracked drainpipes, sneaking into sagging gutters. It creeps like a prowler, cautious, hesitant, before sliding through cracks in windows, worming into keyholes, hovering around dustbins.

Four men stand on the eastern quayside watching in silence as the trawler cuts through the benign waters of the harbour. There's no sign of life on board, just twinkling lights that carve a streak through the mist floating above the black, cold waves.

Dritan Zefi casually checks his watch and *nearly* smiles. 'Francois made good time.'

His English is good, though forever cocooned in a heavy Balkan overcoat.

Stefan, Dritan's younger brother, grins as he pulls a cigarette from his mouth and flicks it into the water, readjusting his grip on the briefcase. The light from the boat catches the long scar on his left cheek.

'I think a small celebration of vodka is called for, Dritan. A toast to our new venture.'

Dritan pouts, contemplates, and finally agrees. 'Yes. Once we have concluded business tonight.'

A clatter—glass on stone—echoes from somewhere behind them.

The four men spin around, alert but not alarmed, hands moving instinctively towards jacket pockets.

An empty wine bottle spins in ever-decreasing circles on the pavement as a hunched figure shambles into view, hauling two bulging carrier bags. Stops at an industrial wheelie bin—his bin, apparently, from the territorial way he approaches it—lifts the lid with a grunt, peers inside. Pulls out a half-crushed pastry box, opens it, inspects the contents. Takes a bite of something stale, chews methodically.

The men watch in silence.

The figure produces a half-bottle of whisky from his coat—twists the cap off—takes a long swig, wipes his mouth with the back of his hand. Begins humming some old melody, tuneless and repetitive, the sound of a man who's spent too many nights on the street.

Stefan exhales quietly. 'Endacak—homeless.'

The man shuffles past them—ten feet away, never making eye contact, still humming—bags swinging in rhythm with his uneven gait. He pauses at the edge of the quay, stares out at the approaching trawler. Takes another gulp of whisky.

'Cold night for sailors,' he mumbles to no one, his thick Scottish brogue barely intelligible. 'Spent half ma life gutting fish in shite like this.'

Scratches his groin, hacks up phlegm, spits into the harbour.

Dritan watches him for a long moment as a memory stirs.

The man shuffles on, swallowed by the fog, his murmuring fading into the night.

'Let us continue,' Dritan says, losing interest in the man. 'We welcome Francois ashore, then make our first move.'

The men turn as one and head towards the swing bridge with similar casual strides.

*All* in the same black leather bomber jackets.

*All* with one objective.

And *all* with an unwavering loyalty to one another.

As thick as thieves.

3

The stooped figure slouches along, the plastic bags bumping against his legs. He stops and scans the narrow yard.

A decent spot for the night?

Whitby's full of hidden yards like this—quiet, half-forgotten. Empty holiday cottages on either side, old garages between them. Poor lighting. High walls. Not far from the busy thoroughfare of Church Street, but who in their right mind would wander down here after dark?

Only the insane, the criminal, or the homeless.

A four-foot high wall juts from a garage at right angles. A perfect windbreak, it offers a modicum of privacy, and safety.

He empties both bags: two sleeping bags, damp and smelling faintly of mildew. Spreading one out on the flagstones for an under-blanket, he lowers himself with a weary groan, then wraps the other tightly around his body until he resembles a giant maggot—only his head exposed to the chill night air.

Sparking a cigarette, the flare of the lighter illuminates his weathered face—a bulbous red nose, saddlebags under the eyes, a brow furrowed long and deep. Fumbles in his coat pocket. Twists off the cap and takes a long slug.

'Ah, just the ticket,' he murmurs, the whisky anaesthetising his throat, as smoke curls from his lips. Settling back against the wall, he croaks an old Highland ballad, the tune low and mournful. Before long, his eyelids fight a losing battle.

$$4$$

The men pass the pub—music spilling out, a bark of laughter following them—and turn right into Black Horse Yard.

In sync, they move as one, like a well-drilled battalion. Their boots echo off the old brick walls, the sound dull and steady in the night air.

Halfway up the yard, they spot a crumpled heap against the wall and slow their pace.

Dritan nods to one of his men. 'Mika. Check it out.'

Mika takes a suck of his cigarette, nods once, and moves forward while the others hang back. He studies the figure wrapped in a sleeping bag, an empty whisky bottle glinting beside him.

He sneers, turns to Dritan and replies in his native tongue. 'Endacak.'

Dritan raises an eyebrow. 'The vagrant?'

A nod. 'The one we saw earlier. More homeless bums here than in Tirana.' He flicks the half-smoked cigarette at the man with contempt.

Dritan strides up and slaps him hard across the face. The crack echoes in the narrow yard.

Mika reels back, more stunned than hurt. 'What was that for?' he protests.

'Show some respect,' Dritan snaps. 'You know nothing of this man, his life—or why he's here.'

The tramp stirs, groggy. 'Whit's this noo? Can ye not let a man sleep, fur Gawd's sake?'

Dritan bends, taps the smouldering cigarette from the blanket, and nods apologetically.

'I am sorry, my friend.' He studies the man's features—broken veins, unruly whiskers, the permanent squint of someone who's spent a lifetime outdoors. 'Do you have work?'

The man blinks, confused by the question. 'Work? Nah, pal. Not for a long time.'

'What did you do—before?'

'Trawlers. Thirty years, man and boy. Out of Fraserburgh.' He wipes his nose with the back of his hand. 'Gutting, mending nets, whatever needed doing. Then the boats got fewer, the quotas got tighter, and—' He shrugs. '—there wasnae room for the likes of me no more.'

Dritan nods slowly, as if reading between the lines. He pulls a crisp note from his wallet—twenty pounds—and offers it.

'Here, my name is Dritan. Get yourself something warm to eat. It is cold tonight.'

The man takes the note, eyes watery, voice rough. 'Ta, big yin. Very generous. Yer a legend.'

Dritan smiles faintly, then shoots a withering look at Mika.

'Come. We have work to do.'

The homeless man retrieves the discarded cigarette butt, rises slowly, takes a long drag, the ember glowing red in the dark. Watches the men fade to black.

Gathering his bedding, he stuffs them into the plastic bags, and drops back into his shuffle.

> *'Ye tek the high road, and I'll take the low road, and I'll be in Scotland afore ye.'*

Singing tunelessly, he slopes off into the fog—just another invisible soul on the street.

> *'On the bonnie, bonnie banks of Loch Lomond.'*

A lone dog howls in the distance.

Dritan and his men climb the dilapidated stone steps until they reach a rope stretched across the path. A weather-worn **PRIVATE** sign dangles from it, flapping in the breeze.

Dritan turns to his brother. 'Here?'

Stefan tilts his head. 'A garage further up on the left. The shutter will be down, but the side door will be open.'

They straddle the rope and continue upwards. Blues music and the faint murmur of voices drift from the building ahead. Thin blades of light escape through gaps in the rafters.

Dritan pauses, facing his men.

'Tonight we are businessmen,' he says quietly.

Stefan shuffles. 'And if he refuses to do business?'

'Then tomorrow—we are assassins.'

None reply, but the message lands loud and clear.

He turns the handle on the garage door and pushes it open.

Four men stand around a pool table chatting, joking, smoking and sucking from bottles.

The air is thick with a heavy funk of cigarette and weed smoke, stale beer, male sweat, and too much testosterone.

Empty cans clutter the makeshift bar, a few perched on the stereo as Muddy Waters rolls out of the speakers.

A red lightbulb above the pool table throws a murky glow across the room.

In a dark corner, a man with a pudding-bowl haircut and ears too big for his head slouches in a threadbare armchair, sucking on a bong.

Dritan clears his throat.

'Good evening, gentlemen.'

The pool game halts. Eyes turn.

A big, muscular man with tattoos climbing his neck grips the cue tighter and steps forward.

'Who the fuck are you?'

Dritan nods in deference. 'My name is Dritan, and these are my business associates. Which one of you is Mr Tompkins—Typhoon?'

One of the players jerks a thumb towards the man in the chair, clearly confused.

'Typhoon—visitors.'

Typhoon exhales, sets the bong aside and gets to his feet. He grabs a beer, takes a long swallow and saunters forward.

'Gents,' he says evenly. 'You have five seconds to turn around and get the fuck out of my gaff before I set my boys on you.'

Dritan holds his hands up. 'Apologies. I understand. No one likes uninvited guests. But before I go, I have something for you.'

Stefan steps forward and lays the briefcase on the pool table.

Dritan gestures towards it. 'Open it, Mr Tompkins.'

Typhoon hesitates, glances at his crew.

The room seems to hold its breath.

He reaches out, thumbs the latches—*click, click*—and lifts the lid.

A low whistle escapes the muscle-man, Blagger.

Stacks of cash fill the case.

Typhoon's voice drops. 'How much?'

'Fifty thousand,' Dritan says. 'Used notes.'

'For me?'

'Yes.'

'Why?'

Dritan looks around the grimy garage, the bottles, the overflowing ashtrays.

'Because I'm a businessman, and this is a business deal.'

Typhoon stands tall and narrows his eyes. 'I don't know *anything* about a deal. Who sent you?'

'No one. I am my own man.'

'Fucking take it,' Blagger urges, eyes wide. 'Fifty fucking big ones.'

Typhoon snaps at him. *'Shut it, Blagger!'* He raises a hand for silence and takes a step closer to Dritan. 'What's this business deal exactly, Polak?'

Dritan smiles at his own men. 'I am not Polak. I forgive your ignorance. I buy your business. Fifty thousand.'

Typhoon laughs—a short, sharp bark—and looks back at his crew.

'Hear that, lads? Old Dritan here wants to buy my business.'

'Tell him he's dreaming,' responds Blagger, standing tall, tensing his pecs.

A few uneasy chuckles ripple through the room.

Dritan's men don't move, don't blink.

Typhoon swigs his beer. 'And what *business* do you think I run exactly... Dritan?'

'You're a distributor. You control Hull up to border of Scotland.' Dritan pauses, eyes steady. 'You use freelance dealers for street trade. Smart, but messy. Your production line suffers from supply issues. Your dealers take from you without you knowing. You are sitting on goldmine but don't have the equipment to reach rich seams. That's where I come in.'

Typhoon's grin fades. 'You seem to know a lot about me.'

'Of course. If you plan a takeover, you study your competitor. Although I prefer to call it a merger. You stay on. Keep your crew.' He nods towards his brother and Mika. 'Stefan oversees day-to-day operations. Mika eradicates any threats, and I smooth out the supply line. The difference is, you work for me, and I'll pay you very well for your loyalty. Everyone's a winner. So—do we have a deal?'

Typhoon stares at the money, then at Dritan, then back at the case. He slams the lid shut, picks it up and shoves it hard into Stefan's chest.

'Listen, you Polak wanker, take your cash and piss off on the first illegal boat back to wherever you fucking came from. This is my operation. Understand?'

Dritan's tone doesn't change. 'It's a lot to think about, Mr Tompkins. I'll give you time to reconsider.'

'Go on—fuck off!' Typhoon waves them away, his men advancing with pool cues raised.

Dritan turns, as calm as someone who knows how this ends. His men follow him out, their footsteps measured, deliberate.

Shouts and curses chase them into the night.

'Foreign bastards—who the fuck do you think you are?'

'Stick to growing beetroot, not running drugs!'

Typhoon stands in the doorway, bottle in hand, watching the silhouettes vanish into the darkness.

Blagger sidles up behind him. 'What do you think all that was about?'

Typhoon shrugs. 'A bunch of amateurs chancing their arm. They obviously don't know who they're dealing with.'

Typhoon bids farewell to Blagger and the rest of his crew, then pushes the door shut and slides the top and bottom bolts across. Moves quickly to the bar fridge, the smell of weed and sweat still heavy in the air. Cracks a fresh bottle of beer. Pulls out his phone, opens the WhatsApp private group named *Lieutenants*. Types a message:

*Whatever the fuck you're doing. Stop right now. Need a group video call with both of you. ASAP!*

He slumps onto the sofa and stares around the room. He's not a man to be easily spooked, but the uninvited guests have made him edgy. It's the nature of the game he's in. No matter your reputation, there's always someone somewhere who fancies their chances at being king. He's dealt with pretenders before trying to muscle in. He's always dealt with them with a show of strength and swift retribution. But he also knows turf wars are bad for business. It gets messy. People get injured, or dead, or simply disappear. And the cops don't like that sort of thing. Makes them look bad. Like they've lost control of the streets—which they did forty years ago—but they'll never admit as much.

Still, he's done well to keep a low profile. He pays kickbacks to a couple of officers in the Drugs Squad. A business expense. But these guys tonight—well, they were different. Maybe he could have handled it better.

Pretended to enter negotiations. Found out more about them, and *then* dealt with the problem. Shouldn't have had the bong, smoked the weed. It relaxes him, but he loses his edge.

He leans back on the sagging sofa, the cold Heineken sweating in his hand. His phone vibrates on the armrest—incoming WhatsApp video call: Gasket, and Wiggy—the green bar pulsing at the top of the screen.

He taps JOIN.

The familiar boop-boop-boop connection tone echoes in the tiny space. Two black tiles.

Then one comes alive.

Gasket appears first, camera far too close, half an eyebrow and the top of his head filling the frame.

'I'm on,' Gasket mutters, shuffling back to get the right angle. 'What's the problem?'

Typhoon takes a quick swig of beer. 'Hang on, Gasket. Wait until Wiggy has joined. Don't want to repeat myself.'

A second tile stabilises, glitching once before resolving.

Wiggy is bare-chested and sweaty.

'Christ, Typhoon, you certainly pick your moments. I was in the middle of banging this bird I've been chasing for weeks. Had to break off halfway through.'

Typhoon laughs. 'You randy little git. Where's your missus?'

'She's gone to Blackpool for a hen party. Not back until Sunday. Anyway, what's so urgent?'

'Can you both hear me?' Typhoon asks.

The two faces nod, each muttering their confirmation.

'Right,' Typhoon says. 'It might be nothing. So, I'm in my gaff tonight with Blagger and the lads—shooting pool, talking shit, having a smoke and a few beers. Then out of nowhere, these four blokes stroll in, bold as brass. Slicked-back hair, bomber jackets, Doc Martens, foreign accents. The lead man says his name's Dritan. Puts a briefcase on the pool table and offers me fifty grand. Says he wants to buy out my operation. And the cheeky bastard tells me *I* can work for him.'

A chorus of disbelief erupts—swearing, muttering, heads shaking across the tiles.

Gasket leans into his camera. 'Were they tooled up?'

'Nah. That's the strange thing. They were polite, respectful, businesslike.'

'What did you do?'

'I told them they were taking the piss and told them to fuck off. As they left, this Dritan guy says he'll give me time to reconsider. That's what made me think maybe they're the scouting party and there's someone else behind them.'

'You should've given them a good kicking and sent them on their way, *and* kept the fucking money. You and Blagger could have handled them all by yourselves.''

'Hindsight's a wonderful thing, Gasket.'

'You said foreign. What nationality?'

'I'm not sure, mate. I'm not great with accents. European, though.'

Wiggy snorts derisively. 'Oh aye, that narrows it down. Russian? French? German?'

Typhoon shrugs. 'None of the above. I thought they might be Polish. Anyway—that's not the point. They seem to know a lot about my business... our business, or at least that was the impression they gave. You heard anything on the street?'

A shake of the head from both associates.

Wiggy is moving around a kitchen. 'All's been running smoothly on my patch, Typhoon. Haven't had any trouble since that Liverpool mob tried it on about a year ago. Business is good.'

'Same here,' Gasket says. 'We've worked hard for this, and we don't want any cocky little fuckers trying it on.'

Typhoon nods. 'I think they're a bunch of wannabes who've watched The Godfather too many times and thought they'd chance their arm.'

Gasket sparks up a smoke. 'What about your contact in the plods? Have you called him?'

'Nah. Too early for that. They need to know what they need to know and nothing else. Keep them at arm's length. All right, cheers, lads. Let me know if you hear anything. By the way, I'm heading to Manchester to visit my mam at the weekend, so don't bother me unless it's urgent. Right, catch up soon.'

The heads disappear one by one.

Typhoon glances up at his championship boxing belt hanging from the wall.

A slow grin spreads across his face.

'If you wanna get in the ring, boys... be my guest.'

# 6

## Friday Morning

Summer is a distant, damp memory, and mid-September is equally uninspiring. Cooler, wetter, and windier than its seasonal neighbour, it occasionally flirts with sunshine and warmth, but it lacks commitment. And with school holidays well and truly over, Whitby has seen an influx of the silver dollar—the retirees.

People assume it's the families with kids who bring the most money into town, but it's not. It's the older folk with their disposable income. Most have worked hard all their lives and now intend to enjoy the fruits of their labour. Although not reckless with their cash, they've grown accustomed to the finer things in life, and don't hold back when it comes to upmarket accommodation, expensive meals out, or overpriced cocktails at the bars.

Today, though, with the cold, blustery conditions, and the occasional squall, even the grey nomads have decided to lie low.

Church Street in Whitby is usually a tunnel of chaos—hordes of holidaymakers meandering as if they've lost their sense of direction.

As the bell from St Mary's tolls ten o'clock, DS Zac Stoker peers out at the quiet street.

He's loitering inside the post office. Been there for twenty minutes, which is far longer than any sane man should endure or reasonably explain away.

The postmaster behind the counter is growing suspicious. Every so often, Zac glances over, offering a polite smile and a nod, to little effect.

He returns his gaze to the other side of the street—Arguments Yard.

His informant, Cleavage, is usually reliable—in fact, he's got an unblemished record for feeding Zac solid information on the lowlifes and ne'er-do-wells that haunt the town. But it's looking like his latest tip-off about a certain individual named Smiler is flawed.

'Come on, you little scrote, where are you?' he mutters, willing Smiler to appear.

'Can I help you, sir?'

Zac spins around and faces the postmaster.

'Ahem—no. Just looking,' Zac replies, plucking a postcard from the carousel and studying it. 'So many to choose from,' he adds with a forced chuckle.

The man peers over his glasses, unimpressed, but shuffles back to the counter.

Zac replaces the postcard of Whalebone Arch and tugs his woollen hat lower. His eyes drift back to the yard.

Movement.

'Come on, bawbag,' he whispers as a figure grows more distinct. 'Gotcha.'

Smiler appears at the entrance to the yard. Above average height, with short cropped blonde hair. An attractive lad with a boyish charm.

He pauses, glances both ways, then buttons his black coat, shiny as wet tar, the shearling collar brushing his jaw. For reasons known only to himself, he smiles—the kind of smile that could win a fair maiden's heart, the sort of grin you wear when life feels good and easy and you're living the dream. Odd, really, given Smiler's a low-level drug dealer who spends his days dodging the police and mixing with the dregs of society.

He finally sets off, turns right, and ambles down Church Street. Zac gives him a decent head start before slipping out of the shop.

The street is narrow and lined with shops, cafes, and holiday cottages. With tourists in short supply, it would be easy enough for anyone to sense if they're being followed.

As Smiler nears the Old Town Hall, he stops and looks around.

Zac ducks into a cafe, pretending to study the menu board. The smell of coffee is heavenly, and his stomach growls—he could murder a bacon butty—but now's not the time.

He pulls out his phone and lowers his voice. 'I'm on him, Frank.'

Finnegan's reply comes sharp and dry. 'About bloody time. I thought your snout said Smiler was regular as clockwork? He's half an hour off the mark.'

'Dealers aren't known for their impeccable timekeeping,' Zac murmurs, peering out of the doorway.

Frank mutes the phone as Jenny leans over the counter and hands him a white paper bag.

'There you go, Frank. One bacon and egg butty to take away.'

He winks. 'Thanks, Jenny.'

'Was that Jenny's voice I heard?' Zac asks suspiciously. 'Are you in Miserly Joe's cafe?'

Frank is flabbergasted at the suggestion. 'Don't talk daft. We're on an operation. Do you think I've got time to feed my bloody face?' he says, sauntering out of Miserly Joe's cafe and peeling back the paper bag one-handed, a skill mastered over many years.

'Hmm... wait, Smiler's on the move again—just turned right onto Market Place. Stand by.'

'Zac?'

'What?'

'Don't let him see you.'

'Really? I never thought of that.'

'I mean, don't get too close. Keep your distance.'

'Aye, will do, but you know Smiler—he's more slippery than a mackerel after a Thai body massage in baby oil. Take your eye off him for a moment and he can disappear up his own bumhole in an instant.'

'You have a very poetic bent to you, sergeant. If you'd turned left instead of right in your youth, you could have been the country's next poet laureate.'

'Thanks.'

'I look forward to your memoirs.'

Zac exits the cafe and ambles down the street with the casual gait of a day-tripper.

Smiler is at the town hall, chatting with three men and two women. Their sallow cheeks, bedraggled clothes, and eyeballs, which protrude from the sockets, are a telltale sign—addicts. Two men and one woman suck on the stubs of cigarettes, making sure there's not a strand of tobacco wasted. Raucous laughter is followed by a few furtive glances as they huddle closer. With clenched fists held out, knuckles skyward, Smiler takes their cash before slipping *something* into their coat pockets with the finesse of the Artful Dodger.

Zac flips his collar up, slides on a pair of sunglasses, and strolls past the group unnoticed, ducking into a sweet shop.

Barely a minute passes before Smiler's on the move again. He bounces along Sandgate with a jaunty spring in his step as if starring in a Broadway musical, the leading man who has just encountered his true love. Stops off at three cafes along the way—in and out in seconds. Pauses to speak with a couple of homeless people sitting in a doorway. A swift exchange, lightning fast, and he's on the go.

Zac trails a hundred yards behind until Smiler turns yet another corner—heading for the swing bridge.

Zac quickens his pace and edges to the corner of Bridge Street for a peek.

'Shit the bed,' he hisses, spotting a trawler chugging up the estuary.

Smiler's put some distance between them.

Near the bridge, it's busier—a natural bottleneck.

The traffic lights flip to red. The bridge operator rattles a bell—a warning. He starts to swing the gates shut, but Smiler skips past him and jogs across.

A moment later, the hydraulics thrum into action, and the swing bridge shudders open to let the trawler through.

7

With one eye firmly fixed on Smiler, Zac lifts his phone.

'Frank, he's crossed the bridge.'

'Righto.'

'Unfortunately, I'm stuck on the other side until the barrier goes up.'

'Kiss my hairy blue arse. Bloody fantastic. Can you still see him?' Frank growls, licking egg yolk from his fingertips.

'I had him, but he's vanished. He took a left onto New Quay Road.'

'Just as we suspected. He'll be heading to the train station. Plenty of customers loitering there.'

Zac heaves a sigh of relief as the trawler passes by and the hydraulics rumble into action.

'Another thirty seconds and I'll cross the bridge,' Zac states.

'Okay. You want me and Dinkel to move into position?'

'Not yet, Frank. Too early. Dinkel would only cause a disturbance and draw attention.'

Dinkel's affronted voice cuts through the ether. 'I *am* here on this group call, you know. I *can* hear you.'

'No offence intended, Dinks, but when God was handing out spatial awareness, you slept in. I'll keep you posted, Frank.'

Eventually, the bridge clamps back together, the gates reopen, and pedestrians start to saunter across.

<hr>

Zac takes up position behind a white transit van parked outside Macy Brown's as he spies Smiler, who is trading his wares outside the railway station across the road.

It's a prime location for dealing drugs. Railway and coach stations are a magnet for the great unwashed—souls who've fallen between the flagstones that pave the long, uneven path of life. Living on the margins means always running away—from a landlord, a dealer, a fist, your abuser. The cheapest escape route is by bus or train.

Zac has no sympathy for the great unwashed.

He's not here to uphold the rights of lawbreakers—he's here to protect those who play by the rules.

Smiler trades a quick high-five with a wizened man—blackened teeth, death circling like a ravenous wolf—then skips across the road, and turns into Loggerheads Yard.

Zac steals behind and glances down the claustrophobic ginnel but doesn't immediately follow, just watches. Smiler ambles down the alleyway before turning right and disappearing from view.

'Frank, Smiler's entered Loggerheads and turned into Mackridges Yard.'

There's a chuckle down the line. 'Snared like a rat in a trap. And from memory, no security cameras down there. Okay, keep calm and carry on. Me and Dinkel are on our way.'

Zac slips the phone into his pocket and steps into the laneway. The air changes instantly—dimmer, colder, a faint echo of dripping water somewhere ahead. Brick walls rise on either side, close enough to scrape a shoulder if he strays.

A few hundred yards in is the entrance to Mackridges Yard—a dead-end, boxed in by three-storey high Victorian buildings, their brickwork patched and botched up in places.

He edges to the corner and peers around.

Smiler approaches a scuffed green door at the end of the yard and raps three times—slow, deliberate—then four quick knocks in succession. A pause.

'Password,' a slightly stoned voice calls from inside.

'Captain Cook,' Smiler replies.

Metal bolts rasp back. The door opens an inch, then wider, as Smiler slips inside.

The unseen male voice grizzles, 'Need to get a spy hole installed in this bloody door,' as the bolts slam home again.

Zac assesses the yard.

To his right, the back door to a fish and chip shop. The reek of beef fat seeps from a grease-caked extractor fan, along with a steady plume of steam. Straight ahead, the green door and a narrow window beside it, half-fogged with condensation. Above, another window glows faintly yellow. To the left, higher still, a set of glass doors opens onto a rusted iron balcony where a Union Jack flaps lethargically in a light breeze. Once upon a time, it must've been a warehouse. The third floor still sports an overhanging beam, once part of a pulley system used to hoist crates through the loft door.

A sudden clang—an emergency door kicks open. A man in a smeared blue apron bursts out, arms loaded with flattened cardboard. He lopes to the industrial wheelie bin, heaves the lid, dumps the stack inside. Without a glance, he vanishes back through the door, leaving the yard empty once more, save for the drifting steam.

Zac treads silently forward. Stops. Peers at the bin, then up at the balcony.

He approaches and raps on the green door—three slow knocks, then four rapid ones.

A muffled curse from inside.

'Password?'

'Captain Cook,' he says, stepping back.

Bolts scrape. The door opens an inch.

'Christ, it's like Piccadilly Circus this morn—'

Zac drives his heel into it. The door smashes inward, hits resistance, then something soft.

A yelp, followed by groaning.

He steps through.

A portly man with a ponytail sprawls on the floor, clutching his face, blood trickling between his fingers.

'Uncool, man!'

Zac hauls him up by the collar, nose-to-nose. 'Keep your voice down or I'll remodel that ugly mug of yours permanently. Where's Smiler?' he hisses.

The man's eyes flick upward.

'Everything all right down there, Blakey?' Smiler's voice echoes down the staircase.

'Yeah, all good, Smiler. Tripped over the bloody cat.'

A door creaks shut upstairs.

Zac releases Blakey, fishes a tenner from his pocket, and tosses it at him.

'Get a coffee. Twenty minutes. I was never here. Understood?'

Blakey hurriedly grabs his coat from the banister and stumbles out.

'Yeah, cool man. You were never here.'

Zac takes the stairs two at a time. Music drifts down—modern jazz, of all things. He passes the second floor and reaches the top. One old door. Brass keyhole. He crouches, peers in—blocked. Slowly turns the handle.

Inside, Smiler sits at a laptop, back to the entrance, fingers tapping the keyboard.

Zac slips in, locks the door, pockets the key. To his right, a retro hi-fi spins *Kind of Blue*—Miles Davis, trumpet, and piano cool as midnight, a fragile calm before the storm.

He lifts the needle—scratch rising through the groove like a plastic zipper.

Smiler snaps his head to the left.

'Fuck! Mr Stoker. What are…'

Zac's already on him before he can move, one hand on Smiler's collar, the other twisting his arm high up his back. He spins him around and slams him into the wall.

'Morning, sunshine,' Zac growls. 'Long time no see.'

Smiler gasps, face to plaster. 'Jesus, Mr Stoker—you can't just—'

'Button it, numpty.' Zac lets go, spins him round, and grabs his throat lightly between his powerful fingers. 'Empty your pockets. Table. Now.'

Smiler, trembling, dumps a wad of notes, a phone, and keys beside the laptop.

'That's all I've got, swear to God.'

'Uh-huh.' Zac quickly checks Smiler's pockets but finds nothing incriminating. 'Looks like you had a good morning. You found honest work since you got out?'

'Not yet. But I'm looking.'

Zac releases him and counts the notes. 'Just shy of a grand. A handsome payday considering you're *looking* for work. Where'd it come from?'

'Benefits. Dropped into my bank account yesterday.'

'My, my, His Majesty's government is generous these days.' He gestures around the tidy flat—hi-fi, widescreen TV, designer labels on the clothes rail, iPhone on the desk.

'And all this? Don't tell me Universal Credit covers Sonos, Armani, and Apple these days?'

'It's old stuff—my grandparents helped me out, that's all.'

Zac's smile fades. He steps closer. 'Cut the crap, Smiler. I tailed you earlier. Quite the little rambler, aren't we? A friend on every street corner and cafe. What are you shifting?'

'Just a bit of weed, nothing heavy.'

'Weed doesn't fit into a clenched fist, Smiler. Try again.'

Smiler straightens, finds some bravado. 'You haven't got a warrant. I want a solicitor.'

'Sorry, Smiler. We're not playing by the rules today.'

He strolls to the balcony doors, pushes them open. The wind gusts in.

'Three floors up,' Zac says. 'Room with a view. Unfortunately, the view is of brick walls and a dead end. How ironic. A bit like your life.' He turns, eyes cold. 'You been dealing fentanyl, Smiler?'

'What? No—no way, Mr Stoker!'

'Over two dozen overdoses in the last eight weeks, fifteen hospitalised, three came within a whisker of losing their lives. All local. All dosed from the same batch. And you just happen to walk free from Hull Prison two months ago. Coincidence?'

'I've got nothing to do with that! I don't deal the heavy shit.'

'Really.' Zac steps forward, grips his arm, steers him toward the open doors. 'I want a name, Smiler. Who'd you get your gear from?'

Smiler thrashes. 'You're mental!'

'A name—now!'

'Please, I swear—'

Zac hoists him half off the ground, legs kicking. 'Name!'

'I don't know his name!'

'A name?' Zac bellows as the balcony beckons.

'Honest to God, I don't know...'

Zac picks him up by the ankles and dangles him over the balcony as Smiler desperately claws for the railings, unable to gain purchase.

'Last chance, Smiler. Give me a *fucking* name—NOW—otherwise, in about three seconds you'll be headbutting concrete. And even with that thick head of yours, there's only one winner in that contest.'

8

Frank powers along, wiping greasy fingers from his bacon and egg butty onto a tissue then drops it into a bin. Lifts the phone to his ear.

'Dinkel, where are you?' he demands.

'On Baxtergate, sir. I can see you coming the other way.'

'Good lad. You know the little archway—adjacent to the Old Smuggler?'

'Yes, sir.'

'Turn down that alleyway. After a few hundred yards, there's a courtyard on your left. That's where the action is. I'll see you there in five... and don't dilly-dally.'

'Wilko, sir.'

Frank turns into the courtyard as raised voices echo off brick—one harsh, unrelenting; the other high-pitched, panicked.

He gazes up.

Barely has time to register what he sees before something dark breaks the skyline—weightless for a second—before gravity takes hold.

'Shite,' he gulps.

The body plummets, flailing through the air like a helicopter hit by a missile—arms and legs spinning wild, uncoordinated, before impact.

A dull thump is followed by a loud wheeze as Zac peers down from the balcony.

'Fuck it!' he snarls.

Frank releases his breath and takes a step towards the blue wheelie bin, and peers inside at the hapless figure cocooned in cardboard.

'Ah, Smiler,' he chuckles. 'New lodgings?'

Smiler looks up and groans, twisting uncomfortably, feeling for broken limbs.

'Very funny, Mr Finnegan.'

'How are your grandma and granddad going? Haven't seen them down the bowls club since you retired to that Hull holiday home a few months back. I think it's the shame. Their only grandson sent down for dealing. And being good, honest folk, I can well understand their reluctance to show their faces in public.'

Frank pauses a moment and jabs a finger into his mouth to extract an aggravating piece of bacon stuck between his wisdom tooth, then spits it out.

'Not right though, is it? They bring you up good and proper. Decent school. Provide for you. Nothing too much trouble. And how do you repay them? You take the path of least resistance—easy money. That's not *their* fault. You're a grown man. Why should they carry the burden of your misdeeds?'

Smiler rolls onto his back, grimacing. 'Mr Finnegan, that sergeant of yours has a fucking screw loose.'

Frank chuckles. 'Aye, he does have a wild side. You're lucky he's in a good mood today.'

'He could've killed me.'

Frank shakes his head dismissively. 'Nay, lad. If he'd intended to kill you, we wouldn't be having this conversation now. All he wants is a name.' He hesitates, cocks his head, glances towards the green door. 'Oh dear—that sounds like the rumble of very angry boots clattering down the stairs. Now, I know you're not a stupid lad, Smiler, so before I let my sergeant at you again, how about you give me a name—who supplies your drugs?'

Smiler tries to sit up. 'I swear I don't know his name.'

Frank pulls a disappointed face. 'It's business. Of course you know his name.'

'I'm not lying, Mr Finnegan. I meet him once a week at the top of the 199 Steps. He gives me a bag, and I pay my cash. Deal done.'

'A bag of what?'

'Weed.'

The front door bursts open as Zac strides angrily towards the bin.

'The little scrote tried to jump for it, boss. Lucky, the bin was there to break his fall.' He dangles a plastic bag from his hand containing at least a hundred or more white pills. 'Found this little lot stuffed into the toe of his Adidas Superstars. Let me at the bastard.'

Smiler rises tentatively and pokes his head above the edge of the bin, but he's a little slow on the uptake. Zac grabs the lid and slams it down on his head, then lifts it up, and slams it shut again. Finally, in a rage, he grabs the handle, and using his body as a counterweight, swings the bin around and around. Once it's gained enough momentum, he releases his grip.

The bin careers across the yard like a pissed-up Dodgem car, slams into a wall, and upturns as Smiler is unceremoniously jettisoned from within.

He scrambles onto his knees, breathing heavily.

Zac marches over, yanks him upright by his jacket, and pulls his fist back.

'A fucking name!'

Eyes wide with terror, Smiler shoots a glance at Frank, hoping for intervention, reason, a modicum of sense.

None is forthcoming.

Frank merely averts his gaze.

Smiler breaks. 'Alright, alright! I'll tell you his name. It's Typhoon—Typhoon Tommy.'

Zac grimaces. 'Typhoon Tommy? What is he—a fucking weatherman?'

Frank steps forward with a puzzled expression. 'Typhoon Tommy, the ex–boxer?'

Smiler nods. 'Yeah, that's him.'

Frank turns to Zac. 'Thomas Tompkins—aka Typhoon Tommy—has that name cropped up on our radar before?'

Zac shakes his head. 'Nah. Never heard of him.'

Frank rubs his chin, thinking. 'Promising southpaw once upon a time. Nippy on his feet, good uppercut. Pundits said he'd be Britain's next light-middleweight champion.'

'What happened to him?'

'Glass jaw. Once the opposition twigged, Typhoon's number was up. He turned to match-fixing—taking dives. Through an intermediary, he laid big bets on himself, picked the round he'd go down, and made a packet. Got away with it for a while until the authorities cottoned on. Big internal investigation by the British Boxing Board of Control—found guilty and banned for life.'

All three are distracted by the clatter of feet on cobbles as DC Dinkel rounds the corner, panting hard.

Zac shakes his head in disgust. 'Fuck me sideways... and here comes blisters. Always appears after the hard work's been done.'

'Sorry, Mr Finnegan, sir. Got waylaid by a little old lady wanting to know where the nearest chemist was. Said her bunions were causing her mischief.'

'Oh, well done, lad. I'm glad it wasn't anything trivial.'

9

Frank and Zac enter the incident room. At the far end, two figures are deep in conversation inside Frank's office—he wasn't expecting either of them.

'Christ,' he mutters.

'What?' Zac asks, following his gaze.

'The ghost of Maggie bloody Thatcher's in town.'

Before Zac can reply, Superintendent Anne Banks emerges from the office—stern, humourless, devoid of any social graces.

'Frank. Zac. My office. Now.'

Zac sniggers. 'Sorry, Frank—but isn't that your office?'

'Piss off.'

⸺◈⸺

Superintendent Anne Banks lowers herself into the chair behind Frank's desk to his obvious irritation as he and Zac enter the room.

By the window stands a tall, narrow-shouldered man in a sharp suit, fingers folded beneath his chin, thumbs pressed together—like a headmaster weighing up whether a schoolboy is telling the truth or not. Heavy-rimmed glasses catch the light as he watches them enter, calm, appraising.

Mid-forties, polished shoes, accountant neat—tidy, cautious, probably dull company over a pint.

Banks performs cursory introductions. 'Frank, Zac—this is Senior Investigating Officer Silas Carmody, National Crime Agency. Silas—DCI Finnegan and DS Stoker.'

As they shake hands, Frank feels an unwelcome flicker of déjà vu. In his occasional dealings with outsiders—whether the NCA or MI5—things had never gone smoothly. In fact, they usually ended in a shitshow.

'Pleased to meet you, Silas,' Frank says, dropping into a chair opposite Banks as Zac props himself against a filing cabinet. 'You up from London?'

'No—I'm based in Leeds.'

'I see. I assume you're not in Whitby to sample the oysters?'

Silas rocks back on his heels. 'Ahem—no. I believe you arrested a young drug dealer earlier this morning by the name of Owen Lister, nickname Smiler.'

Zac straightens as Frank throws him a sideways glance. 'Aye, that's right. And if you know that already, I assume you had him under surveillance?'

His lips flatten, almost a smile. 'Yes. He and many others. Has he been charged?'

'Not yet. I intend to leave him in the cells for a while to reflect upon the error of his ways.'

Silas seems to relax. 'Okay, that's one positive.'

Banks concurs. 'We might still have room to manoeuvre, Silas.'

Frank is losing patience fast. He's Yorkshire-born and bred, likes to speak bluntly and expects the same from others.

'I'm a busy man, Silas. How about you cut to the chase?'

Banks leans forward over the desk. 'Apparently your arrest may have brushed up against undercover work by the NCA.'

Zac emits a low whistle. 'Maybe if the NCA had bothered to tell us about their operation, then we wouldn't have brushed up against it.'

Banks glares at him. 'When I want your input, sergeant, I'll ask for it.'

'Ma'am,' he replies, well used to a ticking off from the Super.

Silas turns and peers out of the window at the pleasure craft drifting in the harbour below.

'What has Smiler said so far?'

'Not much,' Frank answers. 'We know he's a small-time dealer. One conviction—did four months in Hull. He's been out for about eight weeks, which happens to coincide with a string of fentanyl overdoses along the coast. One of DS Stoker's informants tipped us off he was back in business, so we brought him in. He gave us his supplier's name—Thomas Tompkins—or Typhoon Tommy, as everyone calls him. Ex-professional boxer until he was barred for match-fixing. Typhoon's never been in our sights before.'

Silas raises an eyebrow. 'And you've made no further inquiries into Typhoon?'

Frank shakes his head. 'Not yet.'

'Good,' Silas says quietly. 'Then all's not lost.'

Frank folds his arms. 'You want to tell me what's going on?'

Silas turns from the window. 'You almost—unwittingly—jeopardised a critical phase of an ongoing operation.'

'What operation?'

Silas meets his gaze. 'Operation Blackout.'

'I see,' Frank says, recalling his meeting with Hedley Keegan six weeks earlier.

'It's a long-term surveillance exercise,' Silas explains. 'Multi-agency, cross-border. Designed to observe, not interfere. We let people believe they're operating freely while we watch who surfaces, who finances, who connects to whom.'

Frank says nothing.

'At this stage,' Silas continues, 'any overt interest in Typhoon could cause ripples we can't afford. People get nervous. Phones go quiet. Contacts disappear.'

Frank shifts in his chair. 'As Zac said, if we'd been made aware, then it could have been avoided.'

Silas removes his spectacles and massages the bridge of his nose. 'Our cross-border operation has been running for nearly a year, involving numerous law enforcement agencies. We have concrete intel that a foreign drug gang is planning a move into the UK market, specifically the north east coast of England, from Hull to the Scottish border—an area that is currently run at street level by Typhoon. This cartel is highly organised, ruthless, not afraid to make examples of people. Their model is simple—control every link in the chain. Import, manufacture, distribution, street.'

'And who are we talking about?' Frank quizzes. 'Eastern European? South American?'

Silas shrugs. 'We're not attaching a nationality. What matters is the product. They're sourcing fentanyl precursors from Asia—legal chemicals, easy to hide, easy to move. Once they're in Europe, they vanish into legitimate supply chains.'

Zac frowns. 'Why fentanyl?'

'Because it's efficient,' Silas says. 'Synthetic. No fields, no harvests. Our intelligence indicates the cartel will have the capacity to manufacture on an industrial scale, which would flood the entire country.'

Frank rubs his chin. 'And the money?'

'Millions. Many, many millions,' Silas replies. 'High reward, low risk—for them—compared to traditional drug importation.'

Banks leans back, arms folded. 'And you think Typhoon is tied to this foreign gang?'

He edges back to the window, clasps his hands behind his back and peers out.

'And that brings us to the crux of the problem, Anne—at this stage—we're uncertain. You may notice a slight reticence in some of my answers, and for good reason. We have many operatives working undercover, and if they're compromised, it could put their lives in danger. However, I can tell you this: Typhoon could be used as a ready-made distributor network for the cartel. Or...' he pauses and turns glacially to face the three officers. '... he could simply be eliminated. He's certainly no criminal mastermind, but he runs a tight ship, and his team are loyal. Which brings me to my next point—turning a negative into a positive.'

Frank grimaces. 'How do you mean?'

Silas twists a gold ring around on his index finger. 'Scenario one—let's say Typhoon has already hooked up with the cartel. Their distribution network already locked in place. Makes sense. It's now just a matter of time before they smuggle in the precursor and begin manufacture. If you go snooping around, it could spook not only Typhoon, but the cartel. They could delay their move or abandon it entirely. I can't allow that to happen. This is an international operation. I'm sure you're aware of the cost of running such an enterprise.'

Frank nods, understanding the gravity of the situation.

'And scenario two?'

'Let's say the cartel has not yet made contact with Typhoon, and maybe don't intend to. But we need to know one way or another.'

Zac straightens, not entirely following the line Silas is pushing.

'So what's the negative—positive angle you mentioned?'

'Smiler—our way in. From my understanding, he's trusted by Typhoon. He certainly didn't spill his guts when he was arrested last time. Didn't offer up Typhoon in exchange for a suspended sentence, which he could have done.'

Frank has already joined the dots. 'You want to use Smiler to get intel on Typhoon to see what the state of play is?'

'Exactly.'

Frank is uneasy at the suggestion. 'Smiler's a young lad and using him for...'

Silas interjects. 'Smiler is a common drug dealer who brings death and misery to our streets, inspector.'

'Nevertheless, how does he get the truth from Typhoon without raising his suspicion?'

'Obviously, we cannot mention anything to Smiler about the operation.'

'Obviously.'

'We use this.' He pulls an object from his pocket and holds it between thumb and forefinger. 'It's low-tech but reliable.'

All eyes fix on the small USB stick.

'A memory drive?' Zac says, bemused.

'Yes, it's a voice-activated recorder. Smiler places it in Typhoon's headquarters.'

Frank scratches his stubble. 'And what's the incentive for Smiler?'

'Quid pro quo. We drop the charges against him. We explain we're not interested in him, not really interested in Typhoon. We say we're after Typhoon's supplier. We feed Smiler just enough information to make it believable. All Smiler has to do is make an excuse to visit Typhoon at his hangout and secrete the device. As it looks like any other memory stick, it's the perfect cover. But it must be done quickly—tonight. I need to know where Typhoon sits in all this; a player in a bigger, more dangerous game or just another street gangster.'

Frank and Zac glance at one another uneasily.

'And where is Typhoon's place?' Frank asks.

'A converted stable, now a lock-up garage in the bowels of Black Horse Yard, off Church Street.'

'Hmm... I think know the place,' Frank mumbles.

'We leave the device in situ for five days, then Smiler retrieves it and hands it to you... then you hand it to me.'

Banks, who has been unusually quiet, raises a point.

'And what if Smiler agrees but then tells Typhoon about the set up?'

Silas's face tightens. 'Yes, a calculated risk, Anne, but one I believe is worth taking. At the moment we're unsure of Typhoon's role, if any. If Smiler squeals, then we're no worse off than we are now.'

'I don't like it,' Frank states.

'Nor me,' Zac adds.

'And another thing,' Frank says. 'Are you suggesting the cartel intends to use Whitby as the entry point for the fentanyl precursor?'

Silas shakes his head. 'No. That wouldn't make operational sense. We're banking on them moving it via shipping container into a major port, probably Hull or Teesside, our intel suggests.' He raises a finger in the air. 'However, this gang is clever, and they're already running black flag operations, which is spreading our resources thin.'

'Are they aware they're being watched?'

'Nothing suggests that. They're just being smart. They run decoys—boats, planes, articulated lorries entering via ferries. What they're really doing is throwing bait into the water. If we intercept any of the decoys, they'll know they're under surveillance. It's imperative that we don't raise their suspicions. It's hands-off at the moment. It's how they've operated overseas in the past.

'We intend to catch the whole shooting match in one coordinated strike across borders. The kingpin, the cartel, the money men, the chemists, the dealers. If we intercept, we blow our cover, and everyone involved will go to ground. You'll understand that I can't divulge too much due to operational constraints.' He checks his watch. 'So, are we agreed on using Smiler?'

Frank shakes his head. 'Not so fast, Silas. Smiler's a vulnerable twenty-two-year-old that you want to use as a pawn in your game. If it goes tits up, and Typhoon suspects him, then it could end very badly. Men who run drug gangs aren't known for their compassionate nature.'

Banks flicks a small piece of fluff from her jacket. 'Smiler's not a kid—he's a young man who knows the score, Frank.'

'There's virtually no risk,' Silas adds. 'Typhoon trusts him.'

Frank is not backing down. 'I don't like it one little bit. Since when did we recruit rookies from the public to do our job for us?'

'It's our way in, inspector. He plants the device and leaves town for a few days, then returns and retrieves it. You drop the charges. Then he's out of the game. He dodges another prison sentence, and we know if Typhoon's involved or not. It's a win-win.'

Frank turns to Zac. 'Thoughts?'

Zac cringes. 'Smiler is no angel, but I'm with you. Using a civilian to do our dirty work doesn't sit easy with me, and that's before we even get into the legal ramifications.'

Silas huffs, impatient. 'It's already been authorised by people far higher up the food chain than the likes of you and me. There'll be no blowback. I can guarantee it.'

Frank contains his anger. 'I don't care who's bloody authorised it. As far as I'm concerned, it's a no-go. Sorry.'

Silas shoots Banks a pointed look.

She rises slowly. 'We're going ahead with it, Frank. It's my call. You have a chat with Smiler and propose the offer. If he refuses, fine—charge him with possession. If he agrees, give him the recorder and instruct him what to do, charges dropped.'

'Basically, blackmail?'

'Don't be so melodramatic. It's called mutually beneficial cooperation. We need to look at the bigger picture. If we can play a small part in this operation and prevent a flood of drugs hitting our shores, then it's worth it.'

Frank realises he's been shoe-horned into an impossible situation.

'Okay, but let it be noted *on the record* that I'm against the idea. But as you insist on going ahead, then I want some safeguards in place *if* Smiler agrees.'

'Go on?' Banks replies.

'I want eyes and ears on the ground. His every move watched. And we give Smiler a trigger word so if it goes pear-shaped, we move in to rescue him.'

Silas shakes his head. 'No, absolutely not. We don't have the resources. And the more surveillance we have, the more likely someone is to be spotted. At the moment, Typhoon is blissfully unaware of anything untoward. It's business as usual. Our best chance of success is maintaining the status quo. Smiler operates independently.'

Superintendent Banks, impatient as ever, rises and heads to the door, closely followed by Silas.

'Right, end of discussion, Frank. Keep me posted on the Smiler business. I want it sorted today.'

# 10

Frank places two cups of coffee on the table and takes a seat as the fluorescent lights flicker and buzz overhead in the interview room.

'Thanks,' Smiler says, lifting the cup.

'Save your thanks until you've tasted it. I use this stuff to stain my fence if I run out of creosote.'

Smiler takes a sip. 'I've had worse.'

'How are your grandparents?'

A half smile. 'Good. They're in Canada for a month. Staying with my uncle.' He shoots a glance around the empty room. 'So, where's my brief? I've told you I'm not talking until a solicitor is present. I know my rights.'

Frank relaxes back in his chair. 'Let's call this an informal chat. Nothing you say can be used against you, and you only tell me what you want.'

Smiler shrugs. 'Okay. Shoot.'

'I've known you since you were knee high to a grasshopper. You came from good parents. Your gran and granddad are the salt of the earth. How did they react to your little spell inside?'

'They don't say much, but I can see it in their eyes—they're ashamed of me.'

'Where did it go wrong?'

Another shrug, but this time with eyes downcast. 'Not sure.'

'Okay, then why do you do it—deal drugs? You know it's wrong, that it's dangerous, and that what you're selling ruins people's lives. Don't you care about any of that?'

Smiler runs a finger around the rim of the cup but averts eye contact.

'The money, Mr Finnegan. It's as simple as that.'

'The lure of easy gold.' Frank sighs then grimaces as he takes a slurp of coffee. 'I know you lost your mam and dad in tragic circumstances when you were younger—how old, nine, ten?'

'Nine.'

'Can't have been easy. When did you start dealing?'

Smiler finally meets his gaze. 'About the age of fifteen.'

'What was the catalyst?'

He shifts in the chair, picking at a loose thread on his cuff.

'I love my gran and granddad. They sacrificed a lot for me. Gave me somewhere to live, a roof over my head, three square meals a day. But they were never well-off. It was always a struggle for them. All my mates at school had the latest gear—the best Adidas trainers, new iPhone, Nike tracksuits, PlayStation 4. My grandparents couldn't afford that sort of stuff, so I always ended up with the lookalike crap—Primarni Gucci, reps, snide gear.'

Frank frowns slightly. 'Primarni Gucci, reps, snide gear—you'll have to help an old codger out here.'

Smiler grins. 'Primarni—cheap lookalike stuff from Primark for a tenner. Reps—replicas. Snide gear—fakes from the back of the market.'

'Right,' Frank says. 'Got it.'

'Me and my mates started doing a bit of weed, then speed, sometimes coke or ecstasy. But I never really enjoyed it. I like to be in control. And that stuff—drugs, well, it's not reality, is it? And there's always payback, normally feeling shit for the next two or three days. But I realised if I saved up my money I could get better prices from the dealers by buying larger quantities.

'At first I just sold it to my mates. Then, mates of mates. And before I knew it, I had thirty, forty customers. It kept growing. I could turn one hundred quid into three, four hundred. You can't get those returns in any other business; not the stock market, not investing in gold, not speculating on the latest tech boom. It meant I could buy the real Nike, the real Adidas, a legit iPhone, not a knock-off. I didn't intend to do it forever, just until I got a job after leaving school.'

'So what happened?'

'I tried, Mr Finnegan, I really did. I worked in supermarkets stacking shelves, serving at Maccas, a warehouse packer. Thirty to forty hours a week and I'd be lucky to take home two hundred quid. Sometimes a lot less. I could make double that in less than an hour by texting a few customers, telling them I had a good batch of coke or meth on my hands. I only sell good stuff.'

'And where does Typhoon fit in all this?'

'He's my main supplier these days. I'm freelance. I buy in bulk from him and get a better deal, which means a bigger profit margin.'

'And when did the fentanyl start?'

'Not long after I got out of prison. Typhoon said he needed to stimulate the market.'

'You mean sell cheap, get people hooked, then slowly raise the price?'

'Yeah.'

'That's cutthroat, Smiler. Creating an addiction to maximise profits.'

Smiler riles a little. 'It's business, Mr Finnegan. Just like any other. The biggest drug in the country is alcohol. It ruins more lives than all the illegal drugs put together. But you can buy alcohol anywhere, anytime of day or night. And the government profits from it. It's all a sham. Hypocritical. You wouldn't walk up to the landlord of your local pub and accuse him of being cutthroat, would you? You wouldn't say Happy Hour was a way to get people hooked.'

Frank clears his voice. 'No. But the line is clear. There are legal substances and illegal ones. It's not up to the likes of you or me to decide upon the ethics. We live in a society. And society has rules. Break those rules and you're on the wrong side of the law, and with that come the consequences.'

Smiler exhales slowly, sullen. 'You asked how I got into it—I've told you.'

'Yes, and I appreciate your honesty.'

'What happens now—you ready to charge me or not?'

Frank rests his palms flat on the table. 'Maybe. Maybe not. Depends on you.'

'What say do I have in it?'

'Quite a lot, as it happens. I won't beat around the bush. If you do one small favour for me, then I'll do a favour for you.'

Smiler eyes him sullenly, intrigued, but suspicious. 'What favour?'

Frank retrieves the USB stick and carefully lays it on the table between them as Smiler stares at it.

'A memory stick,' Frank begins. 'You see them everywhere. Except this USB is a little different. It's a listening device. I want you... no, I'm *asking* if you'd be willing to plant this in Typhoon's place tonight. In five days, you return and remove the device and hand it to me. In return, we drop charges.

'The alternative is we get you a solicitor and charge you. We have evidence from your flat. Over a hundred fentanyl tablets, a Class A drug. You have a prior conviction for similar offences. I'd say you'd be looking at anywhere between six to eight years. And it won't be a cushy little number in a Category B prison, like last time. With good behaviour, you may celebrate your thirtieth birthday on the outside.'

'And what if Typhoon rumbles me?'

'I won't lie—if he does, then you're in deep shit. Does he trust you?'

'Yeah. We get along fine. He knows I'm clean, and I pay upfront for my gear, so he doesn't have to go chasing his debts.'

'Well then, he's no reason to suspect you. It's all about holding your nerve and acting natural. Just place the recorder somewhere out of sight but also central to where Typhoon usually does his deals.'

'But when you bust him, he's going to suspect me.'

'We won't be arresting him for a long time. This is simply an intelligence gathering exercise to see who his source is.'

Smiler picks up the USB drive and spins it around in his fingers.

'How does it work?'

'You simply press the button on the end and it's live. So, what's it to be?'

Smiler nods thoughtfully, still studying the device.

'No choice really, is there?'

Frank feigns a smile as a deep sense of unease intensifies. He pushes the seat back and rises.

'Let's be clear—is that a yes or no?'

'It's a yes.'

Frank breathes deeply, wishing the lad hadn't agreed.

'Smiler, take this as fatherly advice. Today, you've been given a lifeline. Take it. You may be hooked on money and all it can buy, but nothing outweighs freedom. Use this as a wake-up call and change your ways. Do the right thing, if only for your grandparents. Make them proud of you, not ashamed.'

'Easy for you to say, Mr Finnegan. Once you're on the hamster wheel, it's hard to get off. It's like I'm trapped.'

Frank feels his frustration. 'Sometimes it seems like life has you in its clutches, and there's no way to break free. But there is—it's up to you, Smiler. If you want it bad enough you *can* break free.'

11

Smiler is like a puppy on its second visit to the vet—nervous.

Truth is, he wasn't forced into this. His choice... sort of.

Hobson's choice.

Following the fatherly chat with Mr Finnegan, he spent time reflecting on his life. Initially buoyed by the idea of starting again—going straight—it all seemed so simple.

*Until the doubts crept in.*

How would he make a living? He had twenty grand in cash stashed away in a duffel bag in his flat, but how long would that last? Two years if he eked it out? Then what—back to stacking shelves for a pittance? Living in the boxroom at his grandparents?

But more worryingly, at the forefront of his mind is the *deal*.

Rock up at Typhoon's gaff, make idle small talk, hand over cash, collect the drugs, and somewhere in between—plant the listening device.

*As easy as A, B, C.*

Except Smiler was never good with his alphabet.

Now, as he saunters up the alley towards the rendezvous, he's deconstructing the ramifications if Typhoon *ever* suspects it was he—Smiler—who planted the bug.

At the very least, he'd cop a brutal beating, no two ways about it. Worst-case scenario? Well, there were rumours Typhoon once killed a man.

Half-whispers, insinuations, nods and winks, unfinished sentences. But no corpse ever surfaced, and there were at least half a dozen different names bandied about for the supposed victim.

Smiler reckons it was a smokescreen—something to make Typhoon appear more fearsome than he really is. Bolster his reputation as the local hard man, the ex-boxer. Not to be messed with.

But it's possible he's wrong.

Maybe Typhoon *did* kill a man?

The weather feeds Smiler's unease.

A moonless night, the air icy and damp, drizzle prickling his face, fog creeping like Dracula's ghoul.

Hanging a right into Black Horse Yard, he's immediately spooked by how dark it is.

He's only ever visited Typhoon's place during the day.

Familiar morphs into unfamiliar.

Shadows lurk.

Ominous buildings lean in close.

The air smells of wet brick and decaying vegetation.

Voices drift from the pub—laughter, glasses clinking, the warm thud of music.

It would be nice to be in there now, soaking up the atmosphere, sipping a pint, chatting to an old local, warm and ruddy-cheeked.

Checks his watch.

By the time he gets away from Typhoon, the pubs will have long closed their doors. The merry, the drunks, the loners, the bickering couples, the weird quiet ones will be curling up in a warm bed.

He passes a hopeless drunk in front of a low wall, sleeping bag wrapped around him, singing an old Scottish dirge.

Smiler barely notices him.

Reaching Typhoon's lair, he takes a deep breath, pulls on his mask of youthful optimism, and turns the handle on the side door of the garage—but for once it doesn't give.

He knocks twice.

Tentative at first, he musters courage and gives it a solid rap.

'Alright, alright! Who is it?' Typhoon's distinctive voice.

'It's me—Smiler.'

A clunk. Snap of two bolts. The door swings open.

'Smiler, come in, lad,' Typhoon says, grinning, bare-chested and glistening with sweat.

Smiler hurries inside as the door slams shut.

The air is cloying—warm metal, stale beer, the musty reek of sweat, the faint smell of sick. Scent of the alpha male, primal and heavy—like a bull elephant in musth, reeking its warning across the Serengeti.

Smiler looks around and is grateful.

*They're alone.*

It's normally full of Typhoon's infantry, as he calls them. His yes-men. The sycophants who think that by bathing in Typhoon's past glories it somehow reflects on them.

'Where is everyone?' Smiler asks.

Typhoon plods barefoot back to a metal bar suspended in the corner and resumes his chin-ups.

'The boys went to watch the Newcastle game. Couldn't be arsed going.'

'Ah,' Smiler replies, listening to the huff, hiss, and Neanderthal grunts of Typhoon's exertion.

Typhoon finishes his set, drops to the floor, grabs a towel, wipes his face.

'Beer in the fridge if you want one,' he offers.

Smiler nods, pulls a bottle of Heineken from the bar fridge, cracks the top with an opener, takes a thirsty glug.

'You must be doing well?' Typhoon quizzes, pulling on a T-shirt and jumper.

'Sorry?'

'The fentanyl. You only picked up a batch a few days ago.'

'Ah—yeah, no. I haven't sold them all. Planning a few days in Leeds with some mates. Heading off tomorrow. Thought I'd offload some gear while I'm there. Help pay for a few nights on the lash.'

Typhoon slips on socks and trainers, ambles over, and rests a heavy hand on Smiler's shoulder.

'You watch yourself, lad. There's a couple of mean crews that run the Leeds turf. If they think you're muscling in, you'll end up in the River Aire.'

A grin. 'I can swim.'

'Not with your hands tied behind your back and a couple of house bricks for company.'

Smiler laughs nervously. 'Don't worry. I'll be discreet. In and out before they know I'm there.'

Typhoon studies him—long, searching.

'Yeah... of course you will. No flies on you, eh, Smiler?'

Smiler fidgets with the USB stick in his coat pocket as Typhoon takes a beer from the fridge.

'So, what are you up for?' Typhoon asks, taking a long draw of lager.

Smiler lifts a wad of notes from his pocket. 'A hundred blues, forty Mandy, five of snow.'

Typhoon chuckles. 'Oxy blues, ecstasy, coke? You missed your calling, lad—you should be running a pharmacy.'

'Leeds is a big place. Stag nights, hens, the curious who want to dabble,' Smiler says, counting out the cash. 'What do I owe you?'

'Eight hundred'll cover it. You want the usual mixed bag or separate wraps?'

'Separate. Quicker to move that way.'

Typhoon ducks behind the counter and drags out a heavy toolbox. The padlock snaps open. Lifts the lid, rummages, and starts pulling out plastic bags—powder, pills, wraps—and one unexpected item: a handgun, dull black, resting among the merchandise like another piece of stock.

He rises and sets the bags on the counter beside the gun.

'What's that for?' Smiler asks, a surge of adrenaline flooding his chest.

Typhoon winks. 'What do you think it's for, lad? Protection. Can't be too careful these days. Only last night some Polak wankers tried it on,' he adds, counting out Smiler's order.

'Polaks?'

'Yeah—or some foreigners, anyway. Offered me fifty Gs for my business.' A sniff. 'If they'd offered me a million, maybe I'd have considered it.' He pauses, eyes distant. 'Always fancied living on a remote Greek island in the Med. Laid-back, cruisy. Beach, sun, peace and quiet. The smell of wild garlic and oregano baking in the sun. Who knows, another five years at this game and maybe I'll get there.'

Smiler isn't really listening. He's searching for a spot to hide the USB.

*Pool table? Nah, would stand out like the dog's bollocks. Speaker? Idiot! The music would drown out any talking. Think. Think!*

He scans the room—boxing posters on the wall: Tyson, Hatton, Ali, Lewis, Sugar Ray, and of course Typhoon Tommy himself, belt raised, face battered and proud.

He edges towards the wall and peels off a blob of Blu-Tack. Rolls it between his fingers until it's tacky.

Typhoon's still talking—Greek islands, kleftiko, ouzo, herbs and spices—names Smiler's never heard of.

The bar counter catches his eye—a slight lip at the front. *Perfect.*

He presses the Blu-Tack onto the USB, edges around the counter.

'Yeah, sounds nice,' Smiler says nonchalantly, heart thudding. 'Ibiza's good. Went there once for a weekend rave.'

Typhoon throws him a disparaging look. 'Dickhead—that's Spain. Anyway, too touristy. I like peace and tranquillity. Mix with the locals. They know how to live—slow, relaxed. A gentler pace of life.'

'Yeah, I guess,' Smiler mutters, sticking the USB under the counter with a trembling thumb. Looks around. 'You got a pisser in here?'

Typhoon nods towards a dark corner. 'Over there. If you're taking a shit, open the fucking window.'

'Just a piss,' Smiler says, crossing the shed towards a badly built, makeshift room.

He opens the door and stares at a sink dead ahead with a dripping tap, then at another door to the side. A cubicle. Tugs a cord dangling from the ceiling.

Nothing.

'Light's gone in there,' Typhoon calls out. 'Don't piss on the floor or seat.'

'Righto.'

He peers through the crack in the door—Typhoon's still at the counter, wrapping coke into neat paper parcels.

*All good. He's no idea. Five minutes and I'm out of here. In the clear.*

Guilt prickles.

Typhoon's a drug boss, sure—but he's been decent to him. Fair. Straight.

*A new start, Smiler. A brand-new start. Think of yourself.*

Opening the toilet door, a shard of light kaleidoscopes through frosted glass.

Smiler takes a moment, breathing deep. Feels his pulse pounding in his ears.

He opens the tiny window, unzips, begins to pee.

Sea air drifts in—cold, clean. Somewhere beyond, waves crash, steady and eternal. As a boy, he used to listen to that sound at night. Comforting, yet also sometimes terrifying. He suffered from a recurring nightmare for a few years after his parents were killed. They died when their boat capsized in the dead of night. He's had a fear of water since. Canals, rivers, lakes. But worst of all is the sea, especially the harbour at night. It seems so unnatural, caged between the piers and the town. It's like it's trapped and spiteful.

A shiver runs down his spine as he pushes the thoughts away.

*Talking. Shit. I don't need this.*

He zips up, hands trembling. Almost flushes but stops himself.

Typhoon's voice rises—angry

A reply—calm and contained.

Smiler sneaks out of the cubicle and peeks through the crack.

Four men, late twenties to thirties, stand near the bar facing Typhoon.

All dressed the same. One places a briefcase on the counter and clicks it open.

Smiler's never seen them before.

Foreign accents.

*What did Typhoon say earlier about foreigners?*

Typhoon snarls. 'I told you wankers last night, I'm not interested.' He picks up the gun and waves it around, all cocky cowboy. 'So, unless you come back with a million, I suggest you fuck off before I put a bullet through your fucking head!'

Smiler swallows hard, frozen to the spot.

*Should I help? Walk out? No, it's Typhoon. He's killed a man... maybe. He can handle himself. No point getting involved.*

Immobilised by fear, he acknowledges he's never been a fighter. He relies on his disarming smile and genial charm to get by.

More talk.

More shouting from Typhoon.

More reasoning by one man.

*Escalation.*

Smiler tries to swallow... then tries again... without luck.

The group of intruders edge sideways. Like a fan opening out. Encompassing. Enveloping.

To the left.

To the right.

Typhoon points the gun at the forehead of the man talking in hushed tones.

*A click as the hammer is cocked.*

A man at the side shifts—something glints in his hand.

It rises in an arc.

A shadow flickers across the ceiling.

It descends, swift, clinical.

Smiler blinks, not believing his eyes—*refusing to believe.*

Typhoon's head parts from his neck, lands on the counter, and drops to the floor with a dull thunk. It rolls twice... and comes to a stop.

His eyes are still wide open, staring through the gap in the door—straight at Smiler.

12

Miraculously, Typhoon's headless body remains upright for a few seconds as blood erupts in pulses, rhythmic as a heartbeat that hasn't realised it's over. Crimson mist splatters the ceiling. Arms twitch before the corpse collapses and hits the floor with a sickening thump. Blood pumps in ever-decreasing spurts from the neck, creating a Jackson Pollock impression over the concrete.

Smiler's sympathetic nervous system dumps enough adrenaline and cortisol into his bloodstream to last a dozen lifetimes.

Wants to vomit, shit, and piss all at the same time.

Edging backwards, he stumbles into the toilet, closes the door.

Slips the puny latch across.

Stares at his hands, which have suddenly been struck down with Parkinson's.

Yanks his iPhone from his pocket.

Swipes up.

The phone vibrates slightly and shows the message: *Face ID Not Recognised.*

At the bottom of the lock screen:

*Swipe up to try again.*

He swipes as heat flares up his neck. The same failed message appears.

Whispers. *'Shit, shit, shit.'*

Hears their voices—calm, reasoned—discussing something in their native tongue, unperturbed, like they haven't just decapitated another human being.

*'Who the fuck are you?'*

A bead of sweat rolls from his forehead into his eye.

Blinks rapidly.

Swipes his phone again.

Same response.

And again.

*No luck.*

Whimpers, 'Too dark. Come on, you bastard. Open.'

He's not sure who he's going to call.

*Sergeant—mental as fuck—Stoker? No!*

*Mr Finnegan?*

*Yes, Mr Finnegan. He'll know what to do.*

Another swipe.

A new message:

*Face ID is Disabled. Enter Passcode.*

'Passcode—what fucking passcode?'

He entered one at some point, but his mind is a complete blank.

'Oh, sweet mother.'

Scanning the toilet, he looks for a weapon—anything.

A toilet brush and a bog roll.

Great match-up—toilet brush and bog roll, versus machete, gun and four psychopaths.

*The window.*

It's about sixteen inches wide by fourteen high, but some sort of lever prevents it from opening fully.

Smiler plants his feet on the rim of the toilet bowl and grips the frame.

Short, sharp tugs—and the window gives a little.

He inspects the hinges: two of them, old, rusted, screwed into wood that looks rotten. Another yank and one hinge comes loose.

Falters.

Footsteps.

Laughter.

*What the fuck are they laughing at? They've just killed a man.*

He jiggles the frame back and forth like pulling at a decaying tooth.

Slowly, surely, it gives, little by little.

*Come on, come on.*

A clink of glasses—they've helped themselves to beers, raising a toast to their night's work.

He rocks the top of the frame back and forth; the rotten wood creaks and splinters.

*Come on! Please God!*

Readjusts his grip.

One mighty heave is all it will take.

The window capitulates and comes away from the frame as if it never wanted to be attached in the first place.

Smiler is thrown back by his own violent exertion and clatters into the toilet door, the window frame hitting the floor hard, shattering the glass.

Silence.

He doesn't breathe.

Muted voices. Footsteps.

*Shite!*

Leaping onto the bowl, he throws himself headfirst at the opening.

His shoulders wedge.

Pulls back—tries again. Arms first, followed by head and shoulders.

He wriggles like a worm, the outer frame grazing and ripping the thin layer of skin around his ribs.

His coat snags on a screw.

The outer door of the bathroom creaks open.

'Përshëndetje?'

The call is tentative.

The cord for the light is pulled repeatedly.

Squirms, shuffles, squeezes.

Coat rips.

Hips catch tight between the frame.

The handle of the cubicle turns.

'Përshëndetje? Hello?'

In agonising pain, he twists sideways, frees his waist, inches forward.

The door rattles. More voices join whoever's outside.

He tastes blood.

A thundering crack as the cubicle door is kicked off its hinges and dragged out of the way.

All hell breaks loose—violence in the air.

Smiler is woozy, floating.

A hand like a bear trap grabs his ankle.

He falls forward towards the narrow alley, a sea breeze caressing his face like a mother tending a sick child.

The grip around his foot tightens and drags him back.

'Fuck off!' he screams.

Thrashes with his free leg—connects—someone grunts, curses, shouts.

He's free.

Tumbles headfirst towards the cobblestones.

... until...

Two hands clamp around his ankle—and pull.

13

As his torso is dragged back inside, he thrashes, palms scraping brick, trying to brace against the pull. Drizzle, unrelenting and cold, stings his face. The voices grow louder, angrier, and though he cannot understand most of it, one word keeps cutting through—*gun, gun, gun*.

They're tugging violently on his left ankle. If they grip the other, he's done for.

And then what?

They won't let him live after what he's seen.

His strength is waning.

Breath laboured.

This is it.

*Please God, let it be the gun—not the machete.*

Mr Finnegan's voice drifts through his fractured thoughts:

*If you want it bad enough, you can break free.*

One hand loosens. He takes his chance—maybe his last.

He drives his free leg back, heel smashing into bone.

'Aargh! Qen bir qeni! You son of a whore!'

Smiler twists, wrenches free. Using the wall as leverage, he launches himself forward, bounces off a wheelie bin below, clatters into a brick wall, and hits the ground in a crumpled heap.

A head appears at the window—then the muzzle of a gun.

Two cracks split the night. Bullets whistle past his ear.

He scrambles upright, sprints for the corner of the garage. The side door bangs open behind him. He veers left and pelts up a set of ramshackle stone steps, wedged between damp walls and lopsided, towering townhouses.

Footsteps hammer after him—two, maybe three sets.

He risks a glance behind. Shadows gaining. Yes—three men.

One advantage: *this is his town.*

Whitby's in his bones—the alleys, the shortcuts, the hidden yards.

He forces his legs on, lungs screaming, rain adding to his misery.

The steps end.

*Left or right?*

*Right.*

Twenty yards' lead, maybe less. One misstep and he's gone.

The houses fall away to a bleak open space—Donkey Field—the silhouette of the Abbey watching on in morbid curiosity.

He vaults the wire fence, barbs snagging his jeans. Lands with a wet slap in the paddock. A startled horse rears, whinnying in alarm, hooves thudding the mud.

Runs on, leaps another fence, drops into a narrow lane.

*Left to St Mary's Church or turn right, back towards town?*

Hesitation.

Movement in the field behind—two figures closing.

*Where's the third man? Must've gone right to cut me off.*

His decision is made.

He cuts left, running blind.

Light shimmers from the replica gaslights at the top of the 199 Steps. The Abbey looms right, the graveyard ahead, the steps falling away to Church Lane.

*The Steps it is.*

One pursuer behind him now.

*Where's the other guy?*

He grips the rail. Takes steps two at a time, half sliding, half tumbling, his footsteps echoing... but they're not his footsteps.

A glance over the steep drop to his left.

Ten feet below, a figure barrels down Donkey Road, adjacent to him, hoping to cut him off.

It's a race with only two possible outcomes.

He risks everything—legs on fire, boots skidding on treacherous stone.

The town rushes up at him.

Jumps.

Hits the cobbles hard, slides, almost goes down, then lurches upright.

One second lost forever. That's all it takes.

His pursuer bursts from the lane too fast, grasping for Smiler's head, but Smiler jerks back.

Momentum carries the man forward—he slams into a shopfront with a grunt, winded.

Smiler doesn't hesitate.

He sprints down the street, lungs straining but strength returning. The man who chased him down the steps is still tracking him.

He darts past the Duke of York, cuts down Tate Hill, heading for Colliers Hope—the irony lost on him.

Near the beach, he hooks onto a side path, slips into a narrow, suffocating alley, and ducks behind a bin.

'What the fuck is it with me and bins lately?' he mutters between gasps.

Rubs the wet from his face, sucking in air as quietly as possible.

A shadow jogs past the mouth of the alley thirty feet away, voice low and sharp into a phone, unintelligible.

There's only one left hunting him.

He knows a yard nearby—a holiday cottage with a high wall. Beyond it, a small patio area. If he can reach it and lie low for an hour or two, he might just get out of this alive.

Still catching his breath, he sets off up the alley at a rapid jog, heading back towards Church Street.

What he doesn't know is that the bloodhound he dodged at the bottom of the 199 Steps is also racing—down Church Street.

Like two freight trains meeting at a blind intersection, they collide, tumble, and roll across the unforgiving cobbles.

The man sits up, dazed.

Smiler props himself on an elbow, bruised, head ringing from the impact. His phone slips from his pocket. Unnoticed, it slides into the gutter.

For a moment, predator and prey stare at each other.

The man drops to his hands, trying to push himself upright.

Smiler shakes off the fog and staggers to his feet.

The man's still down, winded.

Smiler's never thrown a punch in his life—violence isn't in his wiring.

But now isn't the time for faint hearts.

He seizes the moment and drives a boot into the man's ribs; a sharp crack—air bursts from the man's lungs with a throttled groan.

He collapses face-down as Smiler takes off.

Rounding a bend, he sees his original pursuer heading straight towards him.

*'Christ! Where are they coming from?'*

A change of plan.

He zips into Arguments Yard, vaults the steps, and hurls himself at the locked wrought-iron gate at the far end.

Sliding over the top, he snags on the railings as the assassin bounds after him, gun in hand. The man slows, watching his quarry—trapped like a rabbit in a snare.

Smiler wriggles and squirms. One vertical bar has pierced his leather coat, wedging into the shoulder piece.

He yanks his left arm free and dangles for a second before his right arm slips from the trapped sleeve.

Crashes to the ground.

A shick-shack of the pistol—one clean motion, one breath from death.

Smiler twists around.

Behind him, the inky, fog-smeared outline of the quay, and beyond it the silent swell of the harbour.

His worst nightmare—*until now!*

He bolts as the pistol cracks, bullets cleaving the night in two.

Reaches the edge of the quay.

Swallows the fear.

Arms speared above his head.

He dives into the cold, black water.

# 14

Shivering like a daffodil in a spring hailstorm, he knocks again—harder this time. A light flickers in the window, followed by grumbling and cursing.

'Who the fuck is it?'

'It's me—Smiler.'

'For fuck's sake. Password?'

'Captain Cook.'

A bolt snaps back, a lock turns, and the door inches open. Smiler rushes through, teeth chattering.

Blakey, perturbed by his appearance, quickly locks the door and leads the lad into the kitchen.

'Christ almighty, Smiler—you're soaked,' he says, flicking on the kettle. 'What happened?'

Smiler can't even speak. His body, still in shock, is in pure survival mode.

Blakey fetches a blanket and drapes it over his shoulders, then makes a cup of packet soup and hands it to him.

'Get this down you.'

'Th... tha... thanks.'

Blakey studiously rolls a spliff as he eyes his young lodger.

'You're getting in too deep, Smiler. First the filth roll up here, now this. You need to reassess. Dealing a bit of weed now and then is one thing, but you've ratcheted it right up. You're moshing with the big boys now. Want my advice? Go straight. Get a job. Leave this life behind you. Okay, not as lucrative, I get that—but, jeez, man, you'll sleep a lot easier at night.'

Smiler sips the tomato soup and shakes his head, staring at the cracked linoleum flooring.

'Bit late for that,' he murmurs.

Blakey chuckles, lights the joint, takes a long drag, and exhales a greyish plume.

'It's never too late.'

'It is this time, Blakey. It's bad. Really bad.'

Blakey nods, not really understanding. 'So how come you're soaking wet?'

'Dived into the harbour.'

He stiffens. 'Are you fucking mental?'

'No choice when someone's pointing a gun at you.'

Blakey's unease grows despite the weed taking hold.

'A gun? Whoa—that's heavy shit, man.'

Smiler finishes the soup and wipes his mouth on a damp sleeve.

'You know Typhoon, don't you?' he asks, raising his head but not making eye contact.

'Yeah, course I do. Was it him after you? No one double-crosses Typhoon. You should know that. You need to keep guys like that sweet. They're not normal—faulty synapses in their brains. Violence is second nature to them.'

Smiler blinks. 'No. It wasn't Typhoon.'

'Who then?'

'Not sure. Foreign. Typhoon's dead,' he adds, finally meeting Blakey's gaze.

Blakey lowers the joint. 'Dead... how?'

Unconsciously, Smiler strokes his throat.

'They cut his fucking head off.'

---

Blakey stumbles down the stairs with a suitcase, a stray sock snagged between two zippers.

Smiler is still sitting on a stool in the kitchen, shivering—though not as violently now.

'Where are you going?' he asks, having never seen Blakey move with such purpose before.

Blakey grabs his jacket. 'I'm out of here. I'll go stay with my brother in Malton until this all blows over—whenever that may be.'

Smiler slips from the stool. 'What are you talking about? You're not in danger, Blakey. Those guys don't know who I am, and they certainly don't know where I live. No one else was at Typhoon's gaff tonight, so no one knows I was there.'

Blakey lights a regular smoke, suddenly averse to the weed.

'Grow up, Smiler. Someone will have seen you. Anyway, that mob sounds hardcore—and you were a witness. What do you think they're gonna do—laugh it off? They shot at you twice. They want you dead, and I ain't gonna be around when they come looking.'

'I'll go to the police tomorrow. They'll offer me protection.'

Blakey snorts. 'Ha! Right on, man.'

'What's that supposed to mean?'

He pulls the smoke from his lips. 'You trust the filth? What if they decide to fit you up for the murder?'

'Don't talk daft.'

'Or what if this gang's already in with the police? You'll walk in there like a lamb to the slaughter.' He saunters over and rests a hand on Smiler's shoulder, the way an older brother might. 'Take my advice—trust no one, especially those you think you can trust. You're on your own now. Good luck, lad. You'll need it. Watch your back.'

—◦—

Smiler makes his way upstairs and into the tiny bathroom.

After warming up in the shower for twenty minutes, he dries himself in front of the mirror, replaying the grisly events in his mind. He's exhausted and desperately needs sleep. Tenderly, he traces a fingertip over the angry graze around his ribs, the bruises on his arms and legs, the scratches on his thigh from the barbed wire.

'What was all that about? If only I could turn back the clock by twenty-four hours,' he murmurs.

Crouching, he prises a panel from the side of the bath, sticks an arm inside, and drags out a duffel bag, then replaces the panel.

In the bedroom he collapses onto the bed, drags the covers over himself, flicks off the lamp, and buries his face deep in the pillow as sleep beckons him with open arms.

As his eyes clamp shut, a thought jolts him awake—he hasn't put his phone on charge.

Then remembers.

He lost it somewhere.

*In the toilet at Typhoon's gaff? Or when I was running? Or maybe it's at the bottom of the harbour? Doesn't matter now. Either way, it's gone. First job tomorrow—buy a new phone.*

<h1 style="text-align:center">15</h1>

## Saturday Morning – 1:18 am

Saltwater laps against the hull of the boat, moored in the entrails of the harbour. The tide is in stasis, neither ebbing nor flowing. Nothing stirs in town; even the fog has surrendered to inertia and simply hovers.

In the galley, deep in the bowels of the boat, a single lightbulb sways back and forth. The air smacks of diesel, salt air, and the more stringent aroma of fresh mackerel fillets that crackle in a blackened pan.

Arben turns the fish in his casual manner, humming contentedly, belly rumbling.

*Murder sharpens his appetite.*

Dritan Zefi refills the vodka glasses of his crew seated around the cramped table, then raises his glass.

'Fati ndihmon trimat,' he declares as they clink. 'To success!'

His salutation is met with a chorus of approval and cheers as the men neck their vodka in one hit.

The skipper, Francois Langlois, a wiser head on older shoulders, is the only one less than happy with the start of the new operation. He stands aloof, arms folded, leaning against the bulkhead beside the steps that lead to the deck.

Dritan refills the vodka glasses, noticing his French colleague's reluctance to join in the celebration.

'Francois, why the glum face?'

'You really want to know?' he replies.

'Of course, Francois. You are among friends. Speak freely.' Dritan sniggers and adds something in Albanian to his cronies, who laugh along with him.

'And that's another thing,' Francois snaps, stiffening. 'I don't speak Albanian. You don't speak French. From now on, we all speak English when together.'

Dritan's smile slides off his face as he raises an eyebrow.

'Very well. Now, get it off your chest.'

Francois stands tall. 'Decapitating the local drug lord was reckless and unnecessary. A great way to bring attention to ourselves. We were supposed to be discreet.'

Dritan shrugs. 'Don't worry—Arben cleaned up the mess and disposed of the body. The police don't even know we're in town. We have false identities. Anyway, I disagree with you. Discreet to the authorities—yes. To the other gangs—no. Tonight we sent a message to every dealer—we're in charge now. Decapitation instils dread and fear. Yes, messy, but it's saved us many problems down the line. I am not new to this. Trust me. I know what I'm doing.'

The fish sizzles and spits as Arben flips it with a fork, unconcerned.

Francois rubs his cheek, agitated. 'And what about this youth who saw you?'

Dritan shrugs, casual, cool. 'Maybe he saw us kill Typhoon—maybe he didn't.'

'And what if he's already gone to the police?'

Dritan sniffs. 'No. He was doing deal. We found cash and drugs on the counter. He operates outside the law. He will not go to police. Anyway, the boy will not be a problem for much longer.'

'And why's that?'

Dritan glances at his brother, Stefan, hunched over a laptop. A blue glow flickers across his face as his fingers tap at the keyboard.

Francois follows his gaze. 'What?'

'Stefan has many talents.'

Francois frowns. 'And?'

Dritan offers his small, icy smile—the one that only ever reaches his lips—never his eyes.

'Stefan, how's it going?' he asks.

Stefan looks up. 'Ten, fifteen minutes—done,' he mutters, eyes already back on the screen.

Francois frowns. 'What will be done?'

Dritan pours another measure, his tone smooth as glass.

'Very soon, we'll know every single thing about the boy's life—his friends, his contacts, his routes, bank accounts, his favourite porn site and what his sexual fantasies are.'

'How?'

Without raising his head, Stefan grabs something at the side of the laptop and holds it aloft.

'This.'

Francois stares at the object. 'And what good is that to us?'

'His phone will tell us where he lives.'

## 16

The empty streets hold their secrets close. The orange blur from lampposts adds a melancholy hue to the night. No hustle or bustle now. No screeching gulls. No whirring and beeping from amusement arcades. Just a deathly quiet—broken only by the repetitive thump of footsteps slapping damp bitumen.

The three men may as well be invisible. With CCTV on every shop and council building, invisibility belongs to an era that seems so long ago now.

But with hoodies up and faces down, they are undetectable.

Even so, they avoid the main thoroughfares of Whitby, taking a convoluted path through yards and alleys as narrow as a lizard's spine.

There is no talking. No banter. They have orders. They are the foot soldiers—automatons—unquestioning, unfeeling. Reasoning is unnecessary. Empathy and sympathy, is a foreign shore on a distant land never visited.

Stefan touches the inside of his pocket, feeling the cold barrel of the gun. Arben's left arm remains rigid, gripping the handle of the machete sheathed beneath his jacket. And Mika, with hands the size of hams, carries—without thinking—his lethal weapons of choice, but also his switchblade for the quick, silent kill. His ribs ache from the kick he received earlier.

He has a short fuse but a long memory.

The night fog swallows them up, as if the town itself wants to hide its dirty laundry.

———<o>———

Smiler wakes with a start as his heart reacts to another dose of adrenaline. He shoots up in bed, sweaty but cold. Glances at the clock—3:43 am.

For a moment he senses relief until his mind clears, and the images return. Typhoon's head rolling onto the floor. Eyes staring at him. Hitting the black saltwater in the harbour and wondering if he'd ever surface.

Thirst bites at his throat. He reaches out, grabs a tepid glass of water from his desk, and takes a gulp.

Calms.

They didn't get a good look at him. It was dark. They seemed as panicked as he was upon his discovery. The only one who *may* have clocked him was the guy he crashed into on Church Street, the one he kicked. But it was dark. He can't really remember what the man looked like.

Taking a deep breath, he surrenders to the warm, soft bed, safe for now.

Another four hours' sleep and he'll feel better. Clarity will return. He'll figure something out. But the first job is to definitely get a phone. Without one, he's a nobody, hamstrung, useless.

◆

The trio stalk along Baxtergate and turn left into Loggerheads Yard. They pause and gaze into the gloom of the black alley.

Stefan nods imperceptibly, and they continue, slower, cautiously.

Halfway along, Stefan's gaze rises to the sign on the brick wall—Mackridges Yard. His head swivels towards the green door at the end of the courtyard.

Raises a finger to his lips and removes a small leather pouch from his pocket. An ancient cast-iron drainpipe slides up the wall, passing a balcony. A possible access point if he can't pick the lock.

Stefan hunches close to the door, a micro torch gripped between teeth. A brief smile as he recognises the familiar lock. He unfolds the leather pouch to reveal a tension wrench and a half-diamond pick—his preferred tools for cheap Yale locks. He inserts the wrench, applying gentle pressure while teasing the pins one by one. A faint metallic click, and the latch gives. He glances once at the others, then pushes the door open.

Someone forgot to slide the bolt across.

Smiler tosses and turns, fighting with the blankets. Sits up in a huff. His body is exhausted, but his mind won't stop. Round and round and around, a recurring dream about phones. Of everything he's been through, why is his mind focused on a stupid, bloody mobile phone?

He beats his pillow up and slumps back down, rolling onto his side in the foetal position.

With all the other rooms checked, the men stand on the landing of the second floor and stare up at the staircase leading to the loft. Arben tightens his grip on the machete. Mika flexes his fingers back and forth, pulls out his switchblade. Stefan places one foot on the bottom stair. A creak. He edges his foot to the side and presses down. Nothing.

He motions with a hand—keep left. The other men nod.

Smiler's eyes flicker open.

*What was that? I know that sound. The creak of the bottom step.*

A deep sigh.

*Stop it. You're being paranoid. Go to sleep.*

⸻◈⸻

The handle twists. Three shadows morph into the room like apparitions. The only light, a blue haze from a digital clock on the desk. Adjacent to it... a bed. Covers draped over a form huddled up, dead to the world.

Stefan motions to Arben, pulling a finger across his throat.

Arben's grin goes unseen as he steps forward.

He brings the machete down with lightning speed, aiming just below the head. Mika steps forward, yanks the covers back and stabs repeatedly like a crazed maniac, out of control, eyes popping with anger, spittle flying from his mouth. His rage masks a soft sound from outside.

⸻◈⸻

Smiler drops from the drainpipe and slinks to the side of the buildings. With the duffel bag slung over his shoulder, he steals along in the shadows, heart thumping against his breastbone. He has no idea where he's going. Certainly nowhere familiar. If they did find his phone and managed to unlock it, they'll know all his usual haunts thanks to GPS tracking.

At this moment, his only purpose is to put as much distance between himself and the killers as possible.

# 17

## Saturday 9:30 am

Sweat peels from his forehead and creates a tiny rivulet that rolls down his nose. It forms a blob, which eventually succumbs to gravity and drips onto the towel between his legs. He takes a deep breath, hot humid air scorching his lungs.

'Right, that's enough for me,' Zac says to the large, fleshy man seated on wooden slats next to him in the sauna.

'Lightweight,' Frank replies. 'You've only managed twenty minutes.'

'Aye, about ten minutes too long.' His head swims momentarily from the heat. Through the glass door, he can see the pool—a blur of turquoise and echoing shrieks. Somewhere in the chaos are his two boys, Sammy and Tom. 'Some of us have responsibilities.'

'What's on for the rest of the day?'

Zac rubs his face with the damp towel. 'I'll take the lads for a bite to eat, then I have to buy Sammy a new pair of school shoes.'

'I thought you did that a few months back, or is my memory playing up?'

'No, you're right. He's going through a growth spurt. Costing me a bloody fortune. And what about you?'

Frank slumps forward, grimacing with the humidity.

'Got the day *and* the week to myself. Meera's visiting her sister. Thought I'd head back to Whitby, have a wander around town and get myself something nice to eat for tea.'

Zac grins. 'Watermelon, feta, and Kalamata olive salad with chilli-lime dressing?'

Frank eyeballs him wearily. 'I was thinking more along the lines of pork pie and mushy peas with mint sauce. Maybe get myself a Mr Kipling's golden syrup sponge pudding for after.'

'Really? What a surprise. I don't know how you do it, living life on the wild side.'

'While the cat's away,' Frank states with a grin.

'I suppose. Right, I'll see you Monday. Take it easy, Frank.'

'Aye, you too, son.'

The cool air hits him as he steps from the sauna and scans the overcrowded wave pool for his sons. He spots Tom and holds his hand up, fingers splayed, then mouths the words—*five minutes*.

As he plods towards the changing rooms, he stops and gazes out of the window at Scarborough Castle high up on the hill in the distance before his eyes drift to the outdoor infinity pool. A familiar figure effortlessly glides through the water, steam rising into the chilly air.

'Cleavage?' he mutters to himself.

The only other places he's seen his informant are in the pub, at the bookies, or queuing at a fish and chip shop. The sight of him in a swimming pool, exercising, seems somewhat... fucked up. Like an elephant performing the tango.

He studies him for a moment, impressed by his elegance in the water. On dry land, he has all the grace of a corpse with a hangover.

———◆———

Zac's patience is disappearing quicker than a politician's promise after election night.

'What's wrong with them?' he snaps as Sammy pulls a face resembling a plate of congealed scrambled eggs.

'They're dead, dad.'

'Of course they're dead. They're a pair of bloody shoes!'

'Not funny. They're so mid. I can't wear these. I'll get rinsed at school.'

The shop assistant pulls an apologetic smile at Zac. 'I think he means they're not cool. He'll get teased,' she explains.

Sammy wrinkles his nose as he stands in front of the full-length mirror.

'And they're too big. I look like Sideshow Bob.'

'That's a character from *The Simpsons* with ridiculously large feet,' the woman adds.

'Yes, I know who Sideshow Bob is,' Zac replies through gritted teeth. He bends down and jabs his thumb into the toe of the leather. 'Plenty of space to grow into. I don't want to be back here in a few months forking out for another pair.'

Sammy is still staring disapprovingly at the footwear. 'And they're Clarks. That's what the donuts wear. Why can't I get a pair of Doc Martens?'

'Because they cost fifty quid more.'

The younger brother, Tom, sniggers. 'You look proper moist in them.'

Sammy punches him on the shoulder. 'Shut up, you neek.'

'Dad, he hit me.'

The assistant is not helping Zac's cause.

'Clarks is a solid brand, but if you want something that will last a couple of years, then Doc Martens are worth paying a little extra for. They're a good investment.'

Zac growls and glares at her. 'Investments earn money. I can't see a pair of Docs paying for my retirement.'

'Once they're broken in, they're more forgiving. It's the air-cushioned sole. They allow the leather to stretch, which should accommodate any foot growth. And of course, if he does outgrow them, they'll still be in good condition for your younger boy in a year or two. They never go out of fashion.'

'Come on, dad. Please,' Sammy begs, sensing a breach in the dam wall.

'Okay, okay! Let him try on the bloody Doc Martens. I'm losing the will to live.'

Sammy punches the air. 'Yeees!'

'You'll still look like a cringe-bag whatever shoes you wear,' Tom notes, for which he receives another thump on the shoulder. 'Dad, he hit me again.'

'Well, hit him back harder and he'll soon stop,' Zac says as he wanders away, cursing the fact that his wife is working a weekend shift. He saunters past the women's footwear as the bickering of his boys fades. 'Christ, what am I going to do with them for the rest of the day and tomorrow?' he mutters to himself.

'No, no. I'll try the next size up.'

Zac pricks his ears upon hearing the voice. He pokes his head around the corner and spots Cleavage sitting on a chair with an array of wellington boots strewn around him as a frazzled-looking man heads into the stockroom.

'Cleavage?'

Cleavage does a double take as he pulls a boot off his foot.

'Ah, Zac. What are you doing here?'

Zac takes a cursory glance around the store at the assorted boots and shoes.

'I thought I'd nip in for a plate of stew. What the fuck do you think I'm doing in a shoe shop?'

'Snarky,' he replies, tossing the green welly to one side.

Zac sidles up to him. 'Saw you in the pool earlier. I have to say I was surprised.'

'What do you mean?'

'The way you moved through the water with such ease.'

Cleavage chuckles. 'Like a dolphin?'

'Hmm... nah. More like a walrus, but impressive nonetheless. Wouldn't have taken you for a swimmer.'

'Loved the water ever since I was a kid. It's my relaxation and recuperation time. I could stay in there for hours. All my worries just disappear.'

'Is that right?'

'I once swam the English Channel.'

'No! Get out of here!'

'It's true. About ten years ago. For charity. Raised ten grand for Blood Cancer UK.'

'Well, well, well. Who'd have thought?'

The assistant returns, carrying an oversized pair of green wellington boots.

'This is the largest size we have, sir.'

'What size are they?'

'Fifteen. If you want larger, I suggest you try a specialist shop.'

'Size fifteen,' Zac snorts. 'Sasquatch is alive and well and living in North Yorkshire.'

Cleavage takes the boot and slips it on. 'That's better. I normally take a size thirteen, but being on my feet on the trawlers all day, my feet swell—and then there are the woolly socks. I need room for my feet to expand.' He hobbles back and forth, nodding approvingly. 'Yep, perfect. I'll take these.'

'Very good, sir. I'll get them bagged for you.'

As the assistant disappears, Zac takes a furtive look around. He pulls his wallet from his pocket and slides out a twenty-pound note.

'Here you go. That's for the horse racing tip you gave me the other day.'

Cleavage is bemused. 'What horse racing... oh, yeah. Smiler. No problem. Thanks,' he says, taking the money. 'I didn't hear the results. Get a win, did you?'

'Oh, yes. We had a win.'

'That's good to know.'

The assistant returns and begins collecting the discarded wellingtons from the floor.

'You working at the moment?' Zac asks.

'Aye. One of the busiest times of the year. I've just signed up with a new crew.'

'Why's that?'

'Better money. Cash in hand. Don't tell anyone, like. Haven't started yet. It's a bigger boat. The Whitby Rose. Mixed crew, but they need a couple of local lads for their knowledge.'

Zac frowns. 'The Whitby Rose? Haven't heard that name before. Is it a new trawler?'

Cleavage chuckles. 'New to these parts.'

The female shop assistant from earlier rushes around the corner.

'Ahem, you may like to supervise your children, sir.'

'Why?'

'They're rolling around on the floor wrestling with each other.'

18

Foxtrot tugs at the lead, nose to the ground, tail swishing in wide arcs as gulls wheel overhead and the wind from the North Sea scours the clifftop. Frank tucks his chin into the collar of his coat, eyes narrowed against the salt spray. September light slants weakly across the bay, painting the rooftops in dull gold.

This stretch of the West Cliff is usually quieter than the rest of the town—dog walkers, a few joggers, pensioners on the benches—but today there's a racket going on.

Ahead, near the boarded-up lift entrance, a small crowd has gathered. People with phones raised, placards reading "SAVE OUR LIFT", a local camera crew, and someone balancing on a plastic crate giving a speech. The breeze carries the man's voice in bursts—grand, blustering Yorkshire tones about heritage, community, and Whitby's proud past.

Foxtrot growls low in his throat. Frank shortens the lead and strolls closer. He recognises the speaker at once: George Sykes—known locally as King George. Owner of King George Seafood, purveyor of half the scallops, lobster, crabs, and fish that come through the harbour entrance. Plus a lot of other business interests. Flash suits, flash cars, big mouth, and a reputation for buying his way into the town's good books.

He stands tall and broad-shouldered, camel-hair coat open to reveal a waistcoat the colour of English mustard, face ruddy from drink or self-satisfaction—or possibly both. Next to him, a woman in her thirties stands by his side: long dark hair, designer sunglasses, a smile like it's been painted on.

'...and so,' Sykes booms, his voice bouncing off the railings and over the cliff edge, 'it gives me great pleasure to donate this cheque for one hundred thousand pounds to the campaign to keep the Whitby West Cliff Lift operational!'

He holds up an oversized cheque, the kind you see on daytime telly when someone has won a lottery.

'I urge everyone who lives here in Whitby—and the millions who've visited our beloved town over the years—to rally behind this cause. For over a century, this lift has given access to the beach for the elderly, the disabled, and young mothers with prams. We cannot, ladies and gentlemen, stand idly by and see it condemned! I urge you all to sign the petition.'

The small crowd erupts—cheers, applause, phones aloft. A few local councillors nod approvingly, sensing a good photo op. Sykes basks in the glory, turning slightly so the cameras catch his best side. Frank stops at the edge of the group, gripping a plastic carrier bag containing a pork pie and a tin of mushy peas, Foxtrot sitting obediently at his heel, head cocked.

Reporters move in with microphones, asking about his generosity, the importance of civic duty. Sykes eats it up, puffing out his chest. When the questions end, he takes the woman's arm and begins working through the crowd, shaking hands, slapping backs, handing out winks like confetti.

'Good on you, George!' someone shouts.

'A true Whitby man!' cries another.

'Long live the King!'

The pair reach the road where a silver Rolls Royce idles at the kerb, polished to a mirror finish. The chauffeur—a tall man in a uniform with a peaked cap—steps forward and opens the rear door.

Before climbing in, Sykes produces a cigar thick as a child's wrist, pulls out a set of clippers, snips the end off. He flicks a gold lighter, the flame trembling in the breeze. The smell of burning tobacco drifts towards Frank, sharp and sweet.

Sykes exhales a ribbon of smoke, surveying the crowd like a monarch inspecting his subjects. His eyes flick to the edge—to the man with the dog. Recognition flashes, followed by the faintest smirk.

Frank doesn't move. He gives the lead a little slack, the dog's collar jingling. Foxtrot's ears prick forward. The two men lock eyes—Sykes immaculate in his fawn Crombie and Italian designer brogues, Frank in his signature black Chesterfield coat. Like two old-time British gangsters from the 70s sizing each other up.

Both know there's more behind the giant cheque than civic pride.

Sykes lowers the cigar, the ember glowing orange in the chill wind.

He mutters something to the woman beside him—too quiet to catch. She laughs, a brittle sound, then slips into the back seat of the Roller, the door closing with a soft, expensive clunk.

Frank moves forward. 'George.'

The greeting is flat. No malice. No love.

George cracks a welcoming beam. 'Frank bloody Finnegan! Thought it was you. Been a while,' he declares, pulling the cigar from his mouth and holding out the hand of friendship.

Frank gives it a dismissive glance, as if looking at a shitty stick, but doesn't reciprocate.

George Sykes is a man who not only knows how to take plaudits but how to glide past a snub.

It comes with the territory.

Frank nods towards the closed lift and the empty space where, moments ago, a few raucous diehards had gathered.

'Throwing yourself behind another cause, I see.'

George rocks back, takes another suck of his cigar. 'You know me, Frank. I like to do my bit for the community.'

'Aye. Good photo op. Get your ugly mug in the local rag and plastered all over social media.'

George looks out to sea, adopting a slightly hurt expression.

'You've always been the same, Frank. Always had it in for me—even when we were at school together. I've often wondered over the years—why. The only thing I can think of is that I once dated Meera... before you stole her from me. How is she, by the way?'

'Fine.'

'Good to hear. And how are you enjoying retirement?'

'I'm not retired. But you already know that, don't you?'

George performs his well-rehearsed false laugh. 'Okay, you got me. Yes, I did.' He becomes serious. 'If you'd taken my offer of becoming head of security thirty years ago, you'd be a rich man by now.' He taps ash from his cigar. 'What are you on these days? Sixty-five, seventy grand a year? You could've earned double that with me, plus perks.'

'It's not about the money.'

'It's always about the money, Frank.' He chuckles and fixes his gaze back on Frank. 'You know, I think your resentment *actually* stems from the time I gave you a good hiding in the schoolyard when we were about what—twelve?'

'Your memory's playing tricks on you, George. It was me giving you a good belting—until your three mates jumped in to back you up. Even then, I walked away with fewer bruises.' He takes a step closer, nose-to-nose. 'That's the thing with bullies. All the bravado and bullshit—it's just a front. Underneath is a scared little boy. Same as the thugs you see walking the streets today—shaved heads, tattoos up their necks, strutting around. What they're projecting is menace: stay away, don't mess with me. But really, deep down, they're more scared than anyone.'

'Doesn't make them any less dangerous though, does it?'

'True. And that's why I'm still working. Taking scum off the streets... or out of the boardroom. No difference. Bullies exist in every walk of life. Shaved head, or camel-hair coats. Same shit—different bucket.'

Sykes stares, eyes narrowed to slits.

The young woman pokes her head out of the Roller.

'Dad, come on! We've got a meeting with—' she hesitates, glancing at Frank, '—in five minutes.'

George Sykes drops his cigar onto the tarmac and snuffs it out with a roll of his shoe.

'That's my daughter—Clarissa. She's my PA. Takes after her mother, my first wife. A ball-buster. I'd be lost without her.' He steps forward and pulls open the car door. 'By the way, when you *do* eventually retire, look me up. I'm always after a good nightwatchman for my seafood distribution depot. Give my best to Meera. See you around, Frank.'

'Aye. You just might, George. You just might,' he murmurs as the car sedately drives away.

Foxtrot lets out a whine, and gazes up at his master.

Frank smiles down at the dog. 'Yep, spot on, Foxtrot. He is a wanker.'

# 19

## Sunday

The morning settles over Whitby like an old grey coat—soft, frayed at the edges, familiar. The harbour is half-asleep beneath the overcast sky. A light drizzle stipples the water as boats shimmer faintly in the sullen light. Gulls squawk and bicker over the empty fish crates stacked by the quay. Somewhere down by the fish market, a shutter bangs loose in the wind. The tide is half in, nudging gently at the stone pilings, as if testing the town's resilience. A billboard tied to a railing has a hastily written scrawl across it—**HIRING**.

The Whitby Rose rocks like a baby's cradle, moored against the dock wall, her hull scuffed and streaked with salt, name faded but still proud. On deck, the skipper Francois Langlois, moves with the easy grace of habit. Checks the winches, tests the hydraulics, and leans over the gunwale to inspect the nets where they hang drying in loose folds. Every few minutes he stops to make a note in the small ledger he keeps tucked in the pocket of his bright yellow waterproof jacket.

There's no glamour in this life—just repetitive, hard graft, the stench of diesel and fish, and the long wait between tides—but it's all he's ever known. And there is reward, sometimes. When he steers into deep water and the sun breaks through at dawn, exploding over gun-metal sea with a golden dazzle so bright it steals his breath away, like God pulled the curtains aside to take a peep at his creation. Or the occasions when a pod of humpbacks breaches nearby, their white fins rising like ancient monoliths to kiss the sky. The slow rhythm of the sea, those great rolling swells that come with a deep low-pressure—higher than a double-decker bus—reminds him he's nothing but a puny, inconsequential creature in the vast scheme of things. To know you are not important, less than a speck in the universe, brings a strange kind of liberation. A calm that seeps right through you. Nothing matters—not really.

When the end comes, he hopes it's at sea. Swept overboard in a raging storm. Or a sudden heart attack—gone before he hits the water. That would be a good death. Better than wasting away in a hospital bed, breathing the stench of disinfectant, surrounded by people in white coats who couldn't care less. And certainly better than being buried deep in cold, dead earth, or set alight in a gas-fired furnace in some chintzy crematorium.

And of course, there is another reward—the camaraderie of a good crew. Brothers in arms. A tight unit.

Like soldiers in battle. Only they can know the dangers and privations they endure. Outsiders could never understand.

He pauses, glancing across at Dritan and Stefan as they haul a crate along the deck, laughing and joking.

There'll be no camaraderie aboard this boat, though. Most of the crew are Dritan's men: cold, surly, humourless unless they're half-sozzled on vodka and jabbering in their own tongue.

He eyes the brothers coldly as they light cigarettes and lean against the railings. A peculiar feeling wriggles in his gut, deep down.

He doesn't trust Dritan. Doesn't trust any of them.

Reckless, cocksure—young men who think they're invincible. But he has a job to do. His biggest payday. Dangerous—true. But when it's finished, he's out. Enough to buy a cottage on the coast of Normandy and a small cabin boat. Along with his modest savings, it will see him through what's left of his years. That will do.

'Oi, pal. You still hiring?'

The gruff Scottish voice slices through Francois's thoughts. He turns slowly to the man on the quayside.

'Pardon, monsieur?'

'A said, you still looking for crew?'

Francois studies him.

Medium height. Stocky. Greasy, matted hair curling at the edges. A grey face with a red nose and heavy jowls. Dishevelled clothes buried beneath a filthy overcoat.

Unwashed. Unkempt. Unwholesome. And definitely unwelcome.

Obviously a drifter.

Despite his own shady dealings, Francois is at heart a decent man. He tries to treat people with respect, whatever their lot. He'll send this one on his way politely—let him keep what dignity he has left.

'Yes, we're still hiring,' he says. 'We need one more hand. You've worked trawlers before?'

'Oh aye, right enough. Out of Fraserburgh mostly—some time in Peterhead when the quotas shifted.'

'Deck or engine?'

'Deck. Gutting, hauling, mending nets, whatever needed doing.'

'What were you fishing for up there?'

'Whitefish mostly—cod, haddock, whiting. Bit o' monk and ling when the grounds were right. Came down south in summer and autumn. Dogger Bank, Forties, Viking.'

'Can you splice rope? Mend a torn net?'

'Could do it blindfolded, pal. Even skippered a boat once or twice when the boss had one too many snifters of whisky, if you know what I mean,' he adds with a cackle.

'How old are you?'

'Fifty-four.'

'You look older.'

The man snorts. 'Cheers, pal. I had two milk rounds as a lad. That would explain it.'

Francois can't help but grin. The man's got spirit, at least. 'Sorry, but you don't look fit enough. We are sometimes away four, five days or more. We need strong, younger men. Maybe try one of the lobster boats.'

'Come on, pal. Give me a chance. I'm desperate.'

Francois sighs. 'Exactly. And desperate men on a boat are never a good mix. Sorry, but it's no.'

The Scotsman's shoulders sag as he turns to go.

'Wait,' Dritan calls out. He steps forward, voice sharp with authority. 'Hire him.'

Francois blinks. 'What?'

'You heard.'

Francois grips his arm, steering him aside. Dritan jerks free with a scowl.

'This man's totally unsuitable,' Francois says quietly. 'He's a tramp—a derelict—and he reeks of drink. And he's not local. I want men who know these waters.'

'You already have one—Cleavage. One is enough. This man has experience of Dogger. He will do. Now we have our crew.'

'I'm the skipper,' Francois snaps. 'I pick who sails.'

Dritan fixes him with that cold, black stare. 'There are many cogs that turn the wheel, Francois. You are just one small cog. I am the wheel.'

He turns back to the stranger on the quay.

'What is your name?'

'Danny. Danny—'

Dritan cuts him off and holds a hand up. 'No need for last names, Danny. We sail Tuesday night, at high tide—eight o'clock—be one hour earlier, yes?'

Danny nods. 'Got yer. Tuesday, seven o'clock.'

'One hundred fifty a day. Cash. If you perform well and we take you on again, then you get a cut of the catch.'

The man's face lights up. 'Aye, too right—cheers, pal.' Then a pause. 'I... I don't have any gear. Waterproofs.'

'Don't worry,' Dritan says. 'We have spares. We'll fit you out.' He crouches slightly, eyes narrowing. 'We know each other, yes?'

'Do we?'

'I gave you money the other night. Don't you remember?'

The tramp's eyes shift left and right before he forces a laugh. 'Oh, aye. That's right. Much appreciated it was, too.'

Dritan studies him a moment longer, then nods. 'Hmm. Okay. See you Tuesday, Danny.'

The man hesitates, awkward. 'I don't suppose you could stretch to a bit in advance, could ye?'

Dritan grins and pulls out his wallet. Slides out two fifty-pound notes. He holds them out, then draws them back before the man can snatch them. His voice drops to a whisper.

'Trust is a priceless crystal vase—once shattered, it can never be repaired. Do we understand each other, Danny?'

The man nods quickly. 'Oh, aye. Loud and clear.'

Dritan hands over the notes. 'Go. Get digs, get clean, eat something. You'll need your strength.'

'Aye, will do.'

'And if you turn up drunk, or with drink on you, you don't step aboard. Understood?'

'Righto, got it, pal.'

Dritan smiles thinly. 'Good. Don't let me down, my friend.'

'No chance, pal. You can count on me. By the way—what's your name?'

'Dritan.'

'Good on yer, Dritan. Yer a real champion.'

He tucks the money into his coat and shuffles off along the quay.

Francois Langlois watches him go, uneasy.

'Ten minutes from now he'll be blind drunk in some alleyway, swigging from a bottle of cheap whisky,' he growls.

Dritan chuckles, slapping a hand on his shoulder. 'The problem with you, Francois, is that you have no faith in humanity. Give a man a break and he'll be loyal for life.'

He pauses, watching the latest and last crew member shuffle into the drizzle, coat hunched, head low. His smile hardens.

'Either that, or he'll kill you with a knife in the back when you least expect it.'

# 20

Frank pulls his collar up against the biting wind that cartwheels down Church Street straight off the sea. He's regretting his decision to spread his wings and be more adventurous, if you can call visiting a bookshop for an author event on a Sunday afternoon, adventurous.

But the moment he steps inside the shop, the doubt evaporates.

Warmth. Soft light. The murmur of gentle chatter from the modest crowd gathered between the shelves. And another smell—one that sits beneath the coffee and damp coats.

An elixir. Freshly printed books.

Ink, paper, glue...whatever alchemy it is, it hits him straight in the chest and transports him back to his childhood.

Those physical Christmas book vouchers from aunts and uncles, grandparents. His mam escorting him on a special day trip to York a few weeks later. In a department store, she'd drift towards the clothes bargains while he made a beeline for the book section. Racks of shiny new titles, covers that promised entire worlds. And although enticed by the vivid designs, what he really loved was the thought of what waited inside. To step into someone else's mind—to see, hear, taste, and feel what they once imagined alone at a desk is a kind of magic.

Quantum physicists can argue all they like about time travel being impossible. For Frank as a boy, a book *was* time travel. It transported him to a different world. A world better or worse than his. But always, *always* more exciting.

Opening one meant stepping back to the moment the author hammered the keys on a typewriter, or scribbled the first draft into a tatty notebook by candlelight. It meant crossing a boundary into someone else's life... for a while—and emerging changed, even if only a little.

Adventures with villains and heroes; ghosts, ghouls, and werewolves. Navigating the Amazon or the Nile in a battered canoe with your best friend. Flying a Spitfire with a Messerschmitt on your tail, or firing a machine gun from the cover of a dense Norwegian pine forest. Stepping into a wardrobe and pushing through a row of fur coats, only to feel snow underfoot and realising it opens into a land of lions, wolves, centaurs, and gryphons. Magical places so far removed from the humdrum of his normal existence.

All of it flickers through his mind in a few seconds of pure, uncomplicated bliss.

If time travel were possible, he'd go back to that day in York with his mam, and lose himself for a perfect hour in the book aisles, the world on pause, his future not yet written.

And yet, if his working life were condensed into a single book, maybe a novella, he's lived many of those adventures—heroes and villains, monsters and angels, betrayal and loyalty, and some events he still can't quite explain.

Funny, really. As a boy, he wanted to escape into stories. And yet, somewhere along the line, he ended up living one.

'Tea, coffee, bottled water, sir. Also, a small selection of cakes and biscuits.'

His reverie breaks. A young woman stands in front of him, offering a leaflet promoting the author and his new book, then gestures towards a table at the back of the room where the refreshments are laid out.

'Ah, thank you,' he says.

He heads straight for the table—an inviting spread of glass coffee carafes on hotplates and pure white china teapots steaming gently. Plates of biscuits sit in neat rows: Bourbons, chocolate digestives, Garibaldi.

He pours strong black tea into an elegant cup and saucer, adds a drop of milk, one sugar... then sees it.

To one side, a large platter of fruitcake, cut thick, the slices packed with glossy cherries and plump raisins. Beside it, a plate piled high with crumbly Wensleydale cheese—pale, cool, slightly damp at the edges where it's just been cut.

*No contest.*

He takes a slice of cake and a generous slab of cheese, presses them together, and bites. Sweet, dense fruit gives way to the sharp, creamy crumble.

*It's perfect.*

Maybe *not* quite as good as sex, but pretty damn close. Then again, that depends on the quality of your sex life. He closes his eyes for half a second, then washes it down with a hot, clean sip of tea.

'Hello, stranger.'

He spins around and nearly chokes. 'Hellfire, Prisha! What are you doing here?'

She tops up her coffee cup, picks up a Garibaldi and takes a nibble.

'Silly question. I could ask you the same. If I'd bumped into Meera, fair enough—she's into her history. But you? I didn't have you down as the author-signing type on a Sunday afternoon.'

Frank sets his plate and cup on the table. 'Meera's away for the week. I had time to kill. Read about this in the Gazette, and it piqued my interest.'

'I see.'

A pause.

'Strange, really,' he adds.

'What is?'

'When you live with someone as long as me and Meera have, you end up taking each other for granted. As though the other half will always be there. No one's fault. We're all caught up in our own little worlds. Then, when they're

not around, you realise you were only one half of a whole...
if you know what I mean. It's the little things you miss.'

Prisha gives him a steely stare for a second before
softening. 'Yes. I guess.'

Frank instantly realises his faux pas. Prisha only recently
split from her long-term boyfriend, Adam—in the most
acrimonious of circumstances.

He coughs. 'So how was your week in Madrid?' he adds,
changing the subject.

'It was a fortnight in Madeira.'

He winces and reaches for his tea. 'Are you sure?'

The stare intensifies. 'Pretty sure. I was there.'

He laughs weakly. 'Haha! Madeira, Madrid. Easy
mistake to make.'

'Not really.' She relaxes. 'It was the perfect tonic, Frank.
Up at five every morning. Two-hour run along the beach
and up into the hills. Then a leisurely breakfast—fresh
rolls from the bakery with ham and cheese. Down to the
beach: sunlounger, umbrella, good book, headphones on,
the odd dip in the water. Back to the apartment for lunch
and a prego no bolo do caco.'

'A what?'

'Steak sandwich marinated in garlic and sage and
served on a flatbread—my absolute favourite. Then a cool
shower, maybe a catnap. Wake up, read on the balcony,
swim in the pool, another shower.'

'You certainly like to keep clean.'

'Get ready for the evening with a Coral—that's the local beer. Then visit a bar for a couple of ponchas, flirt with the barmen. After that, a nice restaurant by the harbour for espetada or grilled fresh tuna. No dessert—just a half-bottle of chilled Sercial.'

Frank scratches his head. 'Do they serve full English breakfasts?'

She shrugs. 'Probably. I didn't go looking for them.'

'Guinness? Tetley's? Timothy Taylor?'

'When in Rome, Frank.'

Grimacing, he ruminates for a moment. 'I think I'll give Madrid a miss.'

'Madeira.'

'Aye, that as well.'

Movement ripples across the room as attendees move towards their seats.

Prisha sets her cup down. 'What's been happening at work?'

Frank funnels the last of the fruitcake and cheese into his mouth.

'Ah—funny you should ask. We've got a curly one.'

Prisha's interest sparks. 'Really?'

'Aye. We've been dragged—unwittingly—into a large undercover operation. Foreign drugs gang. Planning a move into the UK market. Very hush-hush.'

Prisha's eyes brighten. 'Perfect. I could do with a proper case to get my teeth into.'

Frank lifts a hand, already shaking his head. 'No.'

She blinks.

'You're not on this one, Prisha. You've got a fifty-year-old cold case waiting on your desk. That's your assignment. Me, Zac, and Dinkel will run this.'

'Aw, come on, Frank—'

'No.' His tone stays calm, but it hardens. 'You were hand-picked by the Chief Constable for Operation Torchlight. If he finds out you're dividing your time, he'll have my guts for garters. You need to focus.'

Disappointment flickers across her face, edged with irritation. 'You know cold cases aren't exactly where my strengths lie.'

Frank softens—just a fraction. 'I tell you what. I'll keep you informed. And if I need a second set of eyes, I'll ask. Okay?'

She pulls a small, sulky pout. 'Whatever.'

Frank glances around as people settle into their chairs and offers his arm. 'Shall we?'

Her mood lifts as she slips her arm through his. 'Lead on, good sir. And—for what it's worth—I've missed you.'

'Aye,' Frank says. 'Likewise.'

***At the front of the room is the host standing alongside local author Arthur Jarrow, looking every inch the old salty sea dog dredged up from another century. A rumpled Captain Birdseye.

White beard, full and bushy, frames a face etched with deep lines. Eyes brown, warm and steady. A thick cream cable-knit gansey hides under a dark navy blazer, an old captain's cap perched low on his brow. A curved wooden pipe sits at the corner of his mouth, unlit but clearly a fixture.

Fawn corduroy trousers are tucked into battered Wellington boots, thick woollen socks rolled up, hugging his shins. He's only five-five, maybe five-six, but radiates a becalmed kind of authority—quiet power, weathered resilience. On the table beside him sits a squat tumbler of whisky, catching the room's dull light like a signal flare.

Frank and Prisha take their seats near the back as the event host rattles through her introduction.

'As many of you know, Arthur has written many non-fiction books about Whitby, Robin Hood's Bay and the north east coast of Yorkshire. Born and bred not more than a five minute walk from where we are sitting. Arthur has explored every thread of Whitby's story—from its centuries-old fishing and whaling heritage, to the shipbuilding yards and alum-mining cliffs, to St Hilda's founding of the monastery and the great abbey's later dissolution—all the way through to the modern town we know today, still one of Britain's most beloved coastal holiday resorts. And today he's here to launch his new book, a work of fiction, *The Last Leviathan*. So please—put your hands together and give a warm welcome to Arthur Jarrow.'

As the applause dies down, Frank glances around at the gathered guests and realises that—aside from Arthur—he's the only man in the entire place.

The old man rises and nods in appreciation, lifting his book from the table. 'Thank you, everybody. I'll kick this off with a short reading.'

The room falls silent, a hush settling in anticipation.

'This is from Chapter thirteen,' he says. 'Titled Whale Cemetery. Although the book is mostly fiction, this chapter is based on real-life events lifted from the journal of the one who came back—but never spoke again.'

He opens the pages. The room leans in. Even the wind outside seems to abate.

'They sight her far out to sea, just beyond Dogger Bank—a black mountain rising from the water, slow and solemn, heading north with the steady grace of something ancient. They call her the *Last Leviathan*. Larger than any recorded, and moving with the weary dignity of a creature who knows she is the last of her kind.

'Three whaleboats drop from the mother ship—three of Whitby's finest: The Esk Rover, Maiden's Wrath, and Saint Hilda's Lance. Between them, they have dragged home more than a thousand whales. They have lit a town with oil, fed their families on the wages of blubber and baleen, carved a living from the suffering of giants.

'The chase is fierce. Oars bite the sea. Foam turns white as torn linen. Harpoons rise—iron prayers hurled by desperate men. They strike her. Deep.

'But she does not rage.

'For an hour she tows them across the water, the lines creaking, the hulls shuddering. Before at last she slows.

'And when she knows it's over, she sings.

'A sound like the aching of the world. Long. Low. A tremor that threads through the rigging and settles deep in the marrow. Not a cry of pain, but of sorrow. Of betrayal. The lament of a gentle giant—older than our kingdoms—undone by a cruelty beyond her comprehension.

'And the men... the men fall still. Oars slacken. Hands falter. Hardened whalers bow their heads and weep. Others sink to their knees and pray for forgiveness. They have faced death a thousand times. But never have they felt such shame.

'The captain calls for fresh irons. More ropes. More hooks.

'And still she sings.

'Her blood stains the sea. Her breath grows thin. Yet she will not die—not until the last note leaves her.

'Then the fog rolls in. Thick. Unnatural. White as polished bone. The wind dies. The ship drifts, helpless. The ropes hold fast.

'The Last Leviathan turns—once—to look back. Not in anger. Not in vengeance. But in sadness... and in forgiveness.

'And then she dives.

'Sinks without a struggle taking them with her.

'All three whaleboats. Eighteen men. Drawn deep into the dark.

'Only one survives, found days later clinging to a barrel, tongue bitten through, silent as the grave. He never speaks again. But he writes. He writes the tale with a trembling hand until the ink runs dry.

'And in every version, one line remains:

'We believed we chased her that day. But she was the one who bore witness to us—saw what we'd become. Her dying gaze stripped us bare. Each man glimpsed inward and saw the truth—the devil was never in the deep—it was within us.'

Arthur takes a sip of whisky before continuing.

'They say there is a place in the North Sea—blank on charts, cold and still—where the boats, the men, and the whales lie together at last, their violence spent, debts repaid. They call it—Whale Cemetery.'

Arthur closes the book. His voice fades like the last note of a hymn. No one claps. It feels wrong.

Prisha sits still, glassy-eyed. Frank stares at the floorboards, jaw tight. The silence is heavy. Sacred.

A single cough. A murmur. A shifting of chairs.

Arthur offers a wistful, weary smile. 'We like to pretend those days are gone. That the barbarity died with the old fleets. But it hasn't. It still happens today—draped in comforting words like "scientific research" and "cultural tradition." Sad thing is... the whales don't know our excuses. They only know the harpoons.' He pauses, gaze sweeping the room. 'We're all judged by what we chase.'

A woman near the front clears her throat. 'Is Whale Cemetery... a real place?'

Arthur hesitates, then nods. 'There are grounds in the North Sea old fishermen still mark but don't talk about. Blank patches on charts. Nets come up torn. Engines fail for no good reason.'

A faint smile. 'Superstition, of course.'

The woman offers a weak smile as Frank recognises her from yesterday.

Clarissa—the daughter of George Sykes.

# 21

## Monday

The day has already taken hold above Whitby's West Cliff, a pale gold wash spreading over the rooftops and the becalmed sea. PC Malone sits in the patrol car, unwrapping his bacon and egg McMuffin with the reverence of a man who's survived a long night shift. Beside him in the passenger seat, PC Claire Bolden nurses a hash brown and a bitter takeaway coffee, doom-scrolling her phone with her thumb.

Their shift ends at seven.

It's 6:25 am.

Breakfast is the finish line.

The radio chirps, then crackles.

'Control to Sierra Two-One, are you available for an attempted theft at Costcutters on The Parade? Suspect still at the scene.'

Malone closes his eyes and sighs.

Claire stares at her breakfast as if in mourning. 'You've got to be kidding.'

Malone keys the radio. 'Sierra Two-One, received. En route.'

'Thanks, Two-One,' Control replies. 'Grade Two. Shop staff detaining. No further details.'

Malone tosses the bag onto the dash and starts the engine.

'Costcutters,' he mutters. 'Always bloody Costcutters. Why can't they have normal operating hours from nine until five?'

Claire belts up with a resigned sigh. 'If this turns out to be someone trying to steal a packet of biscuits, I'm lodging a formal complaint with the universe.'

The patrol car performs a quick U-turn, tyres squealing.

Breakfast forgotten.

Duty wins.

<hr>

The blue lights wash across the shopfront as Malone and Bolden pull up outside Costcutters. Through the glass, Mr Patel stands just inside the doorway, gripping a baseball bat like it's the only thing holding his nerves together. His chest rises and falls in fast, shallow bursts.

Malone pushes the door open. 'Mr Patel? It's all right—we're here now. Put the bat down for me, please.'

Patel's eyes dart between them and the man slouched by the chilled alcohol cabinets.

'He tried to steal whisky! He not even try to hide it. Simply pick it up and put it in his coat pocket. I want him arrested and charged.' His voice cracks with frustration.

'We'll deal with it, Mr Patel,' Malone says gently. 'But the bat needs to go. Now.'

Patel hesitates, then lowers it, leaning it against the counter with a muttered curse.

The homeless man—late-forties, unruly stubble, clothes layered and ragged—scratches his groin as though bored by the whole event. His Scottish accent is thick when he speaks.

'Aye, about time. Can we get on wi' it? I've places ta be, like.'

PC Claire Bolden steps forward, calm and professional, brandishing handcuffs.

The vagrant brightens instantly. 'Well, hello there, lassie,' he says, giving her a crooked grin. 'You're a sight for sore eyes.'

Bolden raises an eyebrow. 'Cut the crap. Arms behind your back.'

This only excites him further.

'Oh, I see you're into the weird stuff, are ye? Well, break a leg. I'm sexually adventurous myself. Don't knock it until you've tried it is my motto. I tell you what, once I've sorted out this misunderstanding at the station, how about you and me spend the rest of the day together once your shift finishes? I'll run a comb through my hair, put on a bit of the smelly stuff, turn my underpants inside out, then we can paint the town red together and skip the light fandango.'

'I only understood half of that,' she replies, snapping the cuffs around his wrists. 'And you're old enough to be my father.'

'Don't let that worry you, sweetheart. I fully understand that a lot of younger women fall for the father figure. No need to feel guilty about it. Forget about societal conventions and follow your own desires.'

'You really are a sad old sicko, aren't you? And when was the last time you had a shower?' she adds, scrunching her nose up as she marches him towards the entrance.

'I had a shower on Saturday.'

'Which month and what year?' she asks, escorting him through the doorway. She pauses and glances at her partner. 'Don't be too long, Malone. I don't want him stinking the car out otherwise we'll have to get it valet cleaned.'

'Righto. I'll just get some details from Mr Patel.'

The derelict winks at her. 'You can drop the poker face, lassie. Yer cannae hide those smouldering eyes of yours. I saw you mentally undressing me straight away you clocked me.'

'Do me a favour,' she says, opening the back door of the patrol car.

'So how about it? A few quiet drinks, a nice meal—your shout of course as I'm a wee bit short—then back to your place to play hide the marrow.'

'Put a sock in it.' She slams the car door shut and curses to herself. 'I really should have become a wedding planner.'***

The desk sergeant rubs his tired eyes and tries again. 'Name?'

'I told ye. It's McFuckety-Dingleberry.'

'Really. Is that your first name or a double-barrelled last name, sir?'

The man snorts. 'Don't be ridiculous. Whoever heard of anyone's first name being McFuckety-Dingleberry?'

The desk sergeant glances at the two officers. 'Did you check him for ID?'

'Unfortunately, yes. Nothing on him, sarge,' PC Bolden states, feeling slightly defiled.

The man cackles. 'Aye, she had her hands all over me. Spent a not inconsiderable amount of time searching my groin area. But who could blame her? I'm irresistible to women. It's been my downfall.'

The desk sergeant reels back slightly as the odour hits him. 'Christ, when was the last time you showered?'

The man appears hurt. 'A man could take offence at that line of questioning. For your information, I have two overactive and enlarged testosterone glands. My scent is actually a powerful pheromone. Drives the women wild without them knowing why. I mean, take PC Bolden here; she can barely contain herself. Ogling me with those take-me-to-bed eyes. She has lust dripping from every pore. She cannae help herself, poor wee girl.'

'I think she's trying not to dry retch. Now, are you going to stop playing silly buggers and give me your real name or not?'

The man nods. 'Aye, okay. The joke's gone on long enough. The name's Danny.'

The sergeant scribbles on a pad, head down. 'That's better. Danny what?'

'McFuckety-Dingle...'

'Okay!' the sergeant snaps. 'PC Malone, take him to the cells. Removes his shoes and belt. Maybe twenty-four hours in isolation will jog his memory.'

The man becomes serious. 'Actually, I suggest the interview room. I want to see DCI Finnegan.'

The sergeant places his pen down and eyeballs him suspiciously. 'And why would *you* want to see the DCI?'

'Because he owes me a favour. Oh, and tell Finnegan to bring his boyfriend with him—DS Zac Stoker.'

## 22

Frank enters Interview Room One accompanied by Zac. They stop dead in their tracks and stare at the bedraggled figure drumming his fingers on the table, clearly bored.

Zac groans. 'Sweet holy bollocks. My worst nightmare. DS Danny Beale—Police Scotland's shitest.' Despite the shock of seeing Beale, he's even more appalled at his dishevelled appearance.

Beale rises and slaps Zac on the shoulder, grinning. 'It's been a while. How yer going, yer great big streak of Edinburgh pish?'

'I was going alright until I walked in here and saw your ugly mug.'

Beale drops back into his chair and sighs. 'Fucking charming, that is. And by the way—a technical correction—it's DC Beale now, not DS.'

Zac cannot help but grin. 'You've been busted down again. If you keep this up, you'll soon be back in the Boy Scouts. What was it this time—caught in an illegal brothel? Drugs money missing from a raid? Another suspect tripping over his shoelace?'

Beale sniffs dismissively. 'A simple misunderstanding that could have easily been reconciled if they hadn't involved those weaselly, pen-pushing, bean-counting, slack-jawed compulsive masturbators from the Professional Standards Department. Twats. Every last man Jack of them. Woke, fundamentalist zealots who are more than happy to turn a blind eye to rapists and kiddy-fiddlers in the upper echelons of power but more than ready to come down hard on a diligent, conscientious, loyal officer of the Force. Not that you can call it the *Force* these days. It portrays the wrong image.'

Frank and Zac pull up a seat and sit down opposite.

'So, why did you get demoted?' Zac quizzes, failing to suppress a smile.

Beale appears a tad sheepish. 'Not that it's any of your business, but I urinated in the Chief Constable's car.'

'What were you doing in the Chief Constable's car?'

'Who said I was in it? I just happened to be taking a leak as he drove past. His window was down. It was a blustery day... and well, the laws of physics and all that. Anyway, enough about me. How are you going—still married to the drag queen?'

Zac ignores the bait 'Yep, still married, thanks for asking.'

Beale shakes his head in mild contempt. 'Take my advice, sunshine; transfer all your money into an offshore account before it's too late. The bitch will leave you one day. Probably already shagging some Italian-looking barista experiment from the local caff. You'll wake up one morning and she'll be gone. Taken the kids, and your stash of weed, which is even worse. And after consulting a pencil-necked, bedwetting solicitor, she'll take the house and half your fucking pension. You'll be lucky if you can afford the rent on a slop bucket. Face it, Zac, you and me are the same. We're white, working class, and male... which these days means—we're fucked—right up the clacker. No lube. No condom. We're the lowest of the low now.'

He stops and reflects, as if in a daydream.

'If it happened to me, it could happen to you.' A pause followed by a smile. 'And how are your two wee girls? Started their periods yet?'

Zac grits his teeth but doesn't bite. 'I have two boys.'

Beale grabs his testicles in a twisted display of male triumph. 'They always say it takes a real man to produce a son. A few strong swimmers in the sperm pool. Probably doing breaststroke.' He grimaces and doubles over in pain. 'Shite the bed. I shouldnae have done that. I have a nasty lump on my left testicle. I've been meaning to get it looked at.' He straightens. 'I did Dr Google my symptoms. The AI fuckwit suggested the cause could be too much wanking, but I don't think twice a day is too much.'

He bends over and fumbles with his socks before retrieving a cigarette. Rising, he sticks his hand down his pants.

'Now where the fuck is it? It's down here somewhere. Ah, there it is. Between my arse cheeks.'

He pulls out a lighter.

Zac scowls 'You can't smoke that in here?'

'And who's going to stop me?'

Grinning, he lights the ciggy, heaving heavily on it before releasing a plume of smoke with a satisfying sigh.

'Oh, aye. That's the ticket. Anyway, it's *just* a wee cigarette. Tobacco is a plant. I'm not smoking plutonium. You anti-smoking zealots make me laugh. The planet is overheating. Ocean temperatures rising. The ozone layer's fucked. They're mowing down the rain forests like a pensioner with dementia cutting the lawn. Big business is dumping shite and poison into the rivers and lakes. The tech giants watch our every move. The world's overrun with murdering dictators. There's a fuck-knuckle in the Kremlin and an even *bigger* fuck-knuckle in the White House, both a cock's length away from a big red button which says—*Game Over*—once they press it. The Middle East—well, it's the fucking Middle East—end of discussion. And a meteorite could slam into us tomorrow. And the only thing the do-gooders are bothered about is poor wee blokes like myself enjoying a quiet smoke, minding our own business. "Ooh, you cannae smoke that here. I'm passive smoking." Wake up and smell the shite, sunshine, and welcome to Planet Earth. The most fucked up planet in the cosmos.'

Frank folds his arms. 'Okay, Danny, cut the theatrics.'

Zac turns to him, slightly irritated. 'Frank, this isn't theatrics. He's not acting. This is the *real* Beale. In fact, if anything, he's underperforming, something he's good at. I did two weeks undercover with the lunatic in Hull. I still have the therapy bill.'

Beale appears wounded as he flicks ash onto the floor and breaks wind.

'Oi, watch it, pal. I have feelings, you know.'

Frank tries again. 'Danny, why exactly are you here?'

Beale sucks on his smoke and slumps back in his seat. 'Operation Blackout.'

## 23

'Operation Blackout,' Frank repeats, playing coy.

Beale rubs his weathered face. 'Aye. I'm working deep undercover and wasn't meant to surface, but things are moving quicker than I anticipated. I better fill you in about the op.'

'No need,' Zac states. 'We're already aware of Operation Blackout. We met your boss, Silas Carmody, last week.'

Beale is momentarily surprised. 'Oh, I see.'

'And what exactly is your cover?' Zac continues. 'Because you smell like the inside of my compost bin.'

Beale riles. 'Listen, pal, I've spent the last four weeks living rough on the streets. What were you expecting me to smell like—Liberace's hairdresser? I've been dealing with the flotsam and jetsam of society. The dregs of humanity, the mentally insane, footpads, deadbeats, and the Hare Krishnas.'

'Home from home then?'

Beale sneers and studies him. 'Look at you with your slicked-back hair and manicured beard, smelling like an upmarket ponce. It's me with my neck on the line; me who's putting my life at risk for King and country.' He pauses. 'Not that I agree with a monarchy in a modern parliamentary constitutional democracy. Cromwell and the Bolsheviks had the right idea in my opinion. We have enough baggage dragging us under without a conga-line of inbred, stuttering, chinless wonders dipping their hands into the public purse every year. Mind you, the politicians are just as bad. Don't get me started on that chaff sack of mangled cocks.'

Frank coughs. 'Danny, if you could focus.'

He pulls his gaze away from Zac, a little confused. 'Oh, aye. Now what the fuck were we talking about?'

'The undercover operation.'

'Aye, that's right.' He pulls another smoke from his sock and lights it. 'By the way, you might want to have a word with your plods. Their searching technique leaves a lot to be desired. But go easy on that pretty little PC Boland. I think I'm on a promise once this half-cocked shambles of an operation is over.'

Frank taps the table impatiently. 'The operation?'

The nicotine seems to sharpen Beale's mind. 'Okay, what do you know so far?'

'According to Silas, there's a foreign cartel planning a takeover in the north-east. They aim to flood the market with fentanyl. A local small-time dealer called Typhoon has been selling fentanyl, and one of his runners, Owen Lister, better known as Smiler, was picked up last week. We cut a deal with him, and on Friday night he was tasked with planting a listening device in Typhoon's hangout to see if he's involved with the cartel. Once this foreign gang has set down roots, they'll smuggle in a large batch of fentanyl pre-cursor via shipping container into one of the main ports.'

'And Silas told you this?'

'Yes. We were unaware of Operation Blackout until we nicked Smiler. Silas was worried we might have followed the trail back to Typhoon and set alarm bells ringing.'

Beale leans back, puffing on his smoke, eyes flitting between Frank and Zac. His thumb gently strokes the side of his chin, contemplating, assessing, always distrustful.

'What do you make of Silas?'

Frank shrugs and shares a glance with Zac. 'Kept his cards close to his chest, which is understandable. I suspect he's ruthless, efficient. No room for niceties. But overall, he seemed okay.'

'No disrespect, but Silas is a desk-bound, knobjockey,' he says, showing a hefty amount of disrespect. 'If he stands up too quickly, he suffers a nosebleed. He means well, but as for the harsh realities of what's happening out there in the real world—he's like a teenage virgin at an over-50s gangbang on a Blackpool weekender. Hanging around with his dick in his hand, not sure what to do.'

Frank leans back, drops his head, massages his nose. 'Danny,' he says with a deep sigh, 'if you could stick to the point of your visit and leave the character assassinations for another time, it would be appreciated.'

'Oh, aye. Sorry. I do have a tendency to go off-topic. I get it from my mother. She could talk under wet cement.' Another drag on the Lambert and Butler. 'Okay, like I said, I've been deep undercover keeping my ear to the ground, and there wasn't much to report, just the usual petty thugs and dealers doing the rounds. Nothing big. Then I heard about Typhoon and found out where he hangs out. Did a bit of surveillance. He has a small crew, but they're all chocolate gangsters. He's established an extensive network up the coast, but it's small-time. He doesn't have the brains or ambition to try anything big. And then there's Smiler—strange sort of kid. Reserved. Keeps himself to himself, not like the others. So, up until last Thursday, nothing much to write home about.'

Zac frowns. 'What happened on Thursday?'

Beale raises an eyebrow and squints at him. 'It was a quiet night. I was down on the quayside scrounging in the bins and I noticed this trawler making its way through the harbour entrance. Halfway in, it cuts the engine and just glides along on the incoming tide, nice and slow, which was odd in itself. Then I spot these four blokes, early thirties, I'd guess. Doc Marten boots, cargo pants, bomber jackets. Hair slicked-back, designer stubble. They looked like a fucking boy band from Sicily's Got Talent. They're all standing on the quayside watching this trawler berth. One of them holding a briefcase—another oddity. Let's just say my balls began to twitch.'

Zac leans forward. 'You think they're the foreign cartel?'

Beale shrugs. 'They're foreign and dodgy.'

'Italian?'

'Can't be sure. But definitely from that neck of the woods.'

'Then what happened?'

'They all boarded the boat, and I went to my usual spot for the night, tucked up behind a wall in Black Horse Yard. I get settled down, playing the part of the drunken tramp looking for somewhere quiet to sleep for the night. About an hour passed, and whaddya know—the Mediterranean's answer to the Backstreet Boys came swaggering along, swinging their dicks. One of them checks me out. I'm all cosy in my sleeping bag. Prick flicks a ciggy at me. Then this guy comes up, obviously the leader, and slaps him around the chops. Tells him to show some respect.'

'Any names?' Frank asks.

'Aye. The leader is called Dritan. The missing-link who flicked the ciggy is called Mika. Fists like fucking anvils. And here's another strange one; this Dritan bends down and has a chat with me. Asks me if I have any work. I tell him no. He asks me what I used to do. I tell him I used to work the trawlers out of Scotland. He gives me twenty quid and tells me to get something to eat.'

'Peculiar,' Frank notes. 'Then what?'

'I did like he said. Went and got a kebab and a few cans of Tennent's Super. Anyway, jump ahead to Friday night. I'm in the usual location. About closing time, young Smiler walks past, head down, seemed distant, absorbed.

I cannae say he was full of the joys of spring. About fifteen minutes pass, and the Backstreet Boys come strutting past. Didn't stop this time. Men on a mission. The fog was rolling in at that point, and I needed to get to the homeless shelter before they closed the doors for the night.'

'And over the weekend?' Zac quizzes.

'Saturday—deathly quiet. Then on Sunday I heard on the street there was a new trawler in town and they were looking for crew. It piqued my interest, so I wandered over and, sure enough, there's a sign next to a boat—hiring. The same boat that docked on Thursday night— *The Whitby Rose*.'

Zac raises an eyebrow, recalls his chat with Cleavage, but says nothing as Beale continues.

'I thought I'd do a bit of intel under the pretence of looking for work. I spoke to the skipper. A French guy called Francois, late fifties. Decent enough sort, but I knew he wasn't going to give me a job. Just about to turn on my heels and guess who saunters over from the other side of the boat?'

'Who?' Frank asks.

'Dritan. We have another chat, and he offers me a job. Overrules the skipper. He even gave me wages in advance. Slips me a hundred and tells me to get digs, and be back there Tuesday at 7 pm for the first trip.'

The second cigarette joins the first on the floor.

'Is that everything?'

'Aye.'

Frank shoots Zac a glance. 'Thoughts?'

He's curious. 'Silas did say the gang were running decoy operations. This could be one of them.'

Frank nods. 'Hmm... or they could be legitimate trawler men. What's your gut instinct, Danny?'

Beale spins the lighter around in his fingers. 'Not sure at the moment. That's why I signed on for the trawler work. Get a bit closer.'

Zac can't resist a chuckle. 'And how's that going to work? Being a deckhand is one of the toughest and most dangerous jobs going. You'll spend most of your time spewing up over the side.'

Beale eyeballs him with disdain. 'Let's just say it seemed like a good idea at the time. Anyway, I'll wing it.' He focuses on Frank. 'Has Smiler been in touch since he planted the device?'

'No. I told him not to contact us unless it was urgent. He's made himself scarce for a few days. He's due to return to Typhoon's pad on Wednesday and retrieve the device and hand it over.'

'Bit of a gamble, isn't it—using a dealer to plant a bug?'

Frank bites his lip. 'Yes, but not as big a risk as using one of our own. If that went awry, and Typhoon *is* involved, it could blow the whole Op. Anyway, it was Carmody's idea.'

Zac leans forward. 'Why have you told me and Frank this instead of your contact on the operation?'

'Because it could be a false lead. And...' He hesitates, as if unsure.

'And?' Zac prompts.

'You two are cleanskins. You're not really involved. I can trust you.'

Frank pushes his chair back and rises. 'Do you want us to pass on your information to Silas?'

Beale eyeballs him. 'No. Not yet.'

Zac stands and stares down at him. 'Why not?'

'Let's just say I feel safer if my intel remains between the three of us, for the moment.'

'You don't trust him?'

'I didnae say that.'

'Then what?'

'Something I cannae put my finger on just yet. You may think I'm shite at my job, but I'm not. I'm damn good. Okay, maybe I'm not a model police officer, but I know my onions, and something doesn't quite feel right at the moment. Let's leave it at that.'

Frank nods. 'Okay. We'll keep it between us for now. I'll give you our numbers. Call either of us if you think your life's in danger.'

Beale winces. 'Bit of a problem there,' he adds sheepishly.

Zac shakes his head. 'Don't tell me—you don't have a phone?'

'No, I'm supposed to be a down-and-out drunken bum wandering the streets. It would look a bit odd if I had the latest iPhone and a monthly plan. And using a public phone box always looks sus, if such things even fucking exist these days.' His mind drifts again. 'I have fond memories of the old red telephone boxes. It's where I had my first sexual experience.'

'I assume you were you alone?' Zac replies.

'Oh, still the fucking comedian, eh?' Beale snaps.

Frank heads to the door. 'We'll get you a dumb phone, a Nokia, or something, with prepaid credits. Only to be used in emergencies.'

'Okay. Thanks.'

'I'll square this away with the duty sergeant, then you can leave.'

'Not so fast, Frank.'

'What?'

'I was hoping I could get my head down for a kip in the cells for a few hours. After a hearty fried breakfast, of course.'

'I'll see what I can do. I take it you don't have digs?'

'I do from two o'clock this afternoon.'

'Whereabouts?'

'A run-down boarding house on the corner of Abbey and Hudson Street. Number thirteen. Third floor. Even the cockroaches have moved out, but it's cheap.'

Zac nods. 'I know the place. More of a doss house than a boarding house.'

Frank pulls at the door then closes it again. 'By the way, why did you attempt to steal a bottle of whisky from Mr Patel's?'

'Covering my back.'

'What do you mean?'

Beale chuckles. 'If this mob is an organised crime cartel, they'll be no different from all the others—paranoid cock-smokers. Which means for a couple of days they'll put a tail on anyone involved in their operation. Make sure they're not a stooge.'

'I see. And you couldn't simply walk into a police station of your own volition otherwise it would have raised their suspicions?'

'Exactly. Oh, and Frank, if you could send one of the boys out to get me a couple of packets of Lambert and Butler, it would be appreciated.'

# 24

Prisha is half-hidden in the corner of the incident room, boxed in by dusty archive files from her cold case. The material is digitised and online, but she knows better than to trust that alone. Some details never make it from paper to screen—and if anything's been overlooked, she intends to find it.

Frank strides in from the kitchenette with a mug of tea and stands in front of the whiteboard as Zac finishes updating it.

Frank turns to Dinkel, who has his head buried in paperwork.

'Oi, Dinkel, did you do that homework I set you?' he barks.

'Yes, sir.'

'Good. You can debrief us once Zac's finished bringing us up to speed. Grab a pew.'

'Sir.'

With Frank and Dinkel seated, Zac gestures at the board and begins.

'Operation Blackout,' he says. 'A foreign cartel planning to muscle into the north-east. Entry drug is fentanyl precursor. Their point of access—one of the major ports along the coast. They're known for running decoy operations: spreading police resources thin, creating chaos, while the real shipment slips through unnoticed.'

He taps on the next heading. 'Typhoon Tommy. Local mid-level dealer running a tight operation in the region. At this stage, we don't know whether he's directly linked to the cartel. We're hoping the bug Smiler planted will clarify that.

'Danny Beale—undercover. He's had contact with a group of four, maybe five if we include the skipper of The Whitby Rose, possibly from the southern Mediterranean. Italian. Sicilian. Not confirmed. The apparent gang leader is a man calling himself Dritan.

'The Whitby Rose. Medium-sized trawler operating out of Whitby. Skipper is a French national named Francois. Dritan has a connection to the vessel. Beale has blagged his way onto the boat as a deckhand to gather further intelligence.'

'And what do we know about The Whitby Rose?' Frank interjects.

Zac shrugs. 'From the records I've accessed, it checks out as legit. The vessel's registered to a small French fishing company, skippered by Francois Langlois. Records show it used to operate out of northern France under a different name—Rose de la Manche—then got a license to work British waters, and renamed The Whitby Rose. Paperwork's clean. Permits are in place. Nothing about it screams alarm.'

Zac spreads his hands. 'At this point, we don't know if it's part of a decoy, or a legitimate fishing vessel plying its trade.'

Frank nods at Dinkel. 'Okay, lad. The stage is yours.'

A little nervous, he clears his throat. 'Right, sir. I've titled my research—The Life Cycle of Fentanyl.'

Zac lets out a low groan. 'Get on with it. You're not reading a dissertation to a college professor.'

'Ahem, right. So, it starts with a thing called ANPP—short for 4-anilino-N-phenethylpiperidine. That's the immediate precursor. Think of it as the chemical skeleton. Mostly shipped from China or India in hundred-kilogram loads. A legitimate product for pharmaceutical intermediates.'

Frank frowns. 'I keep hearing this term—precursor. Describe it in layman's terms.'

'Think of precursor as flour, sir. And fentanyl as bread. On its own, flour is not much use. But add yeast, water, salt—and someone who knows how to mix it in the right quantities—the baker, and you end up with a finished product.'

If he was waiting for an admiring acknowledgement of his analogy, he's sadly disappointed.

'Anyway, the criminal networks bring it into Europe first. Ports like Rotterdam or Antwerp. Then it's relabelled, driven across borders, and slipped into the UK via freight hubs.'

Zac leans forward. 'What are the other ingredients it's mixed with?'

'Reactive agents. Catalysts. Solvents. Some of it's common, some of it's regulated. Without the secondary mix, the precursor is an innocuous powder.'

'And is this the sort of thing anyone with a rudimentary knowledge of chemistry could produce—backstreet?'

'Definitely not. The reaction can be volatile. The temperature has to stay within very narrow margins. If it spikes too high, you get side-products that are extremely toxic. If it's too cool, you get incomplete conversion. And then—'

Frank interjects. 'You get a bad batch and people die.'

Dinkel swallows. 'Yes, sir.' He fidgets with his papers. 'Once they've cooked the fentanyl powder, they cut it with filler—usually lactose or microcrystalline cellulose—then press it into tablets.'

Zac tilts his head. 'Industrial scale?'

'Absolutely. A rotary pill press can punch out tens of thousands of tablets per hour. You can buy pill presses online. China mostly. Often disguised as vitamin supplement machines.'

Frank grimaces. 'So this isn't opportunists chancing their arm by making a couple of thousand tablets in the garden shed?'

'Definitely not. A typical shipment—say, two hundred kilos of precursor—could realistically yield a hundred million pills. More if they cut it heavily.'

Zac shifts his weight. 'And the manufacturing process—does it smell, like meth labs do?'

'The solvents give off a sharp odour. Chemical. A bit like nail varnish remover mixed with cat urine. Not as overpowering as meth labs, but in a garage or an outbuilding you'd definitely detect a strong smell.'

Frank leans back in his chair, studying him. 'Who does the actual cooking?'

'A trained chemist, sir. Or someone with enough university-level knowledge to keep the reaction stable. Most gangs either import the finished fentanyl from overseas, or they bring in a specialist cook. The risk of getting it wrong is too high. One misstep and the batch becomes lethal.'

Frank takes a sip of tea. 'Good work, lad. Right—they say a little knowledge is a dangerous thing, and that's exactly where we are right now. We don't know enough yet—whether Typhoon's involved, or what this foreign crew on the trawler is really up to.'

Zac shifts uneasily. 'Couple of things, Frank. First—why are we even involved? This isn't our party, yet we seem to be getting dragged in deeper and deeper.'

Frank fixes him with a cold look. 'This is my town, Zac. And it's my job to know what's happening in it. And you're also forgetting—it was Silas Carmody who pulled us into this with his little fishing expedition with the listening device. That makes it our business. So, we watch. We listen. And no information sharing with anyone outside of this room unless I say so.' He pauses. 'You said a couple of things?'

Zac winces and runs a hand through his beard.

'An ethical dilemma.'

'Go on.'

'My snout. Cleavage. I bumped into him at the weekend. We had a quick chat—work came up. He's worked on the trawlers for fifteen years. Anyway, he mentioned he's starting with a new crew this week.'

Frank's expression tightens. 'Don't tell me he's on The Whitby Rose?'

'Aye.'

'Hell's bells,' Frank snaps. 'That's all we bloody need.'

A sharp snort comes from the corner.

Frank glances back and catches the top of Prisha's head above a stack of archive boxes.

'You got something to say, Prisha?'

She steps out from between the boxes. 'Actually—yes.'

'Go on,' he says tentatively, wary of the wild look in her eyes.

'I go on holiday for two weeks and come back to a parallel universe. You tail Smiler. Break into his house without a warrant—'

'Who told you that?' Zac counters.

'Dinkel.'

Zac glares at him.

Dinkel stammers and flusters. 'I... she... sort of has a way of... I didn't know it was a secret.'

'I'll deal with you later,' Zac growls.

'No, you won't,' Prisha snaps, pacing back and forth. 'It's you and Frank who are in the *wrong*, not Dinkel. The NCA ran an undercover Op on *your* patch without briefing you first, and then you acquiesced to their demands. You coerce a civilian into planting a listening device. And now Zac's informant is embedded in a crew you *think* might be a foreign cartel.'

Frank exhales slowly. 'Granted—it's not ideal.'

'Ideal?' Prisha shouts. 'It's reckless. This is not how *we* do things around here. If Superintendent Banks finds out, you'll both be for the high jump.'

'Banks knows,' Zac adds sheepishly. 'She signed off on Smiler.'

Prisha's eyes flick between Frank and Zac. 'She what?'

'It's true,' Frank says.

Prisha turns on her heel and heads for the door.

'Where are you going?' Frank calls.

'Somewhere with fresh air—and fewer cowboys.'

The door slams. The windows rattle. A miniature statue of Whitby Abbey falls from Dinkel's desk.

'By 'eck,' Frank murmurs. 'She has one hell of a temper on her.'

Zac tilts his head. 'Do you think she's annoyed?'

Frank stares at him. 'Take a stab in the dark.'

The door swings open again. 'Oh, and one other thing!' Prisha yells. 'You have a glaring omission.'

'What?' Frank and Zac reply in unison.

'MONEY!'

# 25

## Tuesday 6:30 am

He's taken risks. Calculated risks. The plan was to get as far away from Whitby as possible. But slipping out of his lodgings at four in the morning didn't leave many escape options. With a phone, he could have called a taxi and vanished anywhere. But he didn't have a phone.

Still doesn't.

He darted and weaved through back alleys and ginnels until he reached Green Lane by the allotments. It had been easy enough to prise the clasp from the shed door with a spade left outside. Inside was basic to say the least—an armchair and not much else—but it was shelter. More importantly, it was away from *them*.

It had only ever been temporary. He had a key to his grandparents' house—they were in Canada for another month—but going anywhere near their place was too risky. The GPS tracking on his phone would've shown every address he visited regularly. All the psychos needed was one lookout waiting for him to visit his grandparents.

But how long would they have kept that up? A day, maybe two?

They had their own lives. Their own... activities. And what activities exactly—drugs? Enforcers?

And why kill Typhoon? Had he stepped on their patch? Owed them money? Stolen a batch? Whatever it was, he'd pissed them off.

Intimidation has a scale. It starts with a warning. A threat. If that fails, a gentle beating—cuts and bruises. More serious and you end up in hospital with broken bones. And if you keep offending—death. A drive-by shooting. Or bursting into your bedroom in the dead of night and a bullet to the head.

But decapitation? That was something else entirely. And they had a gun—they could've used that instead.

Cleaner. Easier.

But they didn't.

No, decapitation is the top rung of the intimidation ladder. Nothing more terrifying. Sends a clear warning to everyone.

God only knows what Typhoon had been up to. A wheeler-dealer with fingers in too many pies. His influence was growing—from Hull up to the Scottish border. His shopfront. And woe betide anyone who strayed onto it.

But none of that matters now. Only his own welfare. And he still hasn't worked out a plan. His brain is addled.

Escape, of course. But where to?

London, Manchester, Leeds, Edinburgh, Land's End, John O'Groats—anywhere.

But then what? Live on the run forever?

The other option is the police. But Blakey's warning still gnaws at him—what if he *has* been set up? Walk into that station at your own peril. Lamb to the slaughter.

But surely Mr Finnegan isn't bent?

He doesn't know him well, but his granddad thinks highly of him. And he remembers Finnegan buying him lemonade and crisps when he was a kid at the bowls club. A good, generous man.

Finnegan can't be bent.

Can he?

Doesn't even have to be him. Could be someone else. Sergeant Stoker, for example. He's got a screw loose.

No, too risky to go to the station. If he could get Finnegan alone—maybe. But he doesn't know where he lives. Only where he works. And while ever the four amigos are at large, then he's a walking corpse.

More pressing matters now.

He unscrews the top of the empty water bottle and takes a piss. Pulls a wad of cash from his duffel bag, peels off two fifties, and slides them beneath a stained coffee cup. He peers out of the grimy window.

No one around. Good.

The next hour is the most dangerous part—heading into town and getting a disguise; long coat, woollen hat, sunglasses, buying a phone, then finding a room that doesn't want a card or ID. Cash only.

If he can find a place, he'll buy himself time.

Time to think, rest.

And tomorrow, when he doesn't turn up with the listening device, Finnegan may raid Typhoon's place and retrieve it themselves.

He's not sure how much that helps his present predicament, but at least they can't pin Typhoon's death on him. It will all be there, recorded. The truth.

He's about to open the shed door when he freezes.

Breath snags. Adrenaline pulses through him again.

'You stupid, stupid idiot,' he whimpers.

The realisation lands like a ball-peen hammer to the back of the skull.

Friday night in Typhoon's shed—he hid the USB listening device under the lip of the counter.

Good spot.

One problem.

One *massive* fucking problem.

He forgot to switch it on.

# 26

Frank pushes open the allotment gate and saunters up the gravel path dotted with weeds. He checks the lock on his own shed—intact—then slowly spins around and surveys the scene. Like a shanty town surrounded by market gardens, nothing seems different. An oasis of tranquillity. Birds tweet. Sparrows flit between the plots. Gulls screech overhead. The ever-present distant waves are soft, muted. The top of the Abbey peeks over the skyline, serene, ancient.

But there is one sound incongruous to the setting—chuntering on an industrial scale.

He turns and stares at Arthur's shed forty feet away. He sticks his hands deep in his pockets and ambles over.

'Arthur!'

The grizzled old man clatters out of his door, hair like wire wool.

'Bastards!' he declares, as though the entire world is personally conspiring against him.

'I got your message. This is uniform's job, not mine,' Frank says, slightly annoyed the old man called him directly instead of using the proper channels.

'Aye, I know that. I'm not daft, yer know. Call uniform and I'll be waiting until doomsday, if the buggers decide to show up at all.'

Frank gives a tiny grunt and eyeballs the spade propped up against the side of the shed.

'So... when did it happen?' he asks, inspecting the clasp and padlock that's been prised away, splintering the surrounding timber.

'Not sure. I haven't been up here in a week. Been ailing.'

'Oh, aye. What is it this time?'

'Me haemorrhoids have been playing up. Like a bunch of grapes dangling down.'

'Nice,' Frank replies, attempting to dispel the mental image.

'Felt a bit more sprightly today, so thought I'd come up and potter about. Then I find some little sods have buggered the lock and broken in. Can't have owt to yerself these days.'

Frank steps inside.

The hut smells of soil and old wood. All the usual gardening paraphernalia is present, plus an armchair but also sandwich wrappers, crisp packets, biscuit crumbs, empty Coke and water bottles—some filled with a yellow liquid.

Someone's temporary home.

'Anything valuable taken?' he asks before rephrasing. 'Anything taken?'

'Nah. Not that I've noticed. But they've been sleeping here. Pissed in the bottles. God knows where they took a shit. I hope it was in your patch, not mine.'

'Thanks,' Frank mutters, giving the place the once-over.

For a moment, Danny Beale crosses his mind.

*Could he have used this place? Out of the cold, out of danger? Nah. Too far out of town. And Danny said he usually bags a bed at the homeless shelter. But the piss bottles? That I can imagine.*

He pushes the thought aside and tries to reassure Arthur.

'There's not much I can do, Arthur. Put a new lock on, and when or *if* they return, they'll know they've been rumbled and will move on.'

'Bloody typical. Not sure what I pay me rates for.'

'The only damage is a broken lock. Easy fix.'

Arthur pulls a gurney. 'That's not the point. Young buggers need teaching a lesson. Give 'em a choice—five years in the army or a damn good public thrashing.'

Frank's about to leave when he spots the coffee cup and lifts it up. Gently takes the two fifty-pound notes.

'This yours?'

Arthur stares. 'What is it? I haven't got me glasses with me.'

'It's a hundred quid.'

Arthur runs a hand over his mottled head.

'Well, I'll be buggered. Nay, lad. Not mine.'

Frank hands him the money. 'More than covers the damage. Whoever it was obviously had a conscience... and some brass.'

It instantly tells Frank a lot. It wasn't kids messing about in here. Nor a homeless person seeking refuge. Whoever used this place was hiding, on the run.

His phone rings. He steps outside and checks the screen. 'Zac?' he answers.

'Where are you, boss?'

'Up at the allotment. Old Arthur's shed's been broken into.'

'Right, well... sorry to drag you away from the crime of the century, but we have a situation.'

The tone in Zac's voice puts Frank instantly on alert. 'What?'

'A body's washed up on Saltwick Bay. Forensics are on the way. I'm just setting off with Prisha.'

Frank stiffens. 'Any ID?'

'No. Male, and naked is all I know.'

Frank's stomach tightens. Saltwick Bay rarely throws up anything good.

'Age?'

'Not sure. And... he's going to be hard to identify.'

'Why?'

'Feet, hands, and head are all missing. So we can rule out misadventure and suicide.'

The allotment suddenly feels much colder. Frank turns slowly, scanning the plots again. Everything looks the same, but the tranquillity evaporates.

*Something is wrong in Whitby. He can feel it.*

'Oh, and another thing,' Zac continues.

'What?'

'Doctor Whipple is on his way.'

'Bloody champion,' he replies with a weary sigh.

He hangs up and heads back the way he came with more urgency.

'Well?' Arthur calls after him. 'What are you going to do about it, Frank? The buggers need stringing up!'

'Relax, Arthur. Whoever it was won't be coming back.'

## 27

Frank descends the precipitous steps to Saltwick Bay, boots slipping now and then on the gravel. The air carries a fine mizzle that never quite becomes rain, the cold spray settling on his face and shoulders. The sky hangs low—grey on grey—flattening the morning into something dull and morbid.

Halfway down, he pauses, listening. Just the steady hush of the sea and the faint clack of pebbles rolling in the wash. No birdsong. Not even the usual distant caw of a gull.

The imposing rock, Black Nab, looms out in the murk, its shape shifting slightly each time the mist drifts. Waves lap gently around its base, the ebbing tide exposing darker streaks of reddish rock, like bloodstains on stone. The whole bay feels held in suspension—as if waiting for something to show itself.

Frank keeps moving, one step away from an embarrassing fall into the undergrowth at the side of the steps. The wind is light but insistent, threading through the gaps in his coat, carrying with it a salty, ozone scent of sand and seaweed. The beach unfurls below, empty, save for a small knot of figures attending to their duties methodically near the shoreline.

Charlene Marsden's forensics team, a couple of uniformed officers manning the police barrier tape, Zac with hands deep in the pockets of his jacket, staring at a form on the sand.

He feels the unease deepen as he nears. Something about the quiet. Something about the shape on the sand.

———

Frank stares down at the body, or what's left of it.

'Where's Prisha?' he asks Zac.

'She's up top in the car getting a statement from the guy who found the body. He was down here searching for ammonites in the shale. So absorbed, he didn't notice the body for a good twenty minutes.'

'Morning, Frank,' Charlene says as she wanders over and lowers her goggles and face mask.

'Morning, Charlene.' He nods down at the body. 'You won't be able to tell us much.'

'Probably not. Immersion in seawater will have wiped any potential evidence. It's a very effective way to clean a body. Like putting it in a washing machine. We've conducted a sweep of the beach and haven't found any clothing or personal items, or the missing body parts.'

'You think he was dumped in the water naked?'

'Looks like it.'

'And the head, hands, and feet—any chance it could have been a propeller?'

Charlene pulls a grimace. 'Not my area of expertise, but for what it's worth, I think not. I mean, what are the chances? It would be like picking the first five past the post in the Grand National. Odds are astronomical.'

Zac half-turns as a figure edges into his peripheral vision. 'Here we go. The oracle has arrived,' he mutters, watching Dr Bennett Whipple in white forensic gear lumber over the sand like a polar bear forced upright against its will.

Frank points a finger at Zac. 'Oi, don't you bloody wind him up,' he warns.

'Me? As if.'

'I'll leave you to it,' Charlene says, edging away.

Frank turns. 'Ah, Bennett. It's been a while. Hope you're in fine fettle?'

Whipple hesitates. 'Hmm... fettle. If memory serves, its etymology begins as a simple noun in Old English, from fetel—a girdle or belt one fastens before labour. In Middle English, it transmogrifies into a verb, fetlen. To wit—to arrange, to set in order, to make ready. Thus "fine fettle" simply denotes a state of proper preparation.'

*Only Whipple could turn a simple greeting into a lecture,* Frank thinks.

Whipple's face droops like wet parchment. 'I am not in fine fettle nor the best of temper, inspector.'

'Really? That's most out of character, Bennet. What's troubling you?'

Whipple looks out to sea. 'A most vexatious matter in the domestic realm. Most vexatious indeed.'

Zac nods sympathetically. 'Well, you know what they say—a problem shared is a pain in the arse for the person listening.'

Whipple eyes him as one might regard a diseased pigeon. 'I have my nephew lodging at my domicile. Initially, I welcomed the opportunity to take the boy in, educate him, bestow upon him the unfettered benefit of my immense knowledge.'

'Oh aye,' Frank says, mentally preparing for an onslaught of verbosity and archaic terms.

'I commenced with the titans of the world's classical composers—Beethoven, Brahms, Liszt, Wagner, Chopin. Alas, the boy displayed not a scintilla of interest. I therefore deduced he might be more reader than listener, so I furnished him with many of the classics: Chaucer's Canterbury Tales, Dickens, Shakespeare. The Romantic poets—Wordsworth, Coleridge, Shelley, Byron, Keats—veritable behemoths of the English canon.'

'And?' Frank prompts.

Whipple shakes his head morosely. 'A complete blank. At one point I feared the young man might be congenitally simple, and yet his social intercourse with Mrs Whipple is perfunctory, if banal in its lateral progression.'

'I see.'

He pauses before suddenly straightening, shouting, 'Eureka!' and stabbing a finger skyward.

Frank and Zac both flinch.

'Steady on, Bennett. You nearly gave me a heart attack.'

'My apologies, inspector. But that is the word I uttered when I believed I had cracked the enigma. I thought perhaps the boy possessed an analytical mind. So I attempted to imbue him with a sense of wonder regarding algebra, sines, and cosines, complex equations, binary calculus. I expounded on how the ancient civilisations employed geometric mastery to design pyramids, raise colosseums, construct aqueducts, roads, temples.'

'No good?' Frank asks.

Whipple shakes his head. 'None whatsoever. The boy has an absolute absence of interest in anything cerebral. And Mrs Whipple has exacerbated the situation by mollycoddling him to a ruinous degree. At his age, he requires strict guidelines, discipline—as I myself endured at his age. Boundaries. Regimentation. Instead, I find his manner antagonistic, his attitude truculent and surly, his personal grooming substandard, his locutions monosyllabic, and his comprehension of simple instruction virtually non-existent. At times I suspect he wilfully misapprehends me merely to inflame my passions.'

Zac shrugs. 'Sounds like a typical teenager, Doc. Adolescence can be a trying time. My lads are just hitting that age now. The next few years will be... fun. But if it's any comfort, it'll pass. They come out the other side unscathed. Or so I've heard.'

Whipple stares at him as if he's sprouted antlers. 'You are under a misapprehension, sergeant. He is not a teenager.'

'Oh. How old is he?'

'He has just turned but five years of age.'

Zac buries the smirk. 'Buy him an Action Man and a Lego set—that'll keep him out of your hair,' he advises, inadvertently gazing at Whipple's gargantuan bald head straining beneath a woefully inadequate disposable bouffant cap.

'Ahem,' Frank interrupts, nodding at the corpse on the sand. 'Maybe we should get down to business.'

'Indeed,' Whipple concurs.

He lowers himself beside the body with the grave solemnity of a man appraising a relic. Draws a long, deliberate breath through his nose.

'Well, Bennett, what can you tell us?' Frank asks.

'Adult male. Caucasian. Unencumbered by garment or vesture,' Whipple replies with funereal gravity.

'You don't say,' Zac mutters.

Whipple gives him a dismissive, faintly beleaguered look. 'The cephalic extremity is conspicuous by its absence.'

'You mean the head?' Zac enquires.

'That is precisely what I mean, sergeant.'

Whipple motions at the raw ends of the limbs. 'Furthermore, the distal appendicular structures have been removed—sheared away in a single, vigorous stroke by a sharp-edged instrument rather than any surgical procedure, as per the cephalic extremity.'

Frank is already struggling to keep up. 'Bennett, I've already asked this question to Charlene, but is there any chance—no matter how remote—these amputations could have been caused by a boat propeller?'

Whipple snorts, eyes narrowing with academic reluctance. 'At this preliminary juncture, inspector, I would counsel against embracing such a hypothesis. Propeller trauma typically presents with multiple, irregular lacerations—a characteristic patterning of serration, fragmentation, and repetitive impact.'

He gestures delicately at the limb ends. 'What we observe here are singular, decisive transections. Clean in their linearity, yet lacking the refinement of surgical incision. Crude precision, one might say.'

'More like a butcher chopping up a side of beef?' Frank suggests.

Whipple pauses, lips pursed in disapproval at the coarse simile. 'I would not have chosen your phrasing,' he says. 'But the inference of deliberate, forceful intent is not without merit.'

Frank is not uncertain if that's a yes or no. 'So we can rule out a propeller?'

'I am loath to ascribe any definitive causality until a comprehensive post-mortem is undertaken. For now, let us merely say that a propeller is...'

He tilts his head, searching for the least committal phrasing.

'...an implausible agent.'

Zac huffs. 'So that's a no, then?'

'Sergeant,' Whipple warns, 'I did not say *no*. I said *implausible*. The semantics of language is vital—though perhaps not to everyone!'

Frank clears his throat. 'All right, Bennett... any early thoughts on how long he's been in the water?'

Whipple sighs as though Frank has asked him to predict the moon's collapse.

'Inspector, you do enjoy torturing me into conjecture.' He peers down at the waxen skin, the bloating, the pale sloughing across the torso. 'Decomposition in a marine environment is a treacherously capricious process. Temperature, salinity, tidal action, scavenger activity—each plays its own mischievous little part.'

Frank gives him a look. 'A rough idea would be appreciated.'

Whipple relents, albeit begrudgingly. 'Very well. If one were compelled—*compelled*, I say—to venture a preliminary estimate... the integumentary changes, the degree of maceration, and the modest onset of bloating would suggest a submersion period of, shall we say...'

A long, tentative pause.

'...in the order of several days.'

Zac raises an eyebrow. 'Several meaning... two? Four? Ten?'

Whipple bristles. 'Sergeant, several means several. You may select whatever integer best soothes your interpretive anxieties. I shall refine the estimate once we have the controlled environment of the mortuary.'

Frank nods. 'So, ballpark—days, not weeks?'

Whipple rises, his knees issuing a symphony of snaps and pops. 'If you insist on dragging me into the realm of the approximate... yes, days, not weeks. Though I shall deny ever reducing my findings to such barbaric simplicity outside the exigencies of this beach.'

'Any chance you could narrow it down further?' Frank asks, bracing himself for the explosive reply.

Whipple stiffens, wounded by the very request. 'Inspector, you demand precision from conditions that are, by their nature, contemptuous of it—but if one were forced at metaphorical gunpoint to hazard an estimate, then I would surmise a period of immersion in the order of two to four days. But that is conjecture, inspector. Conjecture!' he bellows.

Frank takes a half-step back. 'Okay, keep your hair on, Bennett. No need to shout.'

Whipple's massive chest rises, his voice easing—despite the perspiration tracing a slow descent from his brow.

'And a guess at his age?'

'A provisional estimation: late thirties, perhaps nudging forty. The physique is demonstrably conditioned—pectorals and deltoids well-developed, abdominal definition intact, minimal adipose deposition.

This is not the happenstance musculature of casual labour but the maintained instrument of a man accustomed to disciplined exertion and ascetic dietary practice. In short, inspector, a specimen who has treated his corporeal form with uncommon rigour.'

Frank's at a loss as he scratches his nut. 'In layman's terms, if you could.'

'A fitness fanatic,' Zac says, now disturbingly fluent in Whipplese.

They exchange a look—sharp, loaded, as the same realisation descends.

Frank lifts a hand. 'Charlene—can a couple of your lads turn the body over, please?'

Two SOCO techs in bunny suits step forward. The cameraman circles, shutter clicking in rapid succession. The men take a moment—hands finding purchase at the shoulders, a brief glance to one another—then, with a steadiness bordering on reverence, they roll the corpse onto its front.

Frank drags a hand through his hair.

'Christ... what is going on here?' He turns to Zac. 'I want you and Prisha over at his place now!'

'On it, boss.'

As Zac jogs away across the beach, all eyes fix on the enormous red letters inked across the man's broad back—bold, blocky, a declaration to friend and foe alike.

**TYPHOON**

28

Prisha knocks again, harder this time.

'This is the police! If anyone's inside, open the door—otherwise we'll force entry!'

Silence. She nods to the two uniformed officers. One steps forward with the "big red key"—or, to a passer-by, a battering ram.

As the man takes up position, Zac emerges from the side alley.

'There's a toilet at the side. Window's missing.'

'A break-in?'

He shrugs. 'Possibly. Bloody narrow though.'

The uniform swings the ram back like a pendulum. It crashes into the lock, and the door shudders open.

'Wait here,' she orders the officers.

'Ma'am.'

Zac kicks the door wider open and steps into a gloomy interior, followed by Prisha. She inspects the lock—a drop latch, easy to bust or pick. More interesting are the heavy bolts top and bottom—both pulled back. Zac flicks the light switch back and forth to no avail.

182

'Either the power's off or the lights have tripped.'

Weak daylight filters through gaps in the eaves, highlighting a chaotic choreography of dust. Half a dozen Heineken bottles sit forlornly on a counter behind the pool table. In the far left corner, an armchair, and settee. Hanging between two metal pillars: a pull-up bar. The back wall displays boxing memorabilia—signed posters from the greats of boxing, a pair of red gloves, shorts, a championship belt. Above, a larger poster of Typhoon Tommy in his pomp and circumstance: left eye puffed to the size of a golf ball, lips swollen, white mouthguard smeared in blood. He looks utterly spent, but grinning as a vast crowd roars behind him.

Silence—apart from a repetitive click.

Prisha walks over to the record player, lifts the needle. 'Well, the power's obviously on.' Glances at the vinyl. 'Muddy Waters. Must've been into his blues.'

Zac slips on black nitrile gloves. He inspects the bottles—two half-full, the others, empty.

'Not quite a party.'

Prisha treads carefully to the right and pushes open a crude cubicle door.

Sink opposite. A toilet door ripped off its hinges lies awkwardly to one side. She steps into the toilet, crunching over broken glass, and sees the window frame discarded at the side.

'Prisha!' Zac calls.

She heads back into the main room. Zac is kneeling, fingers tracing the concrete. He pulls a torch from his pocket.

'What is it?' Prisha asks.

'Not sure. It's darker.'

The light illuminates the change in colour of the concrete from light to dark grey.

Prisha crouches. 'Hmm... it's been washed recently, absorbed the moisture. Not much air movement in here. Maybe three or four days ago—possibly longer.'

Zac rises and moves behind the counter, lifting the lid on a metal rectangular box on the floor. It screams that something was stored there recently—now gone.

'Thoughts?' he asks.

'It's odd. Typhoon's dead. Everything suggests someone broke in through the toilet window.'

'You sound sceptical.'

'The front door has two bolts—but they're pulled back. The toilet window's been yanked from its frame.'

'And?'

'Why's it inside? If someone broke in from the alleyway, that's where the window should be. And the toilet door is smashed—like it's been kicked in.'

Zac begins searching for the listening device Smiler planted.

'Easy to explain,' he says. 'Someone—or more than one—comes to the door to buy drugs. Typhoon lets them in; that explains the bolts. There's an altercation, things turn nasty. Maybe he can't get to the front door—someone's blocking it. His only escape is through the toilet. He runs in, locks the door, yanks out the window, but before he climbs out they boot the door in,' he says, rummaging through various small boxes under the counter.

Prisha isn't convinced. 'He's a dealer high up the food chain. How many dealers of Typhoon's standing do you know who don't carry a gun? And an ex-boxer; I'm sure he could handle himself. What were the instructions to Smiler about the listening device?'

'Place it in a spot where it'll pick up a conversation, and where it wouldn't look out of place if someone spotted it.'

'Hi-tech.'

He glares. 'Hey, this wasn't mine or Frank's idea. It was the bloody NCA's master plan. And they've got a point. We've got a dozen USB sticks at home—they're everywhere. Shelves, drawers, cupboards, a wicker basket full of crap. They're so common you don't even notice them.'

She huffs. 'This whole thing's been a dog's dinner since day one. It's like you and Frank have forgotten the fundamentals of policing.'

'And what does that mean?' he grizzles, tipping out a tray of tools, screws, masking tape and drawing pins onto the counter.

'This is not an operation—it's a badly coordinated stab in the dark. Like a bunch of six-year-olds playing Cluedo.

Unsubstantiated hunches, an undercover officer who goes off-script, and the NCA—either keeping things tight to their chest, or playing us.'

'And why would they do that?' he mutters, scraping the detritus back into the basket.

She fixes him with a look. 'Never heard of a stalking horse?'

Zac squints. 'A stalking horse?'

Prisha sighs. 'Yes. One outfit makes a big song and dance in full view—in this case, us—while the real operation happens out of sight. We're the decoy. We keep the suspects, the bystanders—even our own team—distracted. The NCA feeds us just enough to keep us busy on the visible line of enquiry while they quietly chase whatever they actually care about. We're the smokescreen. They get their result, and we get to look like amateur knobheads.'

He resists a smile. 'I think you're being a little paranoid, Prisha.'

'Maybe. Maybe not. But I hate being used.'

Zac checks the pockets of the pool table.

'It's not going to be in there, is it?' she snaps.

'You never know.'

'Why not just ring Smiler?'

'We don't have his number.'

She throws her hands up. 'Give me strength. Why am I not surprised?'

She turns slowly, taking in the interior. Her recent holiday feels a million miles away as she sheds any residue of relaxation and slips back into hard-nosed detective mode.

'Right... boys' shed, boys' club. Pool table, cues, beer bottles, bar fridge, stereo system, porno mags, bar. Typhoon's runners and dealers hang out here. They talk deals, hand over cash, gear, and make plans. So where do they stand?'

A pause.

She looks at the green baize. 'Obviously around the pool table. That's where the talk happens.'

Spins, faces the bar. The beer bottles. Her eyes drop to the counter.

She crouches, runs a hand underneath. Fingers hit something. She prises it free and stands. Smiles at Zac, holding the USB drive aloft.

He can't help but be impressed. 'I'd have found it eventually.'

'Yeah—eventually.' She pockets it. 'Right. Let's get back to the station and see what this antiquated piece of shit can tell us. But first, call Charlene. I want forensics all over this place.'

'Why? We've got what we came for.'

'In case you missed it, Typhoon had his head, hands, and feet hacked off. That's murder. So where did it happen? You've already found washed concrete.'

'It could've happened anywhere.'

Prisha rolls her neck, releasing tension. 'And it could've happened here. Let's be thorough.'

Her eyes flick open. She stares at the ceiling fan.

Puzzlement—only for a second.

'Shine your torch on the ceiling.'

Zac clicks the flashlight on and raises it.

'Christ,' Prisha whispers. 'Unless I'm very much mistaken—that's blood splatter.'

* * *

Frank blinks. Then blinks again.

'What do you bloody mean there's nothing on it, lad?' he bellows.

Dinkel shrugs apologetically. Not that it's his fault.

'It's blank, sir. There should be an MP3 or a WAV file if it actually recorded anything.'

Prisha rolls her eyes and bites her tongue.

'Let me have a bloody look,' Frank demands.

Dinkel spins his laptop around and points at the empty folder of the USB drive.

'See?'

Frank rubs a hand over his face. 'Is it charged up?'

'Yes, sir. Fully charged.'

'Then it must be broken.'

'Did no one test it first?' Prisha asks.

Zac and Frank exchange guilty glances.

Dinkel pulls the device from the laptop. 'Easy to test.'

He lifts the stick to his mouth, clicks the button and speaks.

'Mary had a little lamb. Its fleece was white as snow; and everywhere that Mary went, the lamb was sure to…'

'For fuck's sake,' Zac groans.

'That'll do, Dinkel,' Frank says. 'We don't need a full recital.'

Dinkel reattaches the drive, clicks his mouse and the recording begins.

*Mary had a little lamb. Its fleece was white as snow; and everywhere that Mary went, the lamb was sure to…*

*For fuck's sake.*

*That'll do, Dinkel. We don't need a full recital.*

Frank takes in the enormity of the situation, suddenly feeling very exposed, and extremely concerned for Smiler's welfare. Those two emotions crash headlong into another feeling—guilt.

He rubs the back of his neck aggressively.

'Why the hell didn't Smiler switch it on? And where the hell is he? If anything's happened to that lad, I'll never forgive myself.'

'It's not your fault, Frank,' Zac states, empathising. 'You were outranked on that one.'

Frank grizzles. 'I should have kicked back more, damn it.'

The others fall silent as Frank paces back and forth.

'Typhoon's dead. At least we assume he's dead—unless someone else with the nickname Typhoon has it plastered all over their back. Extremely bloody unlikely. We've no idea where Smiler is—or if he's still alive. Tonight Danny Beale will be adrift at sea with a bunch of unknowns, along with Cleavage, a total innocent in all of this. And somewhere along the line I feel like I've been played.'

Zac's eyes narrow. 'You think Silas set us up?'

Frank's frustration boils over. 'I don't know what I bloody think! But with the benefit of hindsight, why didn't he at least give us a list of names of who *not* to arrest while his operation was underway? And why didn't he or one of his officers coerce Smiler into planting the bug instead of getting me to do the dirty work?'

Zac shoots Prisha a sideways glance. 'Prisha raised similar concerns earlier, boss.'

Frank halts and stares at Prisha, who is a tad embarrassed.

'Did she indeed,' he murmurs.

A long silence ensues, no one willing to challenge or agree with Frank in case he blows his fuse.

Frank is long in the tooth—an old dog, maybe—but still wily enough to know his limits.

He takes a step towards Prisha.

'Right,' he declares. 'Enough. Time for a reset.'

Prisha cocks her head. 'Frank?'

'You can park your cold case for the moment. You are now on this investigation. We start from ground zero and figure out what the hell is really going on here. Understood?'

Prisha nods, corralling her expression to neutral.

'Understood, boss.'

Frank offers a faint smile as Hedley Keegan's warning—six weeks old now—resurfaces uninvited.

A warning he'd sworn not to share.

And one that weighs a little heavier with each passing hour.

The owner of the holiday apartments is dubious as he studies the young man in front of him. It's unusual for someone to contact him directly and ask to look around. Most bookings are made online. And another peculiarity; most people who rent his accommodation are families or couples—this guy appears to be alone.

'How long do you want it for?' he asks.

Smiler offers him his warmest smile. 'Definitely a couple of weeks, maybe longer.'

'You on holiday?'

'No, I'm local. My flat is being renovated, and the builders are in. It's a bombsite. They say two weeks, but you know what builders are like. It could easily blow out to three.'

The man relaxes a little. 'You got no relatives to stay with?'

*Does this guy want to rent his empty apartment or not,* Smiler thinks.

'No. Anyway, I prefer my own space. You know what it's like when you stay with other people; feels like you're imposing.'

The man nods and pulls out a swipe card and runs it across the glass-panelled door. It's followed by a click. He pulls it open and walks into the small airy entrance adorned with a couple of rubber plants.

Smiler likes it. It's modern, clean, and situated overlooking the river, a good mile or two from the town centre, so relatively quiet. There's also a convenience store a short walk away and an Indian restaurant. Takeaways and microwave meals will do just fine.

He follows the man along a small passageway and waits as he presses the lift button.

'How much is it a week?' Smiler quizzes.

'Six hundred.'

*Shit! That's steep.* 'Right.'

'That a problem?' the man continues.

'No, not at all.'

The lift door slides open, and they both step inside as the man hits the button for the fourth floor.

'What line of work are you in?' the man asks.

'Web design. Freelance. I do everything on my laptop. Can work from anywhere. A digital nomad.'

The man relaxes a little although he's still slightly on edge, mainly due to the lad's attire. A long, old-fashioned Mod parka, and a woollen hat with shades resting on top.

'Aren't you too warm?'

'Nah. My gran always asks the same. She says I must be cold-blooded,' he adds with a chuckle.

'Hmm.'

The lift doors ping open, and Smiler follows the owner down the corridor. They pass two other doors, but it's a slow time of year, so he may be lucky and have no neighbours.

'Two bedrooms. One bathroom and toilet. Open-plan kitchen and living room. Balcony overlooking the river. No pets, no smoking, no parties and we have a quiet policy after 10 pm.'

'No probs. You won't hear a peep out of me.'

Another swipe of the card and they enter the apartment. Smiler wanders around and immediately feels at home.

'Love it, brilliant.'

It's tastefully decorated. Tiled floors, ceiling fans, a fake coal fire, sleek kitchen. Comfy-looking beds and a great view over the river.

'Okay. I'll take it for two weeks. If it looks like the builder is going to take longer than that, I'll let you know as soon as I can.'

'Okay. I'll just need to get some details and your payment and a reimbursable deposit on your credit card in case of damage.'

Smiler pulls a wad of notes from his pocket. 'Cash okay?' *Of course it's okay; it's better than okay. Straight into his back pocket. The taxman won't know about this.*

The man smiles. 'Aye. I'll still need a credit card though.'

Smiler grimaces. 'Ah, bit of a problem there. I either had it stolen or lost it a few days ago. I put a hold on it straight away, and the bank said they'd issued another one, but it hasn't arrived yet. But I'm happy to give you cash.'

Smiler peels off the money and hands it to the man, who folds it and slips it into his pocket. He isn't convinced by anything the young man has said, but he seems genial enough, a quiet type. No trouble. And twelve hundred pounds, no income tax, no VAT, well, it's not to be sneezed at.

The man places the swipe card on the kitchen counter. 'Enjoy your stay, Mr...sorry, I forgot your name.'

'Lister. Owen Lister.'

⁕

Smiler's stomach rumbles as he leaves the curry house with a carrier bag full of goodies. Two onion bhajis, a prawn rogan josh, four chapatis and a carton of pilau rice. It's been days since he ate a proper meal, living off crisps, biscuits, and sugary drinks. He pulls the hood up on his parka and slips his sunglasses on. His mood is a lot better than it's been for a few days. At last, his sympathetic nervous system seems to be settling down. Feels a little safer, less like a hunted rabbit. He has a cheap mobile phone, food, and a comfortable bed to sleep in. Still hasn't figured out what he should do, but he'll sleep on that.

Five minutes later and he's swiping the keycard across the door. It's a cool, but calm evening. Ducks glide effortlessly along the river. A couple of pleasure boats mooring up for the night. He's beginning to breathe again, and the smell of the curry is driving him mad. He jabs at the lift button and waits. Pushes away the thought of Typhoon's headless body. Considers whether he should just walk into the police station tomorrow and spill everything to Mr Finnegan. Maybe, maybe not. No, just lie low for another few days. Regain your composure.

The lift doors slide open, and he steps inside. He presses the number four button. The doors start to close. A disembodied arm thrusts between them. They reopen.

Two men enter, silent. One stands shoulder-to-shoulder with Smiler, the other a step ahead facing the doors as they close. Smiler drops his head, fixes on the rubber flooring. Lift rumbles into action. A faint smell of aftershave, expensive. It's one of those awkward lift moments where no one knows where to look.

The man's expression twitches into a smile that doesn't match his eyes.

'Smells good,' he says, nodding at the carrier bag.

'Yeah. Curry. Rogan josh,' Smiler replies, still keeping his attention fixed on the floor.

The man leans forward and whispers something to his companion. Both men laugh. Private joke.

The lift dings. Doors part. The men step out, moving in a single unbroken line. They turn right. Smiler hangs left.

Swipes the keycard. Door clicks.

The voice echoes down the corridor. 'Enjoy, my friend.'

Smiler gazes over his shoulder at the men about to enter their apartment.

'Thanks.'

The man with a scar on his left cheek pauses a moment as if a niggle has wormed into his brain. Grins, gives a half wave and disappears inside.

# 30

## 7:30 pm

Danny Beale has been a copper for over twenty-five years. He's seen and done it all. It's true that when he arrives at the Pearly Gates, he may have to be economical with the truth when having a recap with St Peter.

It's also true he's bent some rules. Although that depends on your perception of bent. If you consider snapping something over your knee and tossing it away with carefree abandon as bending something, then you're probably singing from the same Danny Beale hymnbook.

It's part of the gig. To get results.

And this gets to the core of Beale's existential dilemma with his chosen profession.

Half the problem is the bigwigs; the career-climbers, the pen-pushing bureaucratic fuckwits, the clipboard-hugging compliance drones, the ethics-committee finger-waggers, the HR holiness brigade, and the Professional Standards puritans.

None of them get it.

For Beale it's simple; there are some really bad people out there, people who rape, murder, torture, rob, steal, exploit. These people have no ethics, no rule book, no crisis of conscience. They don't have to fill out a timesheet or justify their expenses. He doubts they even have a sense of right and wrong, or if they do, they certainly pay no heed to it.

So how do you deal with these types? You play by their rules—which means—no rules. It's the Wild West, and Beale is a sheriff. Best way to catch a bad person—send a bad person after them. A *real* bad person.

He's a hard man who knows how to fight, to snap fingers, gouge eyeballs, kidney punch, headbutt, rupture testicles with his kneecap, and break arms like twigs. He's only once come out on the wrong side of a scrap. He misjudged a Nepalese vegan who looked like a malnourished beanpole and got seven shades of shite kicked out of him. Turned out Sherpa Tenzing was a black belt in jujitsu, or chai latte or some such fucking thing. Whatever it was, it folded him in half. Out of action for eight weeks. Both arms in traction. Had to get a nurse to wipe his arse—so there was an upside. Since then he's treated every quiet, skinny bloke with caution, and thankfully he's yet to cross paths with another Sherpa.

But that was a one-off a long time ago.

He's confident in his ability to come out on top in any situation.

Beale is *not* the nervous type.

So why today, as he steps aboard The Whitby Rose, does he experience a sudden pulse of anxiety?

Beale leans against the guardrail, sucking on a Lambert &
Butler as the boat chugs out of the harbour. Conditions
are good. A small swell—nothing major. Overcast, with a
bit of light drizzle. Seven crew on board including himself.
Francois the skipper. A local lad built like a brick shithouse
who goes by the rather unflattering name of Cleavage. And
lastly, Dritan and three of his gang—Stefan, Mika, and
Arben.

Already there's been a change of plan. It was supposed
to be a two-day trip, but it's now looking like a
twenty-four-hour affair. Something about a low-pressure
system moving in from Norway. The skipper doesn't seem
too perturbed—says it's an opportunity to iron out any
problems and for the crew to get to know one another.

He feels a hand on his shoulder. Dritan.

'How are you going, my friend?'

Beale flicks the cigarette overboard. 'Aye, no too bad.'

'Good.' He removes the hand as the smile slips from his
face. 'Have you managed to keep off the drink?'

'Not had a drop for a few days.'

Dritan nods, serious. 'You may experience the shakes.
Withdrawal—it is a demon that will visit. But you are
strong. I see it in your eyes. Fight through, and it will get
easier. And accommodation?'

'Managed to snag a room at a boarding house. Fifteen quid a night. It's not the Ritz, but it's a bed, toilet, shower. Safe and dry.'

The beguiling smile returns. 'Good. Stick with Dritan and things will improve for you.' He gazes back at the harbour. 'It's a good six hours before we reach the fishing grounds. If you need rest, then now is the time, yes?'

'Aye, you're right. I may go and get my head down.'

⸺ ❖ ⸺

Dritan steps into the wheelhouse where Cleavage is sharing his local knowledge with Skipper Francois.

Cleavage points starboard.

'South of the east pier, you've got reefs. Saltwick Nab runs out a good six hundred metres. Proper bastard of a place—shallow as a paddling pool, sharp enough to open a hull like a tin of beans.'

'This is the one that sank the hospital ship?' Francois asks.

'Aye—the Rohilla. Weather shoved her straight onto it. Snapped her clean in two. Folk onshore said it sounded like a house collapsing.'

Francois studies the chart. 'And the other one—further down the coast?'

'Black Nab.' Cleavage nods. 'Looks like nowt from a distance—just a lump. But it's a big bugger: forty feet high.

At high tide, you only see the tip. Easy to miss. Plenty haven't.'

Francois gives a low whistle. 'These nabs... they are close to the harbour?'

'Close enough you can smell the fish and chips before you drown.'

Francois looks back toward the harbour mouth. 'When I came in, it was calm. Fog rolling in behind me, but calm. I thought it was simple enough.'

Cleavage snorts. 'Aye, you were lucky. Calm hides everything. In a swell, it's like threading a needle in a fistfight. The cliffs bounce the sea back at you, the tide drags you sideways, and if the wind's in the south? Forget it—waves break clean across the entrance. You're flooring it just to keep her pointing the right way.'

Francois taps the chart. 'These shapes—Whitby Rock. It looks... extensive.'

Cleavage laughs. 'Extensive? Mate, it's a suburb. Not one rock—three. Whole chain of teeth under the water. Hit any of 'em and you're not limping home. You're getting craned out in pieces.'

'And the buoy—the yellow one?'

'Whitby Rock buoy. Your big warning sign. Come in from the southeast and go the wrong side of it, you might as well ring the coastguard before the crunch. Local rule: keep it to port or kiss your arse goodbye.'

Francois squints again. 'This course—169 degrees. This is official?'

'Aye. You line up on the leading marks—the white triangle over the dot—and hold it till you catch the pier lights. Easy on a clear day. But sea fret can roll in faster than you can blink.'

'Sea fret?'

'Fog.'

'And the swell?'

'Two hours before high water you get a nasty set pushing you east—right across the entrance. Don't counter it, and you're scraping paint off the pier.'

Francois nods slowly. 'And strong winds?'

'Northwest through east? Forget it. Seen small craft turned into matchsticks. Lost a mate on a day that "looked fine". Never trust how it looks from land.'

Francois exhales. 'Then we follow the buoy. We follow the marks. We respect the tide.'

'We respect everything,' Cleavage says. 'Harbour looks friendly from the pier. But come in blind, in weather, with swell off the cliffs? It'll gut you quicker than a filleting knife.'

Francois nods. 'Good. Then we do what you say.'

Cleavage smirks. 'Now you're catching on. Right, you're out of danger now. Just head east-north-east to Dogger Bank and you can't go wrong. I'm going to get my head down for a few hours. Any issues, and wake me up.'

'I'll be fine from here, thank you, Cleavage.'

'Not a problem. That's what you're paying me for.' He slips from the wheelhouse.

Dritan stands beside Francois. 'Well?'

Francois offers a tight Gaelic wobble of the head. 'He's competent. Still—two unknowns in our midst? I don't like it. Too much risk.'

'You worry too much, Francois. On some trips, we will be returning at night in stormy conditions. That is when Cleavage comes into his own. And we'll time our pick-ups when both men are asleep. They'll be none the wiser.'

Francois isn't convinced. 'I can understand taking on Cleavage for his knowledge. This makes sense. But the tramp to gut fish? Why?'

Dritan chuckles. 'You go to the dog shelter and pick a mutt. It's scared, timid, maybe so scared it's dangerous. You take it home, feed it, walk it, give it a pat and a hug. You make it a comfortable bed in front of the fire. You have a friend for life. That dog will protect you, die for you. People… they're not much different from dogs.' He turns to leave. 'Anyway, Cleavage is short term. After two, three trips, you will have the knowledge.'

'And the tramp?'

'He'll be on a tight leash.'

'But can we trust him?'

He shrugs. 'I think so. If he turns rabid… we euthanise him.'

Dritan studies the nautical chart on the back wall, and stabs a finger at the inked, red circle.

'Have you entered the coordinates?'

Francois glances over his shoulder. 'Yes. Whale Cemetery is our destination.'

31

The wind has sharp teeth as it whips in off the North Sea, daylight dwindling. Frank pulls up the collar of his coat and looks down at Foxtrot, who's happily sniffing the railings along the coastal path overlooking West Beach.

He glances back up the walking track.

The figure is still there—loitering on top of West Cliff.

A gentle tug on the lead. 'Come on, Foxtrot, that's long enough.'

He resumes his nightly routine along the Cleveland Way, but tonight he weaves a more convoluted path—doubling back, pausing to let Foxtrot sniff a lamppost or bench. He pulls out a handkerchief and noisily blows his nose. Another sideways glance. The man is maybe three hundred yards back. Long coat, hood up. Every time Frank stops, the stranger lingers. Pretends to admire the sea view.

'Aye,' Frank mutters under his breath. 'Thought so.'

Foxtrot emits a familiar expectant whimper as Frank hangs a left onto Upgang Lane, the watering hole clearly in sight.

'Patience, Foxtrot. Nearly there.'

They saunter into The White House Inn. The warmth, the hum of conversation, and the smell of beer hit Frank like a blessing.

'Hello, stranger,' the barman calls with a grin.

'Very funny. A comedian on every corner,' Frank says. 'Pint of Theakston's, Jack. And a packet of pork scratchings for Foxtrot.' He steers the dog to a corner. 'Stay.'

Foxtrot sits obediently, eyes fixed on the packet of treats on the counter.

Frank slips out of the bar, through the back doors and into the beer garden. With more difficulty than he'd like to admit, he hauls himself over the waist-high stone wall and cuts up the slope in front of the pub.

He moves fast—and stealthily for a man his size. Two long strides, then grabs the figure from behind, wrenching an arm up between the shoulder blades and spinning him around.

'Right then, sunshine—what's your little game?'

Yanks down the hood of the parka.

Takes a step back, surprised.

'Smiler?'

They've found a deserted nook in the lounge overlooking the golf course. Two comfortable armchairs, tucked away from flapping ears.

Frank takes a hefty quaff of beer. Smiler sits opposite, nursing a coke, hood pulled up like he's trying to retreat inside it.

'We've been worried about you,' Frank says.

Smiler's eyes flick around the room—quick, nervous little sweeps. There's barely a handful of customers in tonight, and all of them are regulars.

Frank follows the lad's jittery gaze. 'You expecting someone?'

'Don't know.'

Frank sighs. 'Why didn't you switch on the listening device at Typhoon's gaff?'

Smiler offers a half-shrug. 'I forgot.'

Frank raises an eyebrow. 'Really?'

'It's true, Mr Finnegan. A stupid mistake. I was that nervous.'

'Did you plant it Friday night as arranged?'

A nod. 'Yeah.'

Frank decides to throw it in early to gauge his reaction. 'Typhoon's dead.'

Smiler's fingers tighten around the glass. He stares at the carpet.

'Yeah... I know. I was there.'

Frank leans forward. 'You were there when he was killed?'

'Yes.'

'Who killed him?'

Smiler looks up, eyes wide, almost pleading. 'I swear to God, Mr Finnegan, I don't know. New guys I've never seen before. Foreign.'

'What did they look like?'

'I... I don't know.'

Frank's tone hardens. 'You just said they were blokes you'd never seen before. Either you saw them or you didn't.'

'It was dark. I was in the bathroom and saw them through a crack in the door.' He swallows hard. 'They... cut his head off. With a machete. Calm as you like. It all happened so fast.'

'Nationality?'

'Don't know. Their voices were low. Typhoon said they were Polaks—assumed he meant Polish. Said they'd been round the night before and offered him money for his business and he could work for them. Course, Typhoon told them to piss off.' His voice cracks. 'They tried to kill *me*, Mr Finnegan. I shouldn't be here.'

Frank studies him. This isn't an act. He knows genuine fear when it's staring him in the face—and Smiler is petrified.

He leans back, steadying himself. 'Right, lad. You'd best start from the beginning.'

---

Frank's barrel chest rises as Smiler finishes his rambling, occasionally tangled account of events.

'I'm scared, Mr Finnegan. I need to get as far away from here as possible.'

'Then why haven't you?'

'Because I needed to speak with you first. When we chatted at the station, I didn't tell you everything.'

'Such as?'

'Typhoon's organisation. I know more than I let on.'

Frank nods once. 'Go on, let's hear it.'

Smiler takes a deep breath. 'Typhoon was organised. Properly organised. He had a tight crew. He's known—was known—as the General. And he had three trusted lieutenants who looked after his territories.'

Frank sips his beer, saying nothing.

'Wiggy ran the southern coastal district—Hull up to Scarborough. Blagger ran the central coast—north of Whitby up to Hartlepool. And Gasket ran the north coast—Sunderland to the Scottish border.'

Smiler rubs his palms against his jeans. 'Each lieutenant had their own group of trusted dealers—Captain's, they're called. Everything flows down the chain of command. If a lieutenant steps out of line, Typhoon dealt with it himself.

If a captain ripped him off or messed up, the lieutenant handled it.'

He looks up at Frank, eyes hollow. 'Like I said... it was all highly organised. Everyone had responsibilities and knew their place in the pecking order.'

Frank nods once. 'All very informative. But why risk hanging around Whitby to tell me this?'

Smiler blinks, almost offended. 'Isn't it obvious? If this new gang is trying to take over Typhoon's business, then the three lieutenants could be next.'

Frank studies him. The lad's rough around the edges, but he's not rotten to the core. He possibly risked his life tonight to save three others who'd never do the same for him.

'Okay,' Frank says, pulling out a notepad. 'You've given me three names—nicknames, I assume. What are their real ones?'

Smiler shakes his head. 'I don't know. Honest. And that's what's scaring me.' He leans in, voice dropping low. 'If the blokes who killed Typhoon hacked my phone, which I'm certain they did, then...'

Frank holds a hand up to calm him. 'Slow down, Smiler. You're a young lad. I'm sure you'll have near to a hundred contacts on your phone. How are they going to know who Typhoon's lieutenants are unless they personally ring every number and pose the question? They can't track these so-called lieutenants from *your* phone.'

Smiler's eyes widen in fear. 'You don't understand.' Takes a nervous sip of coke. 'You've obviously raided Typhoon's lock-up?'

'Yes, today.'

'Did you find his mobile?'

'No. But even if the assailants took *his* phone and hacked it, then they face the same dilemma—hundreds of contacts to wade through.'

'No—it's not the contacts I'm worried about.'

'Then what?'

'It wasn't to watch over them, but to see who was *where* to make deals or receive drugs from suppliers. They're sitting targets, Mr Finnegan.'

*The lad's like a cat on a hot tin roof,* Frank thinks. *Has a tendency to jump ahead in his explanations.*

'What wasn't to watch over them?'

'The GPS tracking app on Typhoon's phone. They'll be able to see exactly where the lieutenants are.'

# 32



The couple walk up the garden path towards the modest three-bedroom terrace house, the moon bright above.

Blagger emits a lager burp. 'Oops. Pardon me.'

'Dirty pig,' Sophie laughs. At the door she wobbles slightly, fishes her keys from her handbag, slots one into the lock. 'Won't your wife wonder where you are at this time of night?'

'Nah. All good. She knows I conduct some of my business late sometimes.'

'Some of your business,' she repeats, giggling as she pushes the door open. 'And what business is it exactly?'

Blagger grins, follows her inside, gives her a cheeky slap on the arse.

'Hear no secrets, tell no lies.' He nudges the door shut.

She loops her arms around his neck, breath warm and sweet with vodka. 'I know what you do,' she whispers, kissing him softly.

'Oh yeah?'

'You're a drug dealer. And high up on the food chain from what I've heard.'

He leans back, wide grin, slightly proud. 'Is that right? For your information, I'm a businessman, actually.'

'Yeah. Whatever.'

His hands slip to her backside. Squeezes. 'Are we going to talk or fuck?'

She half pushes him away, faux insulted. 'Excuse me. I'm a lady and I don't fuck.'

'Oh yeah?'

'I make passionate love... if it's the right man.'

Blagger bows with comic flourish. 'I do beg your pardon, madam. Would you care to talk or make passionate love?'

Another girlish giggle as she grabs his hand and leads him up the stairs.

'Let's fuck.'

⸺◆⸺

She's on all fours on the bed, naked except for the glittery skirt he insisted she keep on.

Blagger—feet planted on the carpet—thrusts back and forth, sweat forming on his hairless chest.

She moans into the pillow. 'Spank me.'

'For real?'

'Yes, do it.'

He smiles. *Right goer, this one.*

Gives her a half-hearted slap across the left buttock. She rocks back and forth so expertly his own efforts feel superfluous to requirements.

'Harder,' she cries.

He grins, obliges. 'You asked for it.'

Another slap.

'Oh *yes*. Talk dirty.'

'What?'

'Talk dirty,' she begs.

He's seen it online, heard lads talk about it, but has never done it. He hesitates, unsure where to begin.

'Give me some ideas.'

'Tell me what a bad girl I am.'

He snorts, trying not to laugh. 'Okay... you're a bad girl. A naughty, dirty girl.'

'Say it like you mean it.'

'You dirty slut.'

A sharper smack.

She responds with increasing fervour. 'More.'

Blagger grips her hips and drives forward with the crude urgency of a rutting animal.

'Okay, you've asked for it, you dirty little wh—'

A sound. A bump.

Something from downstairs.

He slows.

'What was that?'

Sophie glances back, hair in her eyes. 'What?'

'That noise.'

'I didn't hear anything. It'll be Twanky.'

'Who the fuck is Twanky?'

'My cat. He's old. Half blind. Bangs into things.'

He exhales, relaxing. 'Ah.'

'Spank me again. Harder this time. And talk proper filthy.'

He leans back, grinning at his good fortune.

*Christ, I've fallen arse-backwards into the butter here.*

Slap. Thwack. Groans. Gasps.

The squeak of the bedframe in time with his breath.

His face tightens.

*Getting there. Getting there. Getting...*

The bedroom door creaks open.

One frozen second.

Three people locking eyes.

Blagger and Sophie stare at the figure in the doorway—silent, dressed in black, balaclava pulled down, pistol raised.

Sophie's mouth opens to scream.

*Pfft. Pfft.*

Two neat holes appear in Blagger's forehead.

His eyes don't shut instantly.

As if a last shard of thought is still afloat in the porridge the bullets have made of his brain.

But only for a second, maybe two.

He collapses backwards onto the carpet.

The gunman is already gone.

Now Sophie screams.

# 33

## Hull — 11:05 pm

The two friends step out of the Burlington Tavern onto Manor Street, in the old part of Hull near the docks. Moonlight reflects and shimmers on the damp pavers of the narrow laneway.

They turn right, heading towards the city centre, debating what to eat.

'I fancy a curry,' Wiggy says.

His mate is less keen. 'We always go for a curry. What about Chinese for a change?'

'Nah. I always end up with a cracking headache after Chinese. I reckon it's the MSG they put in it.'

'All right, what about we keep it simple—takeaway kebab?'

'Hmm... maybe,' he replies before pulling a pained expression.

'What's the matter?'

'I need a piss.'

'Why didn't you go in the pub?'

'Because I didn't feel the urge in the fucking pub. *Christ*, are we still at school and I need permission to go for a piss?'

He spots a dark lane twenty yards up on the right. 'Won't be a minute. Wait here.'

His friend curses under his breath and pulls out his phone as Wiggy skedaddles down the alley and takes cover behind a pair of industrial wheelie bins, out of sight.

Unzips, pulls his cock out, and leans one hand against the brick wall for balance as men often do when they've had too much to drink.

'Ah yes,' he murmurs as the stream relieves the ache in his bladder.

'We both had the same idea, my friend.'

The foreign voice startles him. He jolts, spraying piss across his shoes as he glances sideways at the man approaching—shortish but solid, bomber jacket zipped to the throat, heavy Docs.

Wiggy replies bullishly. 'What's that, mate?'

'I said—we have both been caught short,' the man replies, chuckling lightly as he scans the alley for somewhere to take a leak.

Wiggy relaxes. 'Yeah. A bad habit of mine. Once I feel the urge, that's it—I've got to go.'

'Me too. Maybe it is a sign of old age—no? Prostate problem.'

The man's words come from behind.

'Cheeky bastard,' Wiggy says, humour edging his words.

Pulls a cigarette from the packet and sparks up. Inhales deeply. Tilts his head back, gazes at the stars and exhales, enjoying the nicotine rush.

Nothing more than a niggling thought

*The voice—Greek, Italian? Typhoon's warning. The visitors.*

Suddenly alert, he shakes, slips himself back in, zips up.

Too late.

The pain hits—bright, shocking, absolute—something cinches tight around his throat. The cigarette drops. His hands fly up.

Claws at the wire, slicing into his skin.

Tight.

Tighter.

Tightening.

Breath snatched away. A wet rasp in his windpipe. He buckles, jerks, shoes scraping on the slimy cobbles as he tries to twist free. The metal only bites deeper. Hot line of agony around his neck.

Vision speckles. Limbs go hollow. Strength waning. The world begins to grey at the edges.

'Come on, Wiggy! Get a fucking move on!' his friend calls from the street.

The garrotte is released.

Wiggy collapses sideways, skull tapping the brickwork with a dull knock as he slumps to the ground.

The assassin is efficient. Doesn't hesitate. Drops to a crouch, grips Wiggy's head in both hands—steady—and delivers one violent, economical twist, like a chiropractor with an evil streak.

A soft crack.

Nothing more.

Plucks up the still-smouldering cigarette, takes a drag, and casually walks away in the opposite direction without looking back.

Another call from his best mate. 'Christ, Wiggy! What are you doing down there?'

Wiggy, for obvious reasons, doesn't reply.

# 34

## Sunderland — 11:23 pm

Gasket sits behind the wheel of his pride and joy—a silver 2014 BMW 330d M Sport, clean lines, tuned enough to give him a kick, subtle enough to avoid traffic cops.

Not flash. Just smart.

His kind of motor. He's always been into cars.

Hip hop music murmurs through the speakers—low bass, soft snare. The lad in the passenger seat is jittery, tapping one knee like he's auditioning for a drum solo.

'Calm down,' Gasket says. 'You're not buying a fucking nuclear warhead.' He produces a small sealed bag of crystal meth. 'Same gear as last time.'

The lad nods, pulls out his phone, thumbs the transfer.

Gasket's handset pings a second later. He checks it.

'Good lad.' Gasket hands over the bag. 'Go steady on it. It's strong gear. A little goes a long way.'

'Yeah, right.'

The lad mumbles his thanks, slips out the door, hoodie up, vanishing into the quiet residential street. Gasket watches him disappear in the wing mirror.

'Jesus. Kids today. Was I like that twenty years ago?'

He switches the radio over to the classical channel—his preferred listening.

Doesn't like to play it with a customer in the car. Doesn't fit his persona.

They might think he's weird. What major drug dealer worth his salt listens to classical music ?

But now he's alone, he lets it come through the speakers, low at first: slow strings, soft steps, something steady that builds in the background without shouting for attention. Samuel Barber's *Agnus Dei*.

He releases a deep sigh as the car moves off. 'That's better,' he mutters. 'A bit of culture.'

The car glides through the estate. Empty roads. Sodium lights. Occasional fox darting between gardens. The music sits in the background—gentle at first, like it hasn't decided what mood it's in.

He sees the 24-hour Auto Car Wash sign glowing at the far end of the retail strip.

'Perfect,' he says. 'Treat the girl.'

Likes to keep his pride and joy clean.

He swings in. The place is deserted. Let's the car idle a moment. A set of headlights appears in his rearview. Watches it cautiously. A small work van. It passes him, and parks in Bay 1.

A man exits in a hi-vis orange vest, overalls on. Moves to the rear of the van, pulls out a toolbox and saunters deeper into the wash bay with all the time in the world.

'Huh, must've had a call out. Certainly in no rush. Probably paid by the minute.'

Gasket slides the car into gear and rolls to the payment terminal of Bay 2.

Taps his card.

Selects Deluxe Wash–£10.

Green light.

Car edges forward.

Checks the windows are shut.

Engine off, but electrics on for the music.

Reaches for a skinny joint.

Lights it.

Suck. Hold. Hold. Hold. Release.

A long, deep sigh as the drug hits his tired brain.

'Nice. Sweet. Chill.'

The conveyor engages, and the BMW is pulled gently into the wash bay.

Water sprays first—flicking across the bonnet.

Foam jets fire, thick white suds splattering the windscreen.

They cling, slide, smear.

Inside, classical strings hum—long, slow, patient.

Melancholy wrapped in Godliness.

He turns the volume up a good notch.

Relaxes into the seat, joint between his fingers, eyes half-closed.

He wonders if he'll ever earn enough to get out of this grind—open a legit garage, re-build engines, work with his hands instead of worrying who's watching him or which little scrote, desperate and out of dough, is going to pull a blade on him. Yeah, he can see himself the proud owner of a garage, a repair shop. Maybe just stick to classic cars. Knows his way around those and the owners are always cashed up. No haggling over the price.

A daft thought, he tells himself. But a nice one. Maybe one day.

Something moves outside.

A shape cutting across the blurred window—only a hint of it through the drifting foam.

He frowns, then relaxes.

'Maintenance bloke.'

Takes another drag.

The music rises a little—violins tightening, deep notes stirring underneath like a warning he doesn't hear.

The wash tunnel shudders.

A mechanical clunk.

Everything stops.

Brushes frozen.

Water cut.

Conveyor silent.

The sudden stillness feels wrong.

'You're kidding me,' Gasket groans.

Soapy lather slides down the glass, carving patterns, thick and streaked, making the outside world look smeared and underwater.

He checks the wing mirror.

*Good.*

The worker is approaching.

Toolbox in one hand.

A takeaway coffee cup in the other.

Gasket taps the window button.

Glass rolls all the way down.

If he'd been switched on, he might've wondered where the bloke got a takeaway coffee from at this hour, in an automated car wash with no staff.

*If.*

Tiny word—massive meaning.

'Hey, mate, what's the go?' Gasket asks. 'I've paid for a deluxe.'

The man steps in close. Expression neutral. Calm. Professional.

'Yeah, sorry about that, my friend,' he says quietly, his accent not raising any concerns. 'Small issue with the pump. Same problem on the other bay. Hang tight, and I'll get it up and running in no time.'

Gasket gives a faint nod.

The worker doesn't move.

Their eyes lock.

Two, three, four seconds pass.

A lazy thought flits through his mind—*what's his fucking problem?*

Eyes drift to the cardboard coffee cup.

A distinctive smell.

Hits him like a punch to the nose—*SHIT!*

He's in trouble.

Brain sends a signal to his body to turn the ignition and hit the accelerator hard.

*Too late.*

The sedative effect of the spliff delays the message by a critical second.

The man hurls the contents of the coffee cup through the window

Gasket jerks backward as the liquid blinds him.

He braces for scalding pain.

Instead, it stings—chemical sharp, biting.

The overpowering reek of petrol hits him.

The worker pulls a small aerosol can from his jacket and a lighter.

A click.

A hiss.

A strip of blue flame stretches out in a fiery lance, igniting Gasket—face, hair, neck, clothes—eyebrows gone in an instant.

*WHOOMPH!*

Fire rips across him—total, unforgiving.

Skin, the first casualty. Blistering, peeling back into scorched, shrinking knots.

Then sight and breath.

Tries to cry out, but the blast of heat cooks the air in his lungs to steam.

Eyeballs melt.

The cabin, a furnace.

A smell.

Burnt pork, sweet but off, riding on a harsh solvent stench.

The music lifts into a slow crescendo—*Agnus Dei*—Lamb of God.

The ethereal voices swell, yearning upward towards a single, blinding point of light.

The worker picks up the toolbox and saunters away.

Thumps the re-start button on the car wash.

Fine spray erupts.

Washers spin and move forward.

The burning BMW glows behind him, a dull orange smudge through the drifting mist, as the angelic choir touches heaven.

**35**

As the boat performs another unexpected heave to the side, Beale is already rethinking his rather hasty enthusiasm for the undercover gig.

Gig? That makes it sound optional. It wasn't. Not an offer, not an opportunity, not even a nudge.

Let's not arse about. It was an ultimatum dressed in weasel words, lacquered with Latin and bureaucratic idioms—the kind of linguistic diarrhoea politicians gush when they're caught trousers-down and desperately prevaricating in front of the cameras.

Or senior officers when they're pretending they're not twisting your arm up your spinal column.

The Assistant Chief Constable had been *clear*—or as clear as an ACC ever gets, which is to say: not clear at all to any sane, oxygen-breathing human.

Opaque is a kinder word.

Deliberately obfuscatory, even better.

Beale has endured years of their interminable gobbledygook: the self-serving, face-saving, cover-your-own-arse claptrap of the shiny shites in the top brass.

He's become fluent in Obfuscaspeak. An expert at reading between the lines—even if those lines resemble an architectural blueprint of the Guggenheim sketched by a chimpanzee with a catastrophic brain injury, wielding a crayon.

And yet, somehow, he'd nodded, smiled, and said *aye, all right then*, like a man volunteering to be a pallbearer at his own funeral.

At the time, anything—*anything*—seemed a damn sight better than another day in the claustrophobic, soul-sapping hamster wheel that is Purgatory Inc, otherwise known as Govan Police Office, Glasgow.

With their HR regulations, community engagement programs, cultural sensitivity courses, and worst of all—*worse* than a rusty corkscrew to the eyeball—the mandatory once a year team-building weekend. He'd rather drink a bucket of warm camel piss and floss the teeth of a corpse with his tongue than endure a single minute of such a pointless, jerk-circle, wank-fest.

Not that he's a man to hold a grudge.

Even though he's a dab hand at deciphering the tsunami of indecipherable management excrement of ACC Malcolm Clutterbuck (or Clusterfuck as Beale refers to him out of earshot), there was one other tiny detail which spray-painted the writing on the wall.

The thick, weighty binder lying on Clutterbuck's desk in plain, deliberate sight.

The heading typed in violent red, bold, uppercase letters:

## HIGHLY CONFIDENTIAL INTERNAL INQUIRY
## ~~DCI~~ ~~DI~~ ~~DS~~ DC DANNY BEALE

The strikethroughs were crude and deliberate, each police rank scored out with the enthusiasm of someone carving lines into wet concrete. A cryptic message to whoever ended up reviewing the mountain of paperwork.

A message that basically said in no uncertain terms:

*Save yourself the bother—this one's already fucked!*

Clusterfuck may as well have propped a sawn-off double-barrelled shotgun on the blotter pad and pointed it straight at Beale's man-titties.

And despite all that—despite every warning sign and every scrap of common sense—Beale is now ruing his decision.

He stands in the bowels of a North Sea trawler, bucking and lurching through vicious swells, shoulder-to-shoulder with two foreigners jabbering away in stereo and a bloke who looks like Grizzly Adams' less hygienic cousin, while he guts an apparently endless supply of stinking fish.

And to add insult to injury, he's feeling a little green around the gills—*which is unheard of* for Beale.

He has an ironclad constitution. A man who lives on a diet of fish and chips, sausage and chips, pie and chips, beans and chips, egg and chips, and—on the rare occasions he treats himself—chips and chips, with a side of chips.

Always washed down with copious amounts of alcohol.

Any alcohol.

When push truly comes to shove, he'll even begrudgingly drink boutique-brewery craft beer with aftertastes of elderflower and juniper berries.

But in the here and now—the mind-numbing monotony continues.

The door above bangs open, spilling in the howl of wind and the truculent sea—then slams shut again.

Footsteps clank down the steel steps.

Dritan's head appears, smiling as he surveys the workers.

'Men, how's it going?'

Cleavage momentarily stops pulling the guts from a cod and glances over his shoulder.

'About another half hour and we'll be done.'

'Excellent work, boys.' He focuses on Arben, the nominated cook. 'Arben, you have food waiting?'

Arben nods. 'All ready, Dritan. It's keeping warm in the oven.'

'Good. Once you finish here, wash and head to the galley. Then we eat. When finish, you boys get your heads down. Francois reckons we should be back in harbour in less than eight hours. Well done, men. A small but fruitful catch, yes? And Cleavage?'

'What?'

'We'll wake you five miles out from port, then you can assist Francois with guiding the boat into the harbour, no?'

'Aye. No worries.'

Dritan turns and clatters back up the steps. The door opens—wind roaring through—then slams shut.

Beale turns to Arben.

'So what's for breakfast?'

Arben grins and performs a chef's kiss.

'No breakfast. This our dinner. Paçe Koke.'

'Pah-chuh koh-keh,' Beale repeats phonetically. 'What the fuck is that when it's at home?'

'It is stew.'

Beale's stomach rumbles again. He's partial to a plate of stew.

'Ah, meat and tatties. Any chips with that?'

'No chips.'

'Ah well, never mind. So—lamb or beef?'

Arben rips the insides from another fish, pauses, thinking. His English isn't the best—something he has in common with Beale.

'It is…' He struggles for the word, then decides on mime. He baas like a sheep.

'Lamb. Excellent.'

'No. Not lamb. It bigger lamb. Mother of lamb.'

'Oh—sheep?'

'Yes, yes. Sheep.'

'Ah, mutton. That'll do nicely.'

Stefan chuckles. 'It is head.'

'Sorry?' Beale quizzes.

'It is head and inside of head.'

'What is?'

'It is brain of sheep. And part of head.'

Beale stops gutting, stares at him. 'Sheep's brain?'

'Yes, yes. This special Albanian dish. Not just brain but tongue, eyes, sometimes teeth—slow-cooked in garlic and vinegar and spices. It is delicacy.' Stefan raises his arm, rigid, punches the air and guffaws. 'It give erection like massive bull, no?'

Beale winces. The thought of sheep-head soup and an angry erection—six hours adrift of female company—doesn't exactly lift his mood.

Suddenly, a team-building weekend involving a raft made from conveniently discarded oil drums, wooden poles, and twine doesn't seem so unpalatable after all. At least more palatable than what's on the menu.

But there is one silver lining.

He now knows their nationality—and they've handed it over without him asking a single suspicious question.

Perfect.

Keeps his down-and-out tramp persona intact.

Gold dust.

⸻◆⸻

Beale stares at the eye in the bowl.

The eye stares right back.

Both appear equally disappointed by the encounter.

He lifts his spoon, slides it into the liquid, scoops.

Slurps.

Not too bad at first—garlic, vinegar—like warm salad dressing.

He dips the spoon back in and feels something clink against the side. Lifts the spoon.

A large, ugly molar peeks out from the broth. Not even pristine white, but slightly decayed, with a scrap of half-chewed grass still wedged in the grooves—proof the sheep had been snacking right to the bitter end.

The Albanians erupt in a cacophony of jubilation.

Stefan slaps him on the back. 'You are blessed, my friend. You got tooth. This sign of good fortune.'

Beale stares at him disdainfully. 'Well, aren't I the lucky boy today—an eye *and* a tooth.'

'Yes. You very lucky man.'

'What's your idea of bad luck?'

He flicks the tooth back into the soup and forces down another mouthful.

Something viscous and gloopy slides down his throat—a lump of slime with ambitions.

His stomach convulses.

A dry retch punches up his throat.

Meanwhile, the others tuck in with cheerful abandon—even Cleavage—who wipes his mouth and announces, 'This is alright. I've had worse.'

Beale grips the edge of the table, desperately trying to keep his insides on the correct side of his ribcage.

He rises.

'Sorry, boys. Been a long day. I'm knackered. I'm going to get my head down.'

Arben is genuinely puzzled and points at the eyeball with his spoon.

'You no eat?'

Beale gives an apologetic wince. 'Unfortunately not. My doctor put me on a low-eyeball diet for a month. Said my retina levels were dangerously high. Night, lads.'

His departure barely raises an eyebrow.

The Albanians are already chatting excitedly in their own language, and Cleavage—clearly ravenous—dives back into the bowl as if competing in an eating contest for overweight, bearded cock-puppets.

Arben scoops up the abandoned eyeball from Beale's dish and bites into it with the contented sigh of a man who's recently enjoyed a relaxing bout of adventurous sex.

## 36

The noise comes again, low, deep. The sort of sound that vibrates in your gut and rattles your fillings. Beale wakes with a thump to the heart. It takes him a moment to regain his senses.

*Where is he? Who is he? Why is he? What's the meaning of life? And more importantly, will Rangers ever win the Scottish Premier League again?*

The great conundrums of existence swirl through his mind. After a few micro-seconds of deep intellectual thought, he concludes he's no closer to solving any of life's eternal mysteries.

The deep, sonic, mournful blast comes again.

It's then he remembers *who* and *where* he is.

On a bed built for a midget, in a cabin the size of a wardrobe, floating around in a steel coffin somewhere in the North Sea.

And that sound is a foghorn.

*The horror.*

A battle-hardened bruiser raised in the back streets of Glasgow, Beale isn't scared of anyone or anything—with *one* exception: thick fog.

Two exceptions, if you include skinny Nepalese vegans.

He blames the fear of fog on a childhood trauma he'd rather forget—if only he could remember to forget. He was four years old, shopping with his grandmother, who desperately needed a new pair of orthopaedic slippers. For reasons he's still unsure of, he became separated.

It was a Glasgow winter, early evening, and the fog was thicker than a spinster's pantyhose. Somehow he wandered down to the canal. Hours later he was found perilously close to a large, deep lock, inches from tragedy, staring into space in a mute, catatonic state.

Over the years he's revisited that stretch of canal a few times in a half-baked attempt at self-therapy. It never helped. Only raised more questions. Like, why was he there? That part of the canal is miles from the shops. And why did his grandmother take him with her in the first place? Was any of it as innocent as it seemed?

Whatever the truth, the whole episode left him mentally scarred, with a lifelong fear of fog—and to a lesser extent, orthopaedic slippers.

The constant drone of the boat's engine is overwhelmed as the foghorn bellows again, rolling through the cabin like a wounded hymn.

He checks his watch and does the maths. Still three hours from safe harbour. Call it roughly thirty miles out.

That's one hell of a foghorn to carry so far from shore. Or maybe it's a lighthouse? Do they even have operational lighthouses these days? Isn't everything GPS and state-of-the-art wizardry now?

Not that Beale trusts modern tech. Nothing beats the human brain.

If he's going to fall out of the sky in a 747 or sink to the bottom of the sea in a trawler, he'd much rather it be down to human error than some technical glitch.

He's not entirely sure why that brings him comfort.

Maybe it's the idea that if he's going to die, then let it be at the hands of some feckless, pot-bellied, cock-trumpet who's taken his eye off the ball, rather than a computer chip invented in America, manufactured in Taiwan, and installed upside-down by Gary from Bradford, who shouldn't be trusted with safety-scissors, never mind critical computer circuitry.

There's something more personal about it.

A low red nightlight barely illuminates the cabin. He's gagging for a smoke, but he's not sure he wants to go on deck and witness the fog.

He attempts to get out of bed and cracks his head on the underside of the bunk.

'For fuck's sake!'

He rolls his legs over the side, sits up, and scratches his testicles through his Y-fronts. Stands, and promptly smacks his head again.

'Sweet merry Jesus.'

He glances around the room, spots his trousers, slips into them. Throws on a jumper. Tugs on a pair of socks. Shrugs into his heavy-duty waterproof jacket. Taps the pocket—smokes and lighter safe and sound. His nicotine urge is becoming intolerable.

Sniffs the putrid air. 'Christ, it smells like a shit-smuggler's rucksack in here.'

Squints into the murky light, searching for his boots.

'Now where the fuck are they? I could've sworn I left them at the end of the bed.'

The noise comes again.

A quick squint at the top bunk where Cleavage is curled up like an elephant seal with period pains.

He experiences a wave of *reloyance*—a mixture of relief *and* extreme annoyance—when he realises the thunderous bass tenor of the foghorn is Cleavage snoring.

He stares at him with utter contempt. 'Yer great big Jabberwocky bawbag.'

Still searching, he bends to check under the bunk for his boots and cracks his head for the third time.

'Kiss my hairy scrotum!'

Rubbing his head, he spots Cleavage's oversized green wellies in the corner.

'They'll do. That witless salami slapper will be none the wiser.'

He pulls the cabin door closed behind him. Stops as the trawler's engine suddenly idles.

Feels the slap of water against the hull.

'What now? Don't tell me some moron forgot to fill up at the petrol station before we set off?'

He pulls out a smoke and puts one foot onto the steel steps. Dritan asked him not to smoke below. But Beale reckons the steps are neither above nor below. A sort of no-man's-land. He sparks up and tentatively climbs the stairs, which is harder than one might think in oversized Wellington boots.

'Hell! The dopey clunt must have feet the size of fucking surfboards.'

———◇———

Beale slouches against the guardrail, mist and spray clinging to him like damp regret. He's deep into his third cigarette when he catches the sound of an engine. Not The Whitby Rose, still idling quietly under him—something else.

'Odd?'

He tosses his cigarette into the rolling sea and makes his way to the stairs.

Freezes as he spots Arben, Dritan, and Stefan at the stern.

Hushed voices.

A smaller boat bobs dangerously close on the starboard side, rising and falling in the strong swell. Too close for comfort. Too close for anything legitimate.

The three Albanians huddle near the gunwale, talking in low, urgent whispers. Shadows in the light. Shapes in the dark.

Arben steps to the hydraulic winch controls. The arm slews out over the side with a mechanical groan. From the smaller vessel, voices carry—muffled, tense.

Beale crouches, tucks into the shadows.

The winch whines. A heavy shape emerges—a wooden crate strapped into two slings, swaying dangerously with every roll of the boat.

It swings inboard and is lowered to the deck with a thud.

Stefan steps in with a crowbar, prises the lid open.

Dritan bends into the crate and lifts an automatic assault rifle with casual ease. Then a second. A third. He inspects each one with calm, professional approval.

Stefan removes a handful of pistols, checks them quickly, and replaces them.

Dritan nods, satisfied.

'Christ almighty,' Beale mutters. 'What is this, the opening act of World War Three?'

Stefan disappears into the darkness and returns with a small sack. Swings it once. Launches it across to the other boat.

Payment?

From here, Beale can't see the faces—just two silhouettes catching the sack in silence.

He retreats behind the stairwell door. Keeps it cracked open an inch so he can see.

The winch slews back over the side again.

A muffled shout from below.

Dritan gives the thumbs-up.

The winch returns, lighter this time.

A figure clings to the straps, legs tucked in, holding on for dear life.

A terrified soul.

Stefan and Dritan haul the man down, steady him on the deck.

Small. Asian. Eyes wide with panic. He looks like he expects to be thrown into the sea at any moment.

Dritan wastes no time, steering him toward the wheelhouse, then through the small door behind it, and into the skipper's private cabin.

Stefan calls something in Albanian, raises a hand in farewell. The smaller boat reverses away into the night as The Whitby Rose's engines crank up.

Arben steps away from the winch, pauses, and shoots a glance towards the door.

Beale winces and eases it shut.

'Shite... did he see me?'

Heart thudding, he scarpers down into the cabin, kicks off the wet wellies, and dives into his bunk, yanking the covers over himself.

A few minutes pass.

Footsteps.

The cabin door creaks open.

Beale squints through the dark and begins his imitation of gentle, innocent snoring.

Stefan steps inside. Watches. Assesses. The man's suspicion feels like a physical weight in the room.

Satisfied—for now—he turns to leave.

Stops.

The wellies.

He bends, runs a hand along them. Glances up at Cleavage, asleep in the top bunk. Looks again at the boots.

A gentle click—the door closes.

Beale lies frozen in his bunk, praying to every deity he doesn't believe in that Stefan doesn't start asking Cleavage awkward questions.

## 37

# Wednesday 6:05am

Beale is standing at the bow, binoculars raised, as The Whitby Rose dips and rises with the elegance of a ballet dancer as dawn breaks. Hand on heart, he never thought this day would come. Twenty-four hours ago, it was unthinkable. But there it is in the distance—England, and the welcoming sight of Whitby Harbour with the Abbey on top of East Cliff. And my God is he ecstatic to see it!

He hates England and the English with a passion greater than he hates Celtic fans... and that's saying something.

But not today.

Today he could kiss an Englishman on the arse—well, perhaps not the arse, but at least be civil to them, possibly even shake their hand. Maybe it's time to forgive and forget the recent Battle of Culloden in 1746 and embrace the English?

Cleavage wanders into view.

*Then again*, Beale thinks.

'How did you enjoy your first trip, Danny?'

'Aye, no too bad. Haven't had so much fun since I was in Thailand and entered a ladyboy brothel by mistake.'

Cleavage struggles with the intent of his response. 'Is that good, or bad?'

'Depends whether you were in my shoes or the ladyboy's stilettos.'

Cleavage is none the wiser and drops the subject. 'You know the best thing about working away from home on the boats?'

'Not seeing the missus?'

'No, it's coming back home.' He stares off, almost misty-eyed. 'I love the open sea—the freedom, the graft, the danger, the crack with the lads. But nothing beats the moment I see the harbour coming into view and knowing I'll soon be back in the loving embrace of my wife and lad.'

Beale wonders if he should refer him to the nearest psychiatric hospital.

'I can well understand you missing your bairn. How old is he?'

'Turns four next week.' Cleavage fishes out his mobile, swipes a couple of times. 'This is him—Fergus.'

Beale squints at the screen and recoils violently.

*Sweet suffering mother of Mary on a pogo stick!*

'Ahem... aye, bonny-looking lad,' he manages to croak. 'Obviously takes after you.'

Cleavage smiles fondly. 'Nah. He's the double of my wife.'

*Jesus wept. Who's he married to—a mad professor's genetic experiment with an orangutan and a root vegetable?*

Cleavage bears the innocent smile of an imbecile. 'Right, I'm going to ring my missus and tell her I should be home in less than two hours.'

'Aye, good idea. Give her chance to kick her lover out of bed.' Then adds under his breath, 'I'm sure the local zoo is missing one of their primates by now.'

As Cleavage wanders off, phone to ear, Beale sparks up and sucks in lustily.

'Dopey sod,' he murmurs.

Half-turning, he spots Stefan a few feet away, silent, eyes firmly focused on Cleavage. When he sees Beale looking at him, he slinks away.

◆

About a mile out, the entrance to Whitby Harbour rises ahead like a pair of welcoming arms—the long stone piers curving inward, their lighthouses standing sentinel against the North Sea. At the very tips, two beacons—more like circular wooden huts on stilted pedestals—keep watch: green to starboard, red to port, guiding seafarers home.

Beale is already dreaming of breakfast. No chance of a full Scottish this far south—no square sausage, no tattie scone, no haggis—so he resigns himself to the full English with a sigh. He'd passed on whatever Arben classed as food—a wedge of cheese and a slab of rock-hard bread. He prefers his cheese melted over a greasy burger, and his bread soft, sliced, and straight from a packet. Instead, he'd made do with a strong black coffee and three cigarettes.

There's a kerfuffle behind him as Dritan and Stefan step out of the wheelhouse, both staring eastward, binoculars raised. Beale turns and squints. A white-and-grey launch is knifing across the swell—fast but steady—blue beacons pulsing against the low sky. High cabin, reflective panels, HM Coastguard insignia clear even at this range.

Dritan watches in silence, jaw set, expression unreadable. Calm but wary. The brothers mutter to each other as Beale joins them.

'Probably just heading into the harbour,' Beale offers.

'Hmm... maybe,' Dritan replies, clearly unconvinced.

The Whitby Rose ploughs on. The coastguard launch closes the gap, then throttles back to match their speed. A moment later, a smaller RIB drops from the launch, slapping into the water before its engine roars to life and drives it straight towards them—three coastguard officers aboard, helmets on, yellow lifejackets strapped tight.

A loudhailer punches through the wind.

'Whitby Rose, this is HM Coastguard. Reduce speed to five knots and hold your heading. Prepare to be boarded for a routine safety inspection. All crew to remain visible on deck.'

Beale feels his heartbeat drum faster, as regret pays him a visit.

*Maybe I should have informed Carmody of my whereabouts, that way the coastguard would have been warned off about intercepting The Whitby Rose. If they so much as glimpse that arms cache, this whole thing's gone tits up.*

Cleavage steps out of the wheelhouse, sipping tea from a white tin cup.

'Nowt to fret about, lads. Just a safety inspection—routine. Sometimes you'll not see 'em for eighteen months; other times, they'll board you three times in a year. Totally random.'

Francoise appears. 'Cleavage, man the wheel. They'll want to speak to me.'

'Aye, righto.'

The RIB comes up on their starboard side. Two officers stand ready at the bow, gloved hands gripping the rail.

'HM Coastguard! Stand by for boarding! Keep clear of the ladder!'

The first officer climbs the ladder, boots hitting the deck with a solid thud. He's dressed in navy-blue, reflective stripes, body-worn radio, safety harness clipped at his waist. A second officer follows, while the coxswain holds the RIB steady against the swell.

'Skipper?' the lead officer asks.

Francois raises a hand. 'Here.'

'We're conducting a safety inspection under the Merchant Shipping Act. Need all crew visible and the vessel kept steady. No one goes below unless instructed. Understand?'

'Understood,' Francois replies, voice level as Arben appears from the galley door.

Beale keeps his eyes forward. The officer's gaze brushes across him—brief, assessing—before moving on to Dritan, then Stefan, the net drums, the winch, the scuffs around the stern.

'How many crew aboard today?' the officer asks.

'Seven.'

He studies Dritan. 'Fine. We'll continue with interior checks shortly. All crew to remain on deck until instructed.'

Francois nods as the second officer moves off, taking a slow circuit of the deck. He checks the life rings, locker seals, the first-aid point, the EPIRB bracket—eyes sharp, face unreadable. A small nod as he goes, apparently satisfied. The Whitby Rose is tidy, everything in its place, deck washed down—shipshape and Bristol fashion, as they say.

'All looks good, Chief,' the junior officer says to the lead. 'We'll head below deck next, and then I'll need to check your flares and fire extinguishers.'

He turns, then pauses—eyes narrowing at the tarpaulin covering something near the gunwale.

'What's under there?' he asks, directing it at Beale, who happens to be closest.

Beale scratches his stubble. 'I'm... not sure, officer.'

Dritan steps forward, takes hold of the tarp, and whips it clear, revealing the rectangular wooden crate underneath.

'Spares for the winch—hydraulic hoses, shackles, pulley wheels. Bit of trawl wire, grease gun, that sort of thing.'

'Open it, please.'

Dritan lets out a sharp laugh and flicks a look over his shoulder at Stefan. The rest of the crew stiffens, Beale included. The officers feel the change in the air; their eyes meet in a quick, uneasy exchange.

'You want me to open it?' Dritan asks, stalling for seconds.

Beale braces himself, mind racing through every ugly outcome.

*Are the guns primed? If they are, this could turn nasty. Coastguard officers—unarmed, no chance if it kicks off. What are Dritan and his men really like? Organised efficient, disciplined. They move with a plan. They've seemed rational so far... surely too rational to start shooting. They've nowhere to run. They can't head back out to sea—low on fuel, and the coastguard would shadow them all the way. Then Border Force would turn up, armed and ready, and the whole thing would end in a bloodbath unless they gave themselves up. They must know the game's over. If they're thinking straight, they'll see it and come quietly.*

Dritan crouches and eases the lid open. 'As I said—spares for winch.'

The crew watches in silence as the officer peers in at the neatly stacked hoses, shackles, pulley wheels and coiled wire.

He relaxes a fraction. 'All right. Though you really ought to keep this sort of kit in a watertight metal trunk, or better still a heavy-duty plastic one. Seawater will chew through untreated pine in no time.'

Francois steps forward. 'Yes, we are aware of that. Our old box rusted out at the bottom. New one on order. This stopgap for moment.'

'I see. Right, let's have a look at your flares and fire extinguishers.'

**38**

Frank is seated behind his desk, staring blankly into space, mind a maelstrom of dark thoughts. The door swings open.

Prisha and Zac saunter in laughing, mid-joke. Normal. Zac tosses a paper bag onto the desk.

'Bacon and egg butty. And a cup of coffee for his Lordship.'

He sets the cardboard cup down carefully, like an offering. Frank doesn't even look at it. The smell of the bacon turns his stomach.

Zac doesn't notice immediately. 'Aye, thanks very much, Zac. Not a problem, Frank. Don't mention it,' he says sarcastically, not receiving a response. Now he clocks it as his grin slips. 'Uh-oh. Something's not right.'

Recent events have killed Frank's appetite—the headless corpse, cold harbour water, fear in Smiler's eyes, the promise he made to Hedley Keegan pressing against his ribs like a bruise, *and* the news he heard thirty minutes ago.

Prisha is studying him now. She always does.

'What's the matter, Frank?'

He exhales. 'Take a seat.'

The mood shifts instantly. Chairs scrape. The air drains out of the room.

'I caught up with Smiler last night.'

'Where?' Zac asks.

'The White House Inn.'

Frank keeps his voice level.

'How is he?' Prisha asks.

'Physically fine. Mentally? I fear he's a wreck. He witnessed Typhoon's execution.'

Zac lets out a breath. 'Jeez.'

'Smiler was taking a leak when four men entered Typhoon's place. Foreign lads. There was a brief exchange, Typhoon waving a gun around acting like King of the Castle, then they decapitated him, casual as you like.'

'Did you ask Smiler why he didn't switch on the listening device?'

'I did. Call it human error—he forgot.'

'And you believe him?'

'Yes. Why would he take the risk of planting it and not switch it on? The lad was obviously in a state of high anxiety.'

'So what happened to him?'

'They rumbled Smiler in the toilet and chased him halfway across Whitby, shot at him a few times, before he dived into the harbour and got away. Some hours later, they turned up at his digs. He escaped again—climbed down a drainpipe.'

Prisha frowns. 'Christ, talk about a cat with nine lives. How did they know where he lived?'

'He lost his phone during the chase. Smiler reckons they must have found it and hacked it—pulled his GPS history.'

Frank tries to push away the ever-present thought, dark and lurking at the back of his brain: this could have been so much worse. Smiler could have been murdered, and Frank knows—quietly, uncomfortably—that his own actions played a part in placing him in the firing line.

'Where is he now?' Prisha asks.

'A swanky Airbnb apartment by the river. Safe for the moment. But we'll need to move him.'

Zac edges forward. 'Did he get a look at the attackers?'

'No, too dark. And thankfully, he doesn't think they got a good look at him.' Frank leans back, steepling his fingers, buying himself a second. 'Did either of you listen to the local news on the radio this morning?'

They glance at each other. 'No,' they reply together.

'Three murders overnight,' Frank states. 'One in Hartlepool. One in Hull. Another in Sunderland.'

Zac shrugs. 'And?'

Frank feels the words lodge in his throat before he forces them out.

'Drug-related, by the look of it. Smiler filled in more detail about Typhoon's business. Three coastal jurisdictions. Each run by a trusted lieutenant.'

Zac swears softly. 'And you think—'

Frank nods as the certainty chills him. 'I do. Typhoon used a GPS tracking app to monitor his men. Business. Control. Paranoia. Who knows? If they hacked Smiler's phone, they could've hacked Typhoon's too. That locator would've led them straight to his people.'

Prisha shakes her head slowly. 'That's four dead already that we know about. Did you get the names of Typhoon's men?'

'Only nicknames. I passed the intel to Cleveland, Humberside, and Northumbria Police last night hoping their officers may be able to locate the men to warn them. A futile effort, by the looks of it. I'm now waiting to hear back if the dead men are the ones Smiler talked about.'

What he doesn't say is that Keegan warned him, that once this started, it could turn ugly, *very* ugly.

He peers down at the untouched bacon butty, grease bleeding through the white paper bag.

As much as he loathes breaking a promise, it's time to fess up.

Shifting uneasily in his chair, he emits a nervous cough.

'There's something I need to tell you—something I should have told you from day one. A while ago, I had a meeting with an old colleague of mine. Someone you both know, especially you, Zac, as you worked on one of his cases in the past.'

Zac's brow wrinkles. 'Who?'

'Remember DCI Hedley Keegan?'

'Aye, course I do. The undercover Op in Hull a few years back. It's seared in my memory. It was the first time I met Beale. A dark day in hell,' he adds in a reflective moment. 'Anyway, what about him?'

'I had breakfast with Hedley about six weeks ago. He's part of Operation Blackout. Head of intelligence. Every piece of intel is filtered through his team. He came to me because he suspects a leak somewhere high up. Zac, the tip-off you received about Smiler from Cleavage was orchestrated by Keegan.'

'Why?'

'To get me into the operation via the back door. That's the reason we didn't obtain a search warrant for Smiler's pad. We had to fly low.'

Prisha nods, now understanding. 'I thought it was uncharacteristic of you, Frank. You're usually so meticulous. Did Keegan mention who he suspects?'

'No.'

'So what does he actually want you to do?'

'Feed any relevant information back him.'

Pulled away from her dusty cold case, Prisha is energised to be in the action again.

'What's our next move?'

'I've arranged a meeting with Silas Carmody at midday. Somewhere quiet. I'll tell him what we know factually, but refrain from speculation. I won't mention Beale or that we know where Smiler is.'

'What do you want us to do?' Prisha asks.

'Chase Charlene. If forensics lifted DNA from the blood spatter at Typhoon's place, I want it prioritised and run against the database.'

'We already have Typhoon's DNA on file. He did six months, ten years back—GBH.'

'Good. That gives us a head start. But I want absolute confirmation the blood matches him.'

Frank turns to Zac.

'Liaise with Cleveland, Humberside, and Northumbria. I want names and photos of the three men killed overnight. Odds are they all have form.'

He pauses.

'Prisha, I'll give you Smiler's address. Take the photos to him. See if he confirms they were Typhoon's men. Then move him to a safe house. Tell him he cannot leave unless I say so.'

'Where do you want him relocated to—well away, I assume?'

Frank strokes his cheek, already four moves ahead.

'No. I want him close. Somewhere I can keep an eye on him.'

'Why?' she asks, clearly puzzled.

'Two reasons: if they're still after him, the last place they'll expect him to be is Whitby. And secondly, young Smiler may come in useful later.'

## 39

Frank and Silas Carmody walk side by side along Whitby East Pier, the midday sun highlighting the bleached concrete beneath their feet. They keep an easy pace, voices low. The sort of conversation that could pass for small talk if anyone cared to listen.

'And you're certain it's Typhoon?'

Frank nods once. 'Positive. The results came back an hour ago. Samples from the body and the blood spatter at his lock-up match what we have on file.'

Silas slides a hand deeper into his overcoat pocket and lets his gaze drift out across the harbour, eyes narrowing slightly.

'And the listening device yielded nothing?'

'No. Either Smiler never switched it on—or Typhoon found it and shut it down.'

'And Smiler himself?'

Frank exhales. 'No idea. We've circulated his photo, checked his usual haunts. So far—nothing.'

Silas slows just enough to make Frank register it. 'Do you think he's dead?'

'Possible.'

Silas stops altogether now and turns, studying Frank's face.

'Would Smiler have been capable of killing Typhoon?'

Frank gives a small shrug. 'Capable of defending himself, maybe. If it came to a fight. But not decapitation. I know Smiler—he's not violent by nature.'

Silas's mouth tightens. He looks away again, resumes walking. 'Which leaves us none the wiser about Typhoon's connection to the cartel.'

'Not entirely. If there was a connection, there isn't anymore.' Frank hesitates. 'And there's more. Three of Typhoon's trusted lieutenants were murdered overnight.'

Silas nods slowly. 'Gang related?'

'Looks that way. Coordinated. All within an hour of each other.'

'Any suspects?'

'Not yet. It's outside our patch, but I'm being kept in the loop.' Frank glances at him. 'Last week you mentioned an undercover operative in the Whitby area.'

'That's right.'

'Mind telling me who?'

Silas allows himself a brief smile. 'Even if I knew their real name, I wouldn't tell you. Operational integrity.' He pauses. 'In truth, I only know their codename.'

'Fair enough.' Frank lets it go. 'Have they been in contact?'

'No. But that's not unusual. If they're doing it properly, they maintain radio silence.'

Frank turns that over as they walk. 'So if there's been no contact, it's safe to say they've got nothing worth reporting.'

'One assumes.' Silas checks his watch, frowns. 'Damn. Time's got away from me. I'd better make tracks.'

He pivots on his heel.

'One last thing,' Frank says. 'How long before you think this operation comes to a head?'

Silas looks back, expression unreadable. 'Imminent.'

'That's vague. Days? Weeks?'

'Possibly days. Maybe a week.'

'And your intelligence still points to one of the major ports?'

'Yes, right, I really must—'

'Of course.' Frank says. 'I'll keep you updated.'

Silas nods once and heads back along the pier, stride purposeful but not rushed.

Frank watches him go, unease settling where curiosity once lived. Silas gives nothing away, and Frank intends to do the same.

He feels a pinch of guilt at holding back Beale's revelations, and that it took Prisha showing Smiler the photographs to confirm the three murdered men as part of Typhoon's gang.

But at the moment—guilt can go to hell. There are bigger things at play.

Such as Silas Carmody.
The truth is, it's not what Silas said that troubles him.
It was his reaction—or lack of it.

## 40

# Thursday

Cleavage is giving Beale a crash course in mending a fishing net, with predictably questionable results. He threads a thick needle through the torn mesh with surprising dexterity for a man his size. With fingers the size of Lebanese cucumbers, it's no mean feat.

'Right, Danny, you fetch the shuttle through here, make a sheet bend, pull it snug, and that's a perfect mend. It's easy once you get the knack.'

Beale watches glassy-eyed, staring at the netting, then at Cleavage, praying that one of them suffers a massive cardiac arrest. At this moment in time, he's not bothered if it's him or Cleavage.

It's the second trip in quick succession and they've been at sea for just over four hours. Predictably, it's grey, overcast, and drizzling. As far as the eye can see, there's nothing but the greenish roll of water, a leaden sky, and the ever-present reek of fish and diesel.

Hell has often been depicted by poets and scholars throughout the ages as a nightmare of fire and brimstone, eternal pain, and torment.

Obviously, none of those nerdy fucks ever spent a few days on a North Sea trawler with Cleavage.

This is the *real* hell.

His mind drifts as Cleavage prattles on. He doesn't despise the man—far from it. Cleavage is a gentle giant, maybe two IQ points above a simpleton, a sausage roll short of a picnic, but harmless enough. And although he has one of those faces you'd happily punch all day long, there's not a bad bone in him.

What grates is his cheerfulness. The relentless, sunny, carefree jauntiness.

It irritates the absolute fuck out of Beale.

He hates optimistic people.

It's unhealthy and unnatural.

Cleavage hands the shuttle and twine to Beale. 'Here, have a go.'

Beale makes an absolute hash of it, which is hardly surprising as he has zero interest in fixing nets, learning a new skill, or pretending otherwise.

Luckily, Dritan strolls up and interrupts.

'Danny, I'd like a word. Below. Private.'

---

As he follows Dritan down into the galley, a prickle of unease crawls up his spine.

Why does he want him alone? Why down here? Was he spotted during the arms drop? If so, his life could be measured in seconds. A bullet to the back of the head, a quick splash, end of chapter.

Then again...

If he is about to be executed, at least it would put an end to Cleavage's relentless mission to "show him the ropes," as he puts it. Neither option is desirable, but the bullet is definitely winning by a couple of lengths at the moment.

Dritan slips on a pair of flower-patterned oven mitts then pours them each a cup of black coffee from the dented metal kettle rattling away on the galley stove. The crew live on instant coffee strong enough to dissolve a titanium horseshoe. He places the cups down on the table and takes a seat opposite Beale.

'So, how are you?' he asks.

Beale offers a fake smile while his eyes dart around the galley, searching for anything capable of maiming a man. Everything is annoyingly neat. Knives locked away in drawers, heavy pots stowed in cupboards, nothing left out where a desperate man might grab it.

The only viable weapon is the kettle, which would mean putting on the oven gloves first. Not ideal when you've got half a second to kill or be killed. And anyway, you can't murder a man while wearing floral oven mitts—it's undignified for both the killer and victim.

His eyes shift to a packet of spaghetti by the stove. Could you bash a man to death with dried spaghetti? Absolutely not. But a tightly gripped handful jabbed into the eye socket? Aye... that would at least buy him some time.

His eyes flick back to Dritan, who's waiting for a response and reading him like a very short children's book.

'Yeah. I'm good, thanks for asking.'

Dritan nods. 'And the drinking... manage to keep off it?'

'Not quite. I allowed myself three pints of bitter, and despite the urge to get into the whisky, I resisted. Got a takeaway pizza and went back to my digs.'

Dritan beams. 'This is good progress. Everything in moderation. Nothing wrong with a few drinks now and again, but know when to stop.'

*Christ... who is this guy, my fucking drugs and alcohol counsellor?*

Dritan leans back in his seat, sipping his brew, his eyes flicking over Beale's face like he's scanning for cracks.

'It is hard being man, no?'

Beale nods. 'Aye. You can say that again.'

'We work and work and work. Like pack horse. And then one day...' A deliberate pause. '...we die.'

Beale urgently reassesses the viability of the oven mitts. 'Very true.'

'We must survive... or die.'

Beale nods in agreement, though it occurs to him Dritan's unlikely to be snapped up by the philosophical lecture circuit anytime soon.

'We must work. We must survive. And why? Because of our loved ones—family, friends, our wives. If we are blessed, our children and our children's children.'

Beale agrees in part. 'Aye, although I'm shaky on the wife part. My ex was a fucking nightmare—still is, and we've been divorced ten years. Even the judge commiserated with me on the way out.'

Dritan chuckles. 'Wife, girlfriend, lover, whatever, no?'

It's true Beale has formed bonds with a few of the sex workers he's frequented over the years. He even knows some of them by their first names, mainly because it's printed on their business cards. But still, he sees it as a clear sign he's maturing emotionally.

Dritan continues, his brow furrowing. 'And so this is our lot in life. A man's life. Sometimes we must do *bad* things to survive. That does not mean *we* are bad men. No?'

Beale's not sure where Dritan's heading with this, but he's watched enough gangster films to detect the warning signs. Any second now the orchestra will kick in—low cellos and double basses rumbling in the background. Strident violins trembling like a nest of angry wasps. A pair of discordant French horns low in the mix. And some maniac with no sense of timing warming up on the timpani. And finally, the ominous sweep of a harp to warn the audience someone's about to get whacked.

'I guess so,' Beale eventually replies, one eye firmly on the oven mitts.

Dritan slaps his hands on the table and lets out a satisfied sigh. 'Good. I am glad we have our little chat. Now, because we are men, it is back to work. But first, you finish your coffee.'

Beale watches him climb the steps, followed by the clank of the steel door above. He removes his woolly hat and scratches his head.

'What in all fuckery was *that* about?'

Beale hasn't been this confused since he was voted *Most Likely Boy to Succeed in Life* by his classmates in high school.

In the end, it turned out to be a clerical oversight. The teachers had run their own poll in the staffroom—*Most Likely Boy to Fail in Life*. Somewhere along the way, the results got mixed up. But for a few days, the Glasgow comprehensive was in a state of consternation and uproar. The headmaster was stood down and put under heavy sedation pending a full enquiry. Even Beale suspected something had gone terribly awry. A week later, a formal apology was issued, and the school promised to review its quality-control processes—which, naturally, it never did.

As he plods up the stairs to the deck, he's got the sinking feeling that Mistress Fate is about to take another swing at him—and she rarely misses.

# 41

Cleavage is still at it, giving Beale another grand tour of the boat as though he's a wide-eyed apprentice on his first day, which basically, he is. He taps bulkheads, names cleats, points out trip hazards, demonstrates how to brace when the deck's pitching underfoot. Beale nods along, absorbing a quarter of it at best, and absolutely nothing at worst.

'Middle of the night, blowing a hoolie, you'll thank me,' Cleavage says, leading him towards the stern. 'When the trawl door swings open, you need to know where *not* to stand, otherwise you'll end up a smear on the deck.'

Beale offers a dry grunt. 'Aye. I'll bear that in mind.'

Cleavage carries on undeterred, explaining the hydraulics, the winch drum, the toe rails—none of it lodging in Beale's bored brain.

'Are you paying attention?' Cleavage asks.

'Oh, aye. I'm honed in like a laser-guided missile.'

Cleavage points at the piece of equipment he explained about a moment ago.

'So what's this?'

Beale stares at the large round thing. 'The rusty insides of a huge washing machine?'

Cleavage purses his lips. 'I just told you. It's the winch drum.'

'That's right, the winch drum.'

'And what does it do?'

Beale's wafer-thin patience explodes. 'What is this, University fucking Challenge? *Beale from King's College Cambridge—your starter for ten.*'

Cleavage shakes his head in dismay at his thick pupil.

'It's the winch to wind the trawl net in.'

'You mean the fishing net?'

'YES!'

'Okay, keep your wig on, Bamber-fucking-Gascoigne. Why not just call it a fishing net and fishing net winch? Why, when we step one foot on a boat, do all the fucking names change? It's not a kitchen, it's a galley. It's not left or right but port and starfish.'

'Starboard.'

'That as well. The front is the bow. The back is the stern. The shitter's called the head. The bottom the hull. A floor is a deck. The walls are bulkheads. A bed is a bunk. A cabin, a bedroom. And why the fuck are stairs called a companionway? Whichever bright spark came up with that name must have been off his crumpet on magic mushrooms at the time. Scuppers are drains, and the wheelhouse is where you drive the fucking boat from, change gears, and look at porn on your phone. You know what this is—exclusionist. A secret society. You lot are as bad as the stonemasons.'

Cleavage sighs but persists. He points aft. 'And what's that large mesh structure?'

'Ah! I know that. It's the cage net.'

'Nearly. It's the net bin. Where we stow the fishing... the trawl net.'

Beale lethargically circles the rectangular cage. He accidentally kicks something and looks down at a large concrete block with an iron eyelet cast into the top. It looks more at home on a building site than on a boat.

'What's that for?' he asks. 'We're not picking up a gang of fucking bricklayers along the way, are we?'

Cleavage hesitates for a second. 'Oh, that'll be an anchor for a buoy. If we need to drop one overboard in a hurry. Slip a rope through the eyelet, fix a bowline and the job's a good 'un.' He pauses, brightening as if struck by inspiration. 'Tell you what—on the way back, if there's time, I'll give you a crash course on the knots we use. What they're for, which one's best for which job.'

'What's wrong with a good old-fashioned granny knot for everything?'

Cleavage lets out a bark of laughter like a hyena with terminal bronchitis.

'You're joking, right?'

He wasn't.

Cleavage sighs, his disappointment evident. 'You'll need to learn the bowline, round turn and two half hitches, anchor bend, rolling hitch, clove hitch, timber hitch, reef knot, sheet bend, double sheet bend, figure-of-eight, trawler's hitch, trucker's hitch, stopper knot, catspaw... whole bloody shooting match. Half the job's knowing your knots in the dark, with wet hands, when everything's sliding about.'

The very thought has Beale considering throwing himself overboard and ending his misery early.

'Aye, well, like you say... only if there's time,' he mutters, edging away.

Cleavage appears a tad contrite. 'Sorry for raising my voice earlier. I'd best get back to net-mending. Fancy another go?' he asks, irritatingly upbeat.

'I'd love to, but Dritan's got a few jobs for me below deck. I'll have a wee smoke, then crack on.'

'Fair enough.'

Beale heads to the stern, as far away from Cleavage as possible, and sparks up. It's only his second trip, and he's already learnt two things. One—avoid Cleavage at all costs unless you fancy having the tits bored clean off you by endless nautical trivia; the man's more tedious than those arseholes who can't shut up about makes and models of classic cars.

And two—he's starting to get a feel for the weather, the sea, the way the conditions shift beneath the boat.

He gazes to the north-east and doesn't much like what he sees. A huge bank of grey is massing on the horizon, sitting there malevolent and swollen, black as a dog's guts.

And the swell—he's noticed it creeping up over the past hour. The further they steam, the more the sea heaves in great slow surges, gathering in strength, testing its weight beneath the hull.

He cocks his head as raised voices spill from the wheelhouse.

'Sounds like Dritan and Francois having a ding-dong,' he murmurs.

The door bursts open, and Dritan storms out, slamming it behind him. He digs out his cigarettes, lights one, then notices Beale.

'Problem?' Beale asks.

Dritan takes a long breath. Beale's never seen him rattled. Even when the coastguard came aboard, he was cool as a cucumber in an igloo.

'It's Francois,' Dritan mutters. 'He is old man... but more like old lady.'

'I see.'

'He thinks we should turn back.' Dritan jerks his chin toward the dark mass on the horizon. 'Another low-pressure system. Forecast says it won't hit for twelve hours. We are three hours from the fishing grounds. That gives us time to get nets down, get a catch, then head back with hours to spare before the worst of storm arrives.'

Beale isn't buying a word of it—apart from the storm. He's convinced there's another rendezvous lined up, probably the drug drop this time. If the stuff's coming in from mainland Europe, missing a handover is serious. It's hard enough dodging Border Force, police patrol boats, coastguard teams, and drones once, never mind aborting and trying again another day.

Francois is worried about the boat and the men; Dritan's worried about the drop. Two very different storms brewing. It's the first real crack Beale's seen in the gang. And although Francois wears the skipper's cap, it's Dritan who's firmly at the helm.

Beale flicks his ciggy overboard. 'Right, you said you had some jobs for me.'

Dritan studies his watch, measuring time with the intensity of a man counting down to something. Eventually he says, 'Yes. Follow me.'

The bleach hits him again—sharp enough to sting his nostrils and sit bitter at the back of his throat. Beale is in the gutting room, sleeves rolled up, scrubbing down the stainless-steel table where fish guts may be flying later—then again, maybe not. He sloshes more bleach across the steel; it runs in clear, harsh-smelling streaks before he works it hard with a stiff-bristled brush, the rasp of it grating off metal walls. The whole place reeks of bleach, brine, and old fish—a punchy cocktail that makes his eyes water.

The Whitby Rose gives a slow, deliberate roll beneath him. Then another. Each one a little heavier than the last, the deck shifting just enough to throw off his balance as he plants his boots wider and keeps scrubbing, wondering—not for the first time—how his career has come to include industrial-strength bleach on a North Sea trawler.

He grabs the hose and rinses the table down with seawater, the cold spray hissing across the steel and sluicing the bleach into the scuppers. He keeps at it for a good few minutes until the worst of the smell lifts. When he finally straightens, he glances at the magnetic knife rack bolted to the bulkhead—half a dozen filleting knives hanging there, thin blades catching the harsh strip-light.

Next job: sharpening the lot with a honing rod.

*Life*, he thinks, *really doesn't get any better than this.*

At least he's alone. Gives him time to think. He knows what his mission is—get an ID on the transfer vessel. A name, a number—anything. Feed it back to the NCA. They won't pounce straight away. They'll investigate who it's registered to, where it's harboured. Rotterdam, Vlissingen, Cuxhaven—who knows? Wherever it ties up, that's where the real players are.

Then it'll be up to Europol to run with it—trace who's supplying the mother ship, then who's supplying them, right up the chain. Like trying to find the source of the Nile or the Amazon: follow every tributary until you finally hit the spring.

His part could end tonight, but only if he gets an ID on the boat. And how the hell is he meant to manage that? If the weather worsens, it might give him cover. The Albanians will be too busy staying upright and hauling in their shipment to be constantly glancing over their shoulders. Still risky, though. If he's spotted... well, if there is a fate worse than death, which he's certain there is after working with Cleavage, it'll be racing his way fast.

And he's alone. No backup. No SOS to armed response. Nothing but thousands of square miles of cold, dark sea.

Right now, putting up with the endless procession of turkeys at Govan HQ feels almost appealing.

He takes a filleting knife from the rack, grabs the honing rod, and draws the blade along it in lazy strokes—his mind miles from the job in hand.

## 42

Cleavage is on deck, perfectly content in his own little world. He's perched on an upturned crate, a tangle of nets pooled around his boots, deft fingers working away as he splices rope, patches mesh, and hums contentedly into the wind. The rising swell doesn't bother him; he rocks with the boat as naturally as breathing, happy as a clam.

Taking out a Mars Bar from his pocket, he demolishes it in seconds and washes it down with a full bottle of water. He knows to keep hydrated and increase the calories. Regular mealtimes on a trawler are hit and miss.

He barely notices the other three—Dritan, Stefan, Arben—huddled at the stern in quiet discussion. Cleavage's mind is somewhere else entirely. He's thinking about what to get his lad for his birthday. Nearly four years old now, old enough to understand what a birthday means, already buzzing about it. Maybe a pedal car... or that little ride-on tractor he saw in the Whitby toy shop... or maybe a train set. Something special.

'Hmm... I think the red pedal car.'

He's already looking forward to getting home. It will be another short trip with the weather closing in. Less pay—not ideal—but Dritan's been more than generous. Didn't have to pay him what he did for the last run. He's assuming this one will be similar. Anyway, that's the life of a trawlerman. Take the rough with the smooth. Won't be long before they're out for a full week, nets bursting, big hauls, and he'll get his cut of the profits. That's how it goes.

The growl of the boat's engine winds down, and the boat begins to slow.

Dritan's voice cuts through the stiff breeze.

'Cleavage! We're thinking of setting the nets like last time—come check the rig with us. Give us your advice.'

'Righto.'

He drops the net he's been working on, stands, stretches, and plods over. The three men subtly spread out as he joins them.

'Right, so what are we thinking?' he asks.

Stefan steps behind him.

'I was thinking,' Dritan begins, then stops. He locks eyes with Cleavage—cold, hard, reptilian. 'I was thinking... that you are dead man.'

The sentence hits Cleavage like nonsense. For a moment, he genuinely thinks he's misheard. Their English can be patchy.

'Sorry—what did you—'

Stefan moves in fast, bringing a wooden marlinspike down hard on the back of Cleavage's skull.

His legs buckle. Drops to his knees, the world tilting violently, his head swimming between consciousness and blackout.

Dritan plants a hand on his chest and gives a firm push. Cleavage falls back, staring up at the sky—grey, shifting—a lone seagull wheels overhead, its cry thin against the wind. He feels the cold whisper of air stir through his hair as the deck rocks beneath him, and for a confused, fading moment, he still can't understand what's happened to him.

'Get the block. Tie his feet.'

Arben moves instantly, looping the rope around the bottom of Cleavage's wellies—two, three, four tight turns.

'Come. Let's lift him.'

They try to haul him upright, but Cleavage is a big lad and a deadweight now. The three of them grunt with effort, failing to get him clean off the deck. Instead, they drag him—boots scraping—across to the guard rails and tip him forward, propping him there, head and shoulders hanging over the side.

'What... what are you doing?' Cleavage manages to groan, a tremor of awareness flickering back. His fingers claw at the metal rail, trying to find purchase, but arms wrap around his legs and he's heaved upward, forced into a sickening angle.

He's staring straight down now—into the violent swell and frothing wake below, the sea rising and falling like a living creature, waiting.

'This is what happens to snitches,' Stefan hisses in his ear.

'I don't know what you're talking about!' Cleavage yells, voice cracked with panic.

Francois appears in the wheelhouse doorway and watches, face as hard as granite. He knew this was coming—that's what the argument with Dritan was about earlier. He doesn't condone it. Doesn't want it. It's messy, unnecessary, and invites questions.

But he's powerless. Outranked. Outnumbered. He turns and steps back inside, closing the door behind him, not wishing to be part of it.

'Arben, have the block ready,' Dritan snaps. 'Stefan—when I say, we lift and push. If he clings on, use the cosh on his fingers. Ready?'

'No! Please—God—what are you doing? I've a wife! I've a kid! Don't do this, I'm begging you.'

His pleas vanish into the wind—and the wind carries on, indifferent, as another man learns what mercy means in Dritan's world.

---

Beale pulls the last knife from the magnetic strip and draws it along the honing rod, steel on steel. His mind's still running on fast-forward, playing out every possible version of what might unfold later. He needs to be on his A-game. Sharp. Alert. Thinking three moves ahead. And he has to be smart—smarter than he's ever been—because tonight there won't be any second chances.

'Ah! You gormless numpty!'

He drops the tools onto the table with a clatter and stares at the blood welling from the slice to the side of his thumb, oozing out like it's delighted to have been released into the real world instead of trapped within Beale's veins.

He glances around, yanking a handkerchief from his pocket and wrapping it around his thumb. The first-aid kit is nowhere in sight—though it is sitting patiently behind a stanchion, just out of view.

'Fucking typical! The one place you're guaranteed to slice yourself open—the gutting room—and there's no bastard first-aid kit.'

He remembers the galley. 'Aye, that's right—fist-aid kit at the side of the stove.'

Making for the steps, the boat gives another slow roll. He keeps the hanky clamped tight to his thumb, the cloth already blooming crimson. He hurries up the stairs and pushes open the door.

Stops dead. For a second, his brain refuses to process what he's seeing.

Cleavage—head and chest draped over the guardrail, limp, hanging like a discarded rag. The three men surrounding him.

*What's happened? Has the big clodhopper had an accident? Seasick? No... not Cleavage.*

Those innocent, predictable internal thoughts vanish in an instant as Dritan barks an order.

'Lift!'

Beale rushes forward. 'Wait! What the fuck are you doing?'

The three men spin around, glaring at him.

'Go back below!' Dritan roars.

Stefan snaps something in Albanian—sharp, urgent—and Dritan fires back, voice rising with fury.

Beale lunges towards them, but halts when Arben pulls a pistol from his pocket and levels it at his chest.

Cleavage finds his voice, raw and terrified. 'Danny! Help me—please help me!'

'He's a snitch,' Dritan says coldly.

Beale thinks of the coastguard stop on the first trip.

'What? No,' he protests. 'It was a random safety check!'

Dritan ignores him.

Beale sways, not only from the swell but from the danger. He suddenly realises what's happened. He has to choose every word with care. A slip of the tongue and he could give the game away. But what can he do—tell them they're all under arrest? That he's an undercover cop. Yeah, right. Then he'd be joining Cleavage in the drink.

'It *was* random,' he growls, inching forward. 'They do it all the time.'

Dritan shakes his head. 'Danny, this has nothing to do with you. Now, *go below!*'

'You can't throw a man overboard because you got stopped by the coastguard,' he pleads.

Dritan's voice hardens, final. 'He knows too much. He cannot be allowed to live. It is for the best. This is not your fight. Now—please—below.'

The world slows.

Beale rocks on his heels, helpless, as Stefan and Dritan give one brutal, decisive heave.

'Nooooo!'

Cleavage disappears over the side without a sound. Arben drops something heavy after him.

Beale runs to the rail and leans out.

Cleavage erupts to the surface—just for a second—face upturned, eyes wide with horror, arms splayed crucifix-fashion as if begging some unseen force to save him.

Then the concrete block drags the rope taut.

Cleavage is yanked down, vanishing into the boiling froth.

<h1 style="text-align:center">43</h1>

Even the weather seems to have gone mute.

Beale has witnessed many things in his time—horrible, gruesome, sadistic things that would leave most men broken for life—but nothing as cold, as deliberate as what he's just witnessed. For once, he's lost for words.

Dritan breaks the stillness, rubbing a hand through his thick black hair.

'Sorry, Danny. He knew too much.'

'Knew too much about what?'

The Albanians glance at one another, a silent conversation passing between them.

'Things are not always what they seem,' Dritan says.

Beale's anger finally boils up, raw and shaking. 'And how the fuck do you think you're going to get away with this? You've just killed an innocent man! He had a wife. A kid. God damn you—you murdering bastards!'

Dritan steps towards him, lays a hand on his shoulder, and gently steers him back toward the deckhouse—an oddly soft gesture that feels all the more sinister.

'On our way back to shore, we raise the alarm,' Dritan says, voice calm. 'We say we noticed Cleavage was missing. By then the storm will be gathering, conditions far worse. He slipped or perhaps a freak wave took him—these things happen at sea all the time. We say we searched but could not see him. We say we are low on fuel and the storm is on our tail. We have to abandon the search for our own safety.'

Beale blinks, still in a state of shock.

'That is the story we all stick to... understand?'

He nods, but doesn't allow himself to speak.

Dritan's gaze drops to the blood-soaked hanky around his thumb.

'You'd best clean that up before you get infection, my friend. Calm yourself. Think things through. It will be for your benefit if you do.' He flicks a glance towards Stefan. 'My brother doesn't trust you the way I do. Now—go.'

Beale pulls at the door, still in a daze.

'And Danny—I will make sure his wife is reimbursed handsomely.'

—◆—

Beale yanks open cupboard doors, clattering through tins and packets.

'Come on, come on... where are you?' He slams one shut and tries the cupboard above the stove. Pushes a couple of sauce bottles aside—then sees it.

'There you are.'

He pulls out a full bottle of cooking sherry and twists off the cap. Sits at the table. Bottle to lips. Drinks like a man punishing himself—three hard swallows. Waits for the warm buzz of alcohol to hit. Checks the label—16% alcohol content. Not whisky, but not bad. Any port in a storm.

He tries to make sense of what he's just seen. Despises himself for standing there, doing nothing. Dritan's last words uncoil in his head—*I'll make sure his wife is reimbursed handsomely.*

Beale sneers, disgust multiplying in his guts. 'What the fuck... like she's getting a refund on a dodgy washing machine or a botched conservatory.'

He recalls Cleavage proudly showing him the photo of his son, Fergus. The little lad doesn't seem quite as fugly now.

'Poor wee mite,' he mutters, sniffing. He wipes the wet from his cheek.

*Cleavage was boring, aye. Annoying at times. No point rewriting history with rose-tinted glasses. But the big lummox was alright.*

And alright, in Beale's estimation, is as high as it gets. On his scale of humanity, *alright* is top of the pops—the absolute pinnacle.

Takes another gulp of sherry. Fumbles deep in his coat pocket and retreats the dumb phone, the Nokia 105. Switched off. Saving the battery. Only to be used in absolute emergencies.

Weighs it in his hand, thinking about calling it in—if he can receive reception this far out. He stares at the tiny blank screen, no bigger than a postage stamp, his thumb hovering over the power button.

'Wait... wait. Think it through.'

If he makes that call, what happens? They'll send out a police patrol or Border Force cutter, armed to the gills. Dritan's mob would spot them miles off—no mistaking a fast-approach response boat. And they wouldn't waste time guessing who tipped them off. Beale's the only one onboard who could have done it.

Then what? Obvious.

Only one choice left to them.

They'd do to him exactly what they did to Cleavage. No witness. No evidence.

And at least for the Albanians, it would give them a fighting chance—two men overboard in a freak wave, storm on the horizon, nothing suspicious on board. No drugs. No contraband. Nothing to charge them with.

And there's the bigger picture.

Beale knows he's one tiny cog in a massive machine. This operation has been running for months—intel overseas, surveillance, dead drops, coded messages, analysts burning the midnight oil. God knows how many people have risked their necks already. Maybe some have died.

One phone call... and he could blow the whole thing out of the water. Now's not the time to panic. It calls for a cool head.

*'Bastards.'*

Presses the power button.

The Nokia crawls to life, its tiny monochrome screen glowing like it's waking from a coma.

He waits.

Waits.

Waits.

Checks the signal bars. Nothing. Not a flicker. Not even the usual "Emergency calls only."

Just a blank corner where the bars should be—the phone's way of shrugging.

Way too far offshore.

'Fuck. What am I thinking? These bricks barely get a signal in the middle of a city.'

He stares at the useless little handset a moment longer, then slips it back into his pocket—decision made for him by the telecom giants and their billionaire overlords.

The door above opens. The weather rushes in—a cold, blustery gust that whips through the galley. Slams shut. Slow, deliberate footsteps follow.

Dritan appears at the bottom of the stairs and studies Beale in silence, eyes drifting to the bottle on the table.

He moves forward without a word, pulls two plastic tumblers from a cupboard, and sets them down. He sits. Notices the band-aid around Beale's thumb.

'How is it?' he asks with a nod.

Beale glances at the throbbing digit. 'Fine. Just a scratch.'

Dritan lifts the bottle. Pours a half-glass into each. Then lifts his own, a silent invitation for Beale to drink.

For a flicker of a moment, Beale considers grabbing the sherry bottle, smashing it on the table edge, and driving the jagged glass straight into Dritan's jugular. One hard thrust, job done. But the thought dies as quickly as it comes.

He stares at Dritan's raised glass. 'What's this? A fucking toast to a job well done.'

Dritan offers, not a smirk, but a look of regret masquerading as a sad smile.

'When we spoke, before, I said that sometimes men have to do bad things. It does not make the man... bad.'

Beale shakes his head in disgust, and takes a gulp of sherry.

'Cleavage was innocent. You killed him for no reason except your own paranoia. That coastguard stop was random. Probably the fifth one they'd done that day. That's what they're there for—to make sure vessels have up-to-date safety gear.'

Dritan takes a sideways glance. 'I cannot take risks. Sometimes there is...' he hesitates, searching for the correct phrase. 'How do the military say—collateral damage, no?' He necks his sherry down in one hit, rises and walks towards the stairs. 'You are upset. Rest.'

Beale glances over his shoulder. 'Why?'

Dritan hesitates, turns slowly, as if the question bores him. 'Cleavage—I already told you why.'

'No.' Beale shakes his head. 'Not Cleavage. Why me? That night we first met, in the alley... you gave me twenty quid and told me to get food. Then when I showed up for a job on the boat, Francois tried to turn me away, but you overruled him. You gave me work. Trusted me—me, a homeless beggar. Even trusted me with advance wages. Why?'

Dritan leans back against the bulkhead, folds his arms. 'Okay. I tell you truth. When I was eight, and Stefan five, we live with our parents in very poor part of Tirana, capital of Albania. We were not rich. Very poor. My father own small grocery shop—vegetables, spices, little things. My mother, father... kind people, loving people. But no money. My father, he not good businessman.' He smiles fondly. 'Once a week, on a Friday, he take a little money from till and give to me and Stefan. Say, "Go, buy sweet. Or ice cream." This was his treat for us.'

He looks down at the floor, remembering.

'One day, same thing. He give money, we go. We get ice cream. Hot day—stinking hot. We take long way home, play around, stupid boys. On way back we smell smoke. Hear sirens. Think nothing. This normal in poor place.' He pauses. 'We turn corner into our street... our home is on fire. Big fire. Whole building. People shouting. Fire trucks everywhere.'

His voice lowers to a whisper.

'My mother, my father... they do not come out. They die inside.'

Beale takes a deep breath, pushing his emotions aside, the way he always does.

'And?' he asks quietly.

Dritan straightens, arms folding tight across his chest. 'And... we go live with my uncle, aunt, in Tirana. Other side of city. Me and Stefan... first time we have separate bedrooms. My uncle not rich but... well-off.' He swallows hard. 'After two, three weeks... my uncle come to my room at night.' He closes his eyes, head bowing under the weight of the memory. 'He touch me. Sexually. Next night, he... rape me.'

'Shite,' Beale whispers.

Dritan straightens, pushing his chest out as he continues. 'This go on many months. Maybe a year. Then one night I wake—need pee. I walk to toilet and see my uncle creeping to Stefan's room. I scream at him. Call him dirty, fucking bastard. I attack him. He drunk. I knock him down. He struggle, Stefan wake, I grab him and we run into the night.'

He shrugs, almost matter-of-fact.

'Long story short, we live on street as orphans. We join small gangs. Learn pickpocket, steal. But this no life for boys. Streets full of drug addicts, paedophiles, men who use you, break you. But I grow up fast. Learn to fight. Join bigger gang—more protection.'

He pauses, then continues.

'Years later—maybe I am twelve, thirteen—a man come. Say he my mother's brother. Another uncle. He take us to live with him and his second wife. She cannot have children.'

Beale grimaces. 'Don't tell me—history repeated itself?'

Dritan chuckles. 'No. Opposite. This uncle, he good man. Try give us education. Private school, tutors. But too late for me and Stefan. We wild boys. Hard boys. He own trawlers. Fishing boats. So he put us to work. Me and Stefan love the sea. We learn fast. Make new life for ourselves.'

'What happened to the uncle who abused you?'

He hesitates as his eyes glaze over. 'When I turn eighteen, I return to Tirana. I follow my uncle home one night from bar. I slice him up middle like fish, then cut his heart out—just like he cut my heart out.'

A small, winsome smile touches his mouth.

'So... this is my story. And this is why I give you money that night. Why I offer you job. I was homeless. You were homeless. I was given chance. I give you chance. Now I am even with the world. Everyone deserve one chance—but only one.'

'But not Cleavage.'

Dritan shrugs. 'That different. I protect us all.' He pulls a small set of keys from his pocket, unlocks a low cupboard, and retrieves a full bottle of vodka. Sets it on the table.

'I know you are upset. Drown your sorrows. Help you forget. When you awake, we back in harbour.'

Beale stares at the bottle. 'Thanks,' he mutters.

Dritan heads for the stairs again. 'One thing you must know about Albanians, Danny. We have strong culture. Brothers, sisters, family, friends. Loyalty is everything. If you remain loyal, six months from now you'll be rich man. Enough to buy one of those half-houses... what you call them? Bungy-low?'

'Bungalow.'

He chuckles. 'Ah, yes. Bungalow by sea. Maybe Scotland, no? You live quiet life. Your own home. Not enough for super yacht—but enough. That's all we need. Enough. Then no more work like pack horse—no?'

His footsteps reverberate off the stairs. Door opens, closes. Silence.

Beale takes a sip of sherry, stands, and pours the rest down the sink. He twists off the vodka cap and empties that too.

'Nice try, sunshine. But you don't catch me out that easily.'

## 44

Beale flicks the light on and steps reluctantly into the cabin. Places the empty vodka bottle on the floor beside his bunk. The bulb hums faintly, throwing a sickly yellow glare over everything.

He gazes around. Cleavage's kit bag sits by the wall—neat, zipped, squared away. A man's life reduced to order. Beside it, Beale's own bag slumps open, clothes spilling out like a confession. Vest, socks, a pair of grubby used underpants he keeps meaning to wash and never does.

He looks at the bunks.

Top one: neat, tidy, blankets tucked tight under the mattress, pillow plumped and centred.

His eyes drop to the bottom bunk—covers mangled like they've been in a fight to the death after a night on the piss, sheets hanging off, pillow abandoned on the floor, dubious stains on the mattress protector.

He doesn't need anyone to spell it out for him. No lecture required. The contrast's loud and clear.

Spots Cleavage's green woolly hat hanging from a drawer handle. Picks it up and sits on the bunk. Twists it around and around between his hands, the yarn rough against his nicotine-stained fingers.

His self-loathing is in danger of overwhelming him. What he'd really like to do is grab one of those razor-sharp filleting knives from the gutting room and open his wrists, neat as you please. Let it all drain out. End his shambles of a life. The only thing stopping him is that he can't be arsed walking up and down those fucking steps again.

He's not got a single friend in the world. Not one. He's universally hated by everyone at the station—in fact, by every copper he's ever worked for, and plenty he hasn't. His reputation goes before him like an advance guard of stinking horseshit.

He tries to think about where it all went wrong. A rough upbringing, sure—but plenty of folk have that and still turn out halfway decent. Can't pin it all on that. Not on his dad, or his mam, not on the estate, not on the teachers who pigeon-holed him as a trouble at the age of seven.

Truth is, he drinks too much, smokes too much, eats shit. His uncouth behaviour, his questionable hygiene, his rude, combative nature, the insults, and endless profanities—those alone can clear a room.

And they're his endearing qualities.

He has his son. Loves him, and—God help them both—he suspects the lad may even love him back. Not that he can be sure. He once toyed with the idea of sticking the lad under a polygraph to find out, but thought better of it. The results are questionable at best. He could have ended up with a false positive, or negative—he's not sure which.

The boy's sixteen. Might as well be an alien amoeba from a distant galaxy. On the rare occasions they spend time together, it's awkward, stilted, both of them counting down the minutes. Neither wants to be there. Not really. He suspects they only do it because it feels like the right thing to do, some dutiful box-ticking exercise between father and son.

The only other person he really speaks to, reluctantly, is his ex-wife—a demented Attila the Hun in a leopard-print fake-leather skirt. And she only ever calls to harangue him about overdue maintenance payments or bleed more cash out of him for some highly dubious excuse about new clothes or computer gear for the lad.

No, he's hit rock bottom. It doesn't get lower than this.

And yet the irony isn't lost on him—*Dritan*.

The only person who's ever given him a chance, ever shown him the slightest flicker of kindness. Dritan actually *likes* Danny Beale.

Dritan, the murdering, paranoid psychopath—of all people—has a soft spot for him.

It beggars belief.

And yet it's all a falsehood. He likes Danny Beale, the homeless tramp, the bloke who's fallen on hard times. And it's all a big fat lie.

Dritan and his gang may have pushed Cleavage overboard, but it's he—Danny Beale—who has blood on his hands.

Those oversized Wellington boots. When Stefan came to check the cabin after the arms drop, he must've noticed they were wet. That sealed the fate of Cleavage.

Beale wore the boots.

He's as much responsible for the brutal death as Dritan.

He can't escape the mental images. Cleavage's yawning, gormless grin. The staccato, braying donkey laugh that could slice cheese. His incessant wittering about weather signs and sea lore, how everything has to be spotless and tidy. His mind-numbingly dull accounts of past fishing trips, like anyone gives a fuck. And yet—he misses the big lummox. It isn't just the swamping guilt. Cleavage was a family man, loved his wife and kid. Maybe Beale was a little jealous. Cleavage had what he could never have because he was a good man, as interesting as a bowl of cold porridge—aye, but decent, alright.

Unlike him.

He knows who he is. He knows *why* he is.

It's a shield, armour. The more that people despise him, the more obnoxious he becomes.

Like two nuclear powers upping the ante—sabre-rattling, daring the other to make the next move.

On reflection, he realises it's a woeful analogy, or metaphor, or whatever the fuck it was meant to be.

The vodka bottle catches the mournful yellow hue of the light.

They'll come and check on him when they're ready—make sure the bum has drunk himself into a comatose stupor, dead to the world.

He knows now how they operate, what they're capable of.

And he knows something else.

Doesn't know how. Doesn't know when.

But he *will* kill Dritan.

It's all he has left—revenge.

# 45



## Twenty minutes earlier...

It's the last word he hears. A negative.

'Nooooo!' Danny's howl splits the air as Cleavage pitches over the rail, wild water surging up to claim him.

The rest is sensation.

The sea hits hard—not a splash, but a flat, brutal slap across his face and chest. Cold detonates through his body, a jolt that steals his breath as a pressurised spike of seawater blasts up his nose. His eyes clamp shut. Limbs convulse.

Then everything softens.

Sound dims under the surface, as if someone has wrapped the whole world in a thick woollen blanket. Everything is muted—the churn of waves above, the distant throb of the engine, the hull's deep metallic rumble. Movement becomes a shove, a drag, a twist. Salt burns his throat. His clothes balloon and twist around him, dragging him deeper. The cold presses in, tight and unforgiving.

He kicks—hard—and bobs through the surface. Air slams into his lungs.

The face of Danny is above him on the rail, twisted in pure anguish.

He's taken the fall. The shocks haven't stopped his heart. He's breathing—gasping—but breathing. The cold bites deep, but he's afloat, head clear enough to think one fractured thought:

*I might actually survive this.*

But it's a mirage, a cruel joke offered by a mocking God.

The rope tightens around his ankles. The tug of the concrete block. And down he goes.

Down.

Down.

Deeper and deeper.

Clamps his mouth shut, forcing himself to hold his last breath.

Stares up, eyes wide in horror. The weak daylight retreats as if offering a last, forlorn goodbye.

It's over, and he knows it.

Soon his lungs will ache, then burn, then revolt. He'll lose the fight to keep the air inside. Instinct will wrench his mouth open. He'll try to inhale.

But it won't be oxygen waiting for him—only saltwater.

The body will take charge, coughing to expel the intrusion, and that reflex will betray him, triggering the urge to drag in another breath. Another mouthful. Another flood. Each reaction feeding the next.

A simple sequence. Unstoppable.

There's no panic now—only the long, slow sink. Limbs loose. Mind dimming.

One last thought of his wife—Raquel. His little boy—Fergus.

The pedal car.

Fergus would have torn around the garden in that thing, laughing his head off.

And his wife—her arms around him every time he came home from a trip. The warmth of that embrace. Smell of her hair. The touch that told him he was loved so much.

*It's coming.*

That deep, primal command to refresh his lungs—to open his mouth and drag in air that isn't there.

A feeling.

The boot on his left foot shifts—slides. He feels it flick free from his ankle. He waggles his toes.

The right Wellington is next. Oversized. Flooded. The rope strains against it, tugging hard.

It gives. A tiny shift. Then another.

He kicks. Drags his leg back and forth, working it loose.

And suddenly—he's free.

He looks up.

A faint sliver of daylight, thin as a smear of milk across a grey slab.

He rises slowly, body angled upward, moving like something huge and heavy lifting from the depths.

No rushing. No wasted effort.

His jacket drags at him, clumsy and waterlogged, hindering every stroke. He can't spare the seconds or the strength to fight free of it.

Sombre daylight wavers above.

He can't hold on much longer. Feels time thinning. The ascent stretching into an eternity he doesn't have.

He's not going to make it. Another five seconds—that's all he'd have needed.

His eyes bulge as his chest locks tight, screaming for release.

*Just two more seconds, please God.*

Explodes through the surface.

Coughs out the stale, stagnant air and sucks in fresh, life-giving oxygen.

Lies on his back, spreadeagled, floating as his lungs hammer to catch up.

A strange sliding sensation takes hold—he's drifting, not sinking.

Turns his head.

He's gliding down the face of a massive swell.

*Don't panic. They're not breakers.*

He rides the slope until the uncanny moment he reaches the trough—weightless for a second—before the sea picks him up again, lifting him like a scrap of driftwood.

He rises with the next wave, higher and higher, until he crests the peak.

Glances left.

That's when panic arrives.

*Shit!*

Five, maybe six waves away, an immense wall of water—ten, fifteen metres high—rears up, coming straight for him. White water frays along its crest, gathering and thickening.

The whole thing is building mass, velocity, anger. Soon its weight will be too great to hold itself together. It will pitch forward and break—millions of gallons of white water, a roiling, devouring vortex that ignores the laws of physics and anything small enough to get in its way.

He kicks himself upright, clothes dragging at him like soaked sandbags.

Not much time.

He yanks the zipper on his waterproof jacket and forces it down.

One arm slips free. Then the other.

Gone.

He sinks briefly as the swell rolls under him, uses the moment to claw at his thick woollen jumper. Arms up. Fingers hooking the sleeves. It clings to him like a second skin, stubborn and heavy, but he fights it off, peeling it inch by inch until it finally drifts away.

Next—cargo pants.

He unfastens them, pushes down, wriggling, kicking, fighting the drag of soaked fabric.

Then—release.

He feels it instantly: the lift.

As if ten kilos have fallen away from him.

He's left in his all-in-one thermal underwear and socks.

That will do. A thin skin of insulation, something like a wetsuit, and at the very least, a barrier against the endless scouring of saltwater.

He rises on the next swell and sees the wall of water again.

Fear grips his throat.

The freak wave.

He has two options—take a chance and hope he can ride it before it breaks.

If he gets it wrong, he's a goner.

It will roll him like a tennis ball in a washing machine on a fast spin. Then the thunderous weight will drive him down and keep him there, pressing relentlessly, a giant boot on his back, until his lungs give out and burst for release.

His other option: swim towards it and at the critical moment—two, three seconds before it folds over itself—dive under and power head-first into the base of it.

If he's lucky, he might slip past the worst of its power.

Yes, it'll still catch him, grab the back of him and drag him along, but he'll be clear of the cascading, whirling spin cycle. Out of the washing machine hell.

One more swell to pass and it will be above him.

He treads water, pulling in slow, deliberate breaths, forcing the air deep into his diaphragm.

Calm. Controlled.

Oxygen in the bank.

No panic.

Panic kills.

He can barely look at it.

The skyscraper of water.

A curtain of misery.

At the trough of the last swell he starts his freestyle—steady, deliberate—arm over arm, head down for three strokes, up for a breath.

Feels himself rising, pushed up by the sea.

Takes one last glance to judge the timing.

The peak is curling over itself now, a hooked beak of water fighting gravity. In seconds, the whole thing will cave in on itself like a black hole.

*Now!*

He dives—deep—kicks hard.

Breaks into a breaststroke, strong, driven, legs hammering through the cold.

The roar swallows him. Above, the water flexes and reaches, grasping, dragging, pulling him backwards into its collapsing heart.

Kicks harder.

Pulls stronger.

Fights the grip of the wave with everything he has left.

Surfaces. Turns. An explosion of frothing white peels away into the distance.

He's done it.

Survived.

At least for now.

But there's no respite. With the sun blotted out, he has no sense of direction.

The boat was heading north-east towards Dogger Bank. Maybe ten, fifteen miles out when he went overboard. That distance is right at the edge of his capabilities in seas like this.

He floats and slowly turns with the swell, carried where the water wants him.

Then—he catches it.

A blur in the distance, glimpsed only in the brief window between each rising and falling wave.

*The Whitby Rose* steaming away.

He now has his bearings and turns, searching for any hint of land, any landmark to ground him.

Nothing.

No faint smudge of coastline. No rocky outcrop. No lighthouse. No passing boat.

Just grey.

Grey sea, grey sky—merged into one indistinguishable daub.

There are no options left. It's simple.

Head down.

Arm over arm.

Three strokes.

Breath.

His last saviour might be the sea itself. Don't fight it. Roll with it.

Surely he deserves at least one break today?

The swell should be rolling inland. The currents may favour him.

Let the water take some of his weight. Let it guide him.

Nice and steady.

And he prays—quietly, desperately—that he spots a boat.

Or, more likely, that a boat spots him.

Focuses and thinks of one thing only—the pedal car.

# 46

The steel steps give the game away. Doesn't matter how carefully they tiptoe down them, they still broadcast someone's imminent arrival.

The cabin tilts in grudging little lurches, a reminder of the conditions outside.

Beale sprawls himself out on the bunk, right arm dangling over the edge, clutching the empty vodka bottle. Head back, mouth open, snoring. A thin ribbon of drool leaks down his cheek—the final cinematic flourish.

He really missed his vocation. Could've given De Niro and Dustin Hoffman a run for their money.

A shard of light cuts across the cabin as the door creaks open a notch. Then wider. He doesn't dare risk opening his eyes, but he feels the presence—someone blocking the light, standing over him.

Whoever it is... waits.

If he's misread the situation, he's in deep trouble. Stefan might've whispered poison in his brother's ear. Maybe Dritan now sees *him* as a liability. Maybe the figure standing there is holding a hammer, weighing up the best angle to cave his skull in.

No. Have faith. Dritan rules with an iron fist. He's the leader, and like most leaders, once he backs a decision, he carries it through to the bitter end. Whether he's right or wrong, he can't lose face.

The unseen intruder shifts. Beale feels the vodka bottle eased from his fingers—slow, careful, like handling a live grenade.

Then, the strangest thing.

A blanket settles over him, tucked lightly at the shoulder. Footsteps retreat. The door clicks shut. Boots tread softly up the steel stairs just as the engine eases down.

*Rendezvous point.*

Beale doesn't waste a second. Slips his boots on, shrugs into his jacket, and creeps past the door.

At the top of the stairs, he waits, listens.

Raised voices, but they offer little meaning as the three men are talking their own language. He assumes the supply boat will follow the same routine as last time, come along starboard side. But only a maniac would bring a boat in close in these conditions. A collision would be catastrophic for everyone.

He has his hiding place all mapped out in his head—behind the net cage. It will offer him camouflage but is dangerously close to the winch that Arben manned last time.

The boat lurches violently from left to right, up and down. He grips the handrails as he's thrown back and forth.

'Christ, what am I doing here? I should have heeded my mother's advice and entered the ministry.'

He hauls the door open and is hit with an icy blast. A small floodlight glows on the starboard side, but the rest of the boat is sunk in darkness—an unnecessary precaution as far as he can see. There won't be any patrol boats out tonight.

He pulls the door shut and, head down, scurries like a sewer rat to take cover behind the net cage. Even better than he imagined—he can make out the silhouettes of the men through the mesh.

A blinding light sweeps across from the sea—the supply vessel, rising and falling like a haunted lantern in the dark.

*What will it be this time?* he wonders. *More guns, drugs... another migrant?*

He pulls his collar up against the chill, and spiteful squalls of stinging rain. Peeks around the corner of the cage to get a better view. Dritan yabbers into a radio, then snaps an order to Arben, who strides to the stern and takes up position beside the winch—only yards from Beale.

Out beyond the guardrail, the supply boat bobs at a safe distance, its lights a hazy smear in the dark. No way are they risking coming alongside in this lot.

After a minute or so, a smaller shape drops from its side—a rigid inflatable, outboard motor coughing into life. It slaps down, then noses towards The Whitby Rose, climbing and falling as it comes in. Two men aboard, and lashed in the bow, two oil drums.

Beale squints, trying to make out the name on the side of the boat, but he's blinded by the spotlight—as if it's pointed directly at him.

The whirr of the hydraulics battles with the roar of the sea as the winch arm swings outwards. Arben works the levers back and forth, and the cable and strap drop over the side. Dritan and Stefan cling to the guardrail, shouting orders as the cable swings wildly back and forth. The inflatable bucks beneath it, men fighting to steady the load. After a few minutes, Dritan throws Arben a thumbs-up. A sharp crack of thunder rolls across the sky, a distant flash flickering above the black horizon.

Beale stares nervously out.

Arben pulls on a lever and the barrel lifts free of the RIB, slung in a wide lifting strap hooked to the cable. It sways dangerously, then pendulums out, and lurches back as the davit arm swings inboard. Dritan and Stefan stand ready, hands out, tracking its movement.

As it nears the deck, they grab hold, muscles straining as they steady the drum. Arben feathers the controls, lowering it the last few inches until it settles with a shuddering clunk onto the steel. Stefan slips the straps free and hauls them clear.

More urgent chatter as the winch starts to repeat the process.

Beale still cannot make out the name or number on the hull of the supply boat.

*Damn it!*

If he's going to get a proper look, he needs to be at the bow—somewhere out of the blinding light. But that's risky. He could be spotted by Francois.

The second barrel begins to rise into view, slung awkwardly beneath the strap. Before the arm can swing it over the deck, one of the straps snaps—a sharp, violent crack.

All hell breaks loose.

Shouting. Arms waving. The barrel swings wildly, a hundred kilos of dead weight pinwheeling above the deck. It sways over the boat, then back over the sea again, tilting dangerously. Arben lunges for the controls, but it's too late. The load tips, topples, and crashes over the side—missing the dinghy by inches.

A burst of furious shouting erupts. Arms flail, men jabbing fingers, each blaming one another.

Beale takes his chance while they're distracted.

He steals forward, keeping low, darting across the deck, up the port side. He crouches beneath the windscreen of the wheelhouse, heart hammering, breath shallow. Edges round the corner.

A sudden flash of sheet lightning floods the world white for a few seconds, turning sea and sky into neon electric.

In that instant, he sees it—the name and number on the supply boat's hull:

*ZEEWOLF ENI 07741066*

Beale is not a linguistic genius by any means. He's barely mastered English. But even he knows that has to be Dutch—or German—for Sea Wolf.

And he has his first bit of luck.

He's terrible at remembering numbers, and he certainly can't risk writing them down. But 0774—are the first four digits of his mobile number. Easy. And 1066 rings a very distant bell. Something to do with history, which he was crap at. An invasion or the Magna Carta, or blowing up the Houses of Parliament or some such fucking thing. Whatever it is, it sticks.

He sees the dinghy making its way back to the supply vessel, tossed around like a toy in a bathtub, the sea becoming more belligerent by the minute. Crouching, he makes his way back, ducking down under the wheelhouse window.

Rounds the corner.

And runs slap bang into Francois.

# 47

## Friday 6:50 am

Zac collects the coffee, and ham and cheese toasty and saunters over to the bandstand near West Pier, settling onto a bench. Another grey morning, but not too cold. He occasionally takes breakfast here. It steadies his mind before the rigours of the day. He demolishes the cheese and ham toastie in no time and chases it down with strong, black coffee, warmth spreading through him, his sluggish body and mind beginning to rouse.

The whoop-whoop of an emergency siren cuts through the harbour air, growing louder.

'Ambulance,' he murmurs, gazing back along the promenade. He rises from the bench and watches the vehicle as it threads the narrow run between the shops and amusement arcades on one side and the harbour on the other. It passes him and pulls up hard near Battery Parade overlooking West Beach.

He swills the last of his coffee, dumps the cup in a bin and jogs over as a male and female paramedic spill out of the cab.

A member of the public reaches the crew first, tugging urgently at the male paramedic's sleeve. Whatever she says sends the man sprinting with her down the steps to the beach, medic bag slung over shoulder. The second paramedic swings open the back doors of the ambulance and yanks the stretcher from its cradle.

Zac arrives as she's manoeuvring it clear. He flashes his warrant card.

'DS Stoker, CID. What's going on?'

'Report of a body washed up,' she says, breath tight with urgency.

'Dead?'

The female, who looks like she should be still in high school, shrugs.

'Caller said he looked dead, but we'll confirm that ourselves.' She nods at the stretcher. 'I need this down there.'

'I'll give you a hand.' Zac grabs the opposite end, and together they start for the steps.

———— ❈ ————

Zac and the paramedic tramp across the last stretch of wet sand, the stretcher bumping between them. A small knot of bystanders hovers around the figure on the ground—concerned, uncertain where to look, but gawping all the same. The first paramedic is kneeling beside the casualty, pulling oxygen tubing from his kit bag.

The stricken man lies belly down, head twisted to the left, covered in a silver thermal blanket. The skin on his cheeks is the colour of old candle wax—pale, translucent. Lips blue. Eyelids slack. Salt crusted in his eyebrows and beard. His chest barely moves, almost imperceptible beneath the blanket.

But at least a sign—a good sign.

Life is not totally extinguished.

'Airway's clear... breathing's shallow,' the paramedic says to his partner.

He works quickly and fits monitoring leads to the man's chest. Checks the carotid pulse—slow, patchy. He slips a tourniquet around the upper arm and tightens it. The vein finally shows—a faint, reluctant ridge—he eases a cannula into the bulge, taping it down before connecting a saline drip.

'His temp's through the floor,' he mutters. 'We need him off this sand.'

The second paramedic angles the stretcher closer.

'Right. On your count.'

Zac steps in to help, eyes fixed on the waxen face, the salt crust, the faint tremor moving through the man's jaw—signs of someone who's been in the water far too long. All typical signs of someone who has come off second best against the sea.

They lift the man onto the stretcher in one swift, coordinated movement.

The lead paramedic shoots a sharp glance at the onlookers.

'Does anyone know who he is?' he snaps.

A low murmur ripples through the group. Heads shake, almost apologetic.

Zac peers closer. His eyes widen as the man's features line up in his mind.

'Oh Christ... it's Cleavage.'

———— ❦ ————

Zac stands just inside the ward as the nurse steps out of the side room, pulling off her gloves.

'He's stable,' she says. 'Under sedation. Severe dehydration, but he'll be fine. We'll keep him under observation for twenty-four hours, then he can go home. A week of rest and he should be right as rain—physically.'

Zac lets out a breath of relief.

'Thank God for that.'

She studies him for a moment. 'You came in with the ambulance?'

He flashes his warrant card. 'Followed them, yes. DS Stoker. CID. You can call me Zac.'

She nods. 'I'm Amara. I'm looking after him for now.'

'Thanks.'

'We didn't get any ID,' she adds. 'You're certain about his name?'

'Definitely. Ryan Harker,' Zac repeats. 'Most people know him as Cleavage.'

Raised eyebrows, as she gives him a dubious look.

Zac winces apologetically. 'Sorry. Not my idea. I think it's the man-boobs.'

'I see. Some people are cruel,' she says. 'We'll try to trace next of kin. If you think of anything useful, let the ward know.'

'I will.'

She hesitates. 'Do you want to see him?'

Zac glances towards the door, contemplates for a second, then shakes his head.

'No. I'll leave you to it.'

She nods once and turns back into the ward.

Zac watches the door close, then pulls out his phone and heads towards the lift.

# 48
## 9:52 am

Zac parks up and locks the car. He stares at the guesthouse on the backstreets of Whitby. Early Edwardian red brick, big bay windows, high ceilings—beautiful once, impossible to heat, now in a state of terminal decay. Its heyday, sixty years ago. These days it's cheap accommodation for whoever has nowhere better to go: drifters, homeless, people on the run from something or someone.

Inside the entrance, a swarm of leaflets clings to a corkboard—helplines for drug and alcohol counselling, a domestic-abuse hotline, a flyer for some Tuesday-night support group. And front and centre, printed in bold, officious letters:

**NO SMOKING**
**Any patron suspected of smoking in this building**
**will be asked to leave immediately.**

He skips up three flights of stairs; on each landing the smell of tobacco smoke grows stronger. He strolls along the corridor, looks both ways, and knocks.

Coughing and muted curses emanate from within.

'Who is it?' a voice croaks.

'It's me—Zac,' he whispers.

'Who?'

'Me. DS Stoker.'

'Whatever it is you're selling, I'm not interested.'

Zac tightens his fists and growls. 'Stop pissing about, Beale, and open up.'

Silence.

'Who is it again?'

'I swear to God,' he murmurs.

A click, and the door inches open. Zac pushes it wider and is met with a fog of choking cigarette fumes.

He storms to the window and rattles it up, allowing a refreshing sea breeze to enter.

'Christ almighty, Beale. You could smoke kippers in here.'

'I'll stick to Lambert and Butler, thanks.'

Dressed only in a grimy white vest and even grimier baggy Y-fronts, he ambles over to a dispirited dressing table, pulls a cigarette from a packet, and sparks up. Grabs a bottle of whisky and a chipped cup. Pours a healthy slosh into it.

'Drink?'

Zac checks his watch. 'It's not even ten o'clock in the morning, for crying out loud.'

Beale is puzzled. 'So what? Have I missed an appointment or something?'

Zac takes a seat in a high-backed, threadbare armchair opposite a single bed with its covers strewn everywhere. He gazes around the room. To call it depressing would be an understatement.

Beale knocks the lighter onto the carpet and wearily bends to pick it up, exposing a pair of bulbous, hairy testicles.

Zac swallows hard and pulls a pained expression. 'Please, Lord, save my soul.'

Beale slumps onto the bed and takes a sip of whisky.

*He's not his usual self,* Zac thinks. *Yes, he's still repulsive, unhygienic, obnoxious—but he seems to have lost a spark.*

'So, what's happened?'

Beale drags on the ciggy, emits a plume of smoke, sighs, rubs at his face. He's tired, jaded.

'I'm about done, Zac. I've one more thing to do, then it's over for me.'

'What are you talking about?'

'I'm finished. I'm going to resign. Those weak-kneed, pasty-faced puss-balls from HQ have been trying to get rid of me for years. If it wasn't for the fact my brother-in-law's high up in the police union and has some clout, I'd be long gone.'

Zac leans forward. He's never witnessed Beale like this before.

'Well, I'm sure you'll be missed.'

Beale stares at him coldly. 'Oh, very fucking droll. Always the comedian, eh?'

'What will you do?'

Beale shrugs and stares wistfully out of the window. 'Thought I'd move to the highlands. See out my time there. The cry of the buzzard, the skreigh of the hawk. The rolling glens, the snow-topped peaks of the mountains. The shimmering lochs and cascading waterfalls. The distant twinkling of oil rigs on a moonless night. The constant throb of those fucking wind turbines.' He sighs. 'Maybe take up water colour painting. Try my hand at poetry. Basket-weave. Get in touch with my feminine side... if the bitch is still talking to me. I'll get on benefits. Do a few odd jobs, cash in hand. Every other fucker does. Why not me?'

Zac smothers a snigger. 'Benefits won't keep you in cigarettes and whisky for a week, never mind food and accommodation.'

Another fierce glare. 'Are you deliberately trying to pish on my rhubarb?'

'Sorry.'

'Thought I might even join the village choir.'

'Poor bastards,' Zac mutters, imagining the pained expressions on the faces of some innocent highland choral ensemble.

'What's that yer say?'

'Nothing.'

Beale gazes at the floor, almost detached. 'They're ruthless, Zac.'

'Who?'

'Dritan and his gang. They kill men without a second thought—quicker than you can say soggy gusset.'

'What time did you get back?'

'About six this morning. A trip from hell.'

'Are you going to tell me what happened?'

Beale knocks back the whisky, then drops his face into his hands. Emotion laid raw. His voice lowers to a sad whisper, tears welling at the side of his eyes.

'They killed Cleavage. Tied a concrete weight around his feet and tossed him over the side like a bag of kittens. Thought he was a grass because on the first trip we were boarded by the coastguard. I'd grown to like the lad. Aye, one could almost call it—love. Brotherly love. And his death, well... it was all my fault, do ye hear, all my fault.'

More sniffles as he wipes snot from his nose, and breaks into soft, tuneless singing.

*'Should auld acquaintance be forgot,*
*And never brought to mind?*
*We'll tak' a cup o' kindness yet,*
*For auld lang syne...'*

*Oh Christ*, Zac thinks. *Please not the singing. Anything but the singing.*

'Ahem...' Zac cuts in gently. 'Cleavage is not dead.'

Beale stops the caterwauling mid-wail and stares at him with pure contempt.

'Of course he's fucking dead!' he snaps, wiping the damp from his cheek. 'We were miles offshore, and the sea was wilder than my ex-missus when she's onto her third bottle of Bacardi. For God's sake, man—show some respect for the recently departed.'

He makes the sign of the cross over his heart.

'Cleavage *isn't* dead,' Zac repeats. 'He washed up on West Beach this morning. Hypothermia, severely dehydrated. Looks like he's been rolled around in a barrel full of grit, but he'll survive. I've just come from the hospital. He hasn't spoken yet. He's under sedation.'

Beale's eyeballs are in danger of popping from his skull. 'If this is some sick joke of—'

'It's true. Cleavage is my snout. Although he knew nothing about what he was mixed up in. Totally innocent and oblivious to everything.'

Beale grabs Zac's arm in a state of excitement. 'You mean... he's alive?'

'Yes.'

'He'll survive?'

'Aye. Doc reckons a week of restful recuperation at home and he'll be right as rain.'

Beale rubs furiously at his forehead and begins pacing back and forth across the cramped room.

'Oh, sweet Jesus. Thank you, Lord, thank you. Next time I'm in church, I'll drop a twenty into the plate.' A moment's reflection. 'Maybe a tenner. Thank you. This calls for a celebration,' he adds, topping up the cup with a generous splash of whisky. He stubs out the cigarette in a jam-jar lid and instantly lights a fresh one.

He spins violently, eyes narrowing into slits of suspicion.

'Hang on, big man—how did that massive turd-burger manage to survive? No one could have lived through that.'

'He once swam the Channel. That's his hobby—swimming.'

Beale ponders, stroking his chin. 'The brainless, empty ball sack never mentioned that to me. Which is highly surprising, as the gobshite never shut the fuck up. Yap, yap, fucking yap. With his bowlines and sheep-shagger's hitch, and aye, aye, skipper, and hard to starboard, Horatio. I'm telling you—he could bore the todger off a bronze statue.'

'What happened to brotherly love?'

Beale snorts derisively. 'Pffft! I'm tired and overly emotional. I wasn't thinking straight.'

'So, wanna go through where we're at?'

'What?'

'The covert operation—give me a debrief.'

Beale tugs on the smoke. 'Oh, aye. Are you sitting comfortably?'

'Not really.'

'Okay—I'll begin.'

# 49

## 10:55 am

The black Doc Martens are immaculate as they squeak along the pavement and head towards the entrance to the hospital.

The man pauses just long enough for the sensor to catch him.

Automatic doors slide open with a soft pneumatic hiss.

Reception is a glass-fronted box of posters and paperwork. The woman is on the phone, eyes on her screen, one hand hovering over the keyboard.

There's no respite for a hospital receptionist.

'No, test results don't come through reception.' Taps a few keys, nodding along to a voice only she can hear. 'Your GP will contact you if there's anything you need to act on. That's okay. Goodbye.'

Doesn't look up but senses a figure approaching, just one of hundreds throughout the day.

Another call flashes. She hits a button.

'Scarborough General Hospital, how can I help? ... I see. Have you spoken to your local practitioner... yes, your doctor... oh, you can't get in for three weeks? Well, if you feel it's urgent, then I suggest you present at A and E... yes, that's right, accident and emergency. Okay, no problem. Bye.'

There's someone at the counter as the phone rings again. She lifts the receiver.

'Scarborough General Hospital, I'll just put you on hold.'

Finally glances at the figure in front of her. Registers details without really processing them: a man standing patiently. A baseball cap with a large rim sits above warm brown eyes. Black leather bomber jacket. A bunch of flowers clutched in one hand, cellophane catching the fluorescent lights—a visitor.

'Yes, sir, how can I help?'

'I have come to see my stepbrother. He was the man who nearly drowned. Found on Whitby Beach.'

The receptionist glances at her notes. 'You must mean Ryan Harker?'

'Yes, yes, Ryan,' he exclaims, overly excited. 'How is he?' His face morphs into anguish. 'Please God, let him still be alive.'

His emotion is natural and it briefly touches her usually detached demeanour—enough to make her notice how handsome he is.

She offers him a reassuring smile.

'He's doing fine. Stable but under sedation. You'll need to speak to the nurse in charge or his doctor, but I believe they're keeping him in for observation for twenty-four hours.'

The man wipes a tear from the corner of his eye and sniffles.

'Providence has smiled upon us. Thank you. Truly. Where is he?'

She glances down at her screen again.

'He's on Lilac Ward, Level 2.' She gestures to her right. 'Take the lift to the second floor. The ward desk is directly opposite the lift. You can speak to the nurse there.'

'Thank you,' he says again, voice thick with gratitude. 'May good fortune visit you.'

He turns and heads for the lifts, flowers tucked under his arm.

The receptionist watches him go for a moment longer than necessary.

*What a hunk*, she thinks. *Even with a scar running down his cheek.*

# 50

## 10:57 am

As Beale labours the point and goes into every detail of his ordeal, and the intel he gathered, a thought niggles away at the back of Zac's mind, but it just won't surface in a coherent manner.

With the cigarette and whisky fumes, and Beale's gravelly, slow Glaswegian drawl, he's feeling a little nauseous.

'The transfer ship is called the *ZEEWOLF* and the boat's number is ENI 07741066.'

'Right,' Zac says, jotting the details down in his notepad.

Beale pours another slug of whisky into the cup, sparks another ciggy.

'Now here's the interesting part. Once I had the boat's ID, I made my way around the wheelhouse to head back to my cabin, or berth, or whatever the fuck it's called. And guess what?'

'What?'

'I ran slap bang into...'

Zac's niggling thought dances naked across his mind and hits him square between the eyes with a sledgehammer.

He leaps from the chair. 'Bollocks!' he yells.

Beale gawps at him open-mouthed. 'You haven't even heard what I'm about to say.'

Zac clutches his head. 'No. Listen to me—Dritan and his men threw Cleavage overboard. Attempted murder. *Attempted*—get it? Except as far as they're concerned, it worked. A body dumped in the North Sea is a problem that usually solves itself.'

'And?'

'But Cleavage survived.'

Beale burps and readjusts his testicles. 'What are you talking about, hair-bear?'

'It will be all over the local media by now, and the talk of the town, especially down by the harbour.'

'What will?'

'That a man found on the beach is alive and in a stable condition in the hospital. Which means Dritan will have more than likely heard the news.'

'Oh, shite,' Beale murmurs. 'They can't afford to leave him alive. They don't know whether he's spoken yet, whether he's identified anyone—but this isn't a gang that leaves loose ends. They finish what they start.'

Zac pulls his phone from his pocket.

'I'll ring Scarborough Police. Tell them to get officers there now. Put a guard on the ward.'

His thumb hovers over the screen.

Every second matters. Dritan could already have someone on the move.

'Wait,' Beale says. 'Think for a moment. Even if they give your call their undivided attention—and that's a gamble—you'd have to explain enough to justify the response. You'd need a senior officer. They may insist on the Armed Response Unit, which means risk assessments and all sorts of shite. And you need to be careful not to expose myself or the wider operation. And all that would take time, sunshine. Fifteen, twenty minutes, at best. An hour or more at worst.'

Zac hesitates 'You're right. Too long.'

He thinks of the nurse.

*What was her name? Tamara? No—Amara. That's it.*

He scrolls through his contacts and dials the hospital.

It rings. And rings.

'Scarborough General Hospital. How can I help?'

'I need to speak to a nurse called Amara. She's on one of the medical wards looking after Ryan Harker.'

A pause. Keys tapping.

'And who's calling?'

'Zac—DS Zac Stoker. She knows me. She'll take the call.'

'She's on her rounds. Is it urgent?'

'Yes. Very.'

Another pause.

'Please hold.'

The line clicks, and he's dumped into music—a murdered, synth-heavy version of Greensleeves, looping without mercy.

Zac is already moving. 'Call me later,' he shouts to Beale.

He hammers down the steps of the boarding house. Through the front doors. Hit by the sudden slap of sunlight and sea air. He jogs across the pavement, fumbling for his keys.

*'Come on. Come on.'*

The car unlocks. He yanks the door open, drops into the seat, slams it shut.

Greensleeves continues like a never-ending migraine.

Engine running. Seatbelt on.

'Hello?'

Amara's voice. Cautious now. Guarded.

'Amara—it's Zac, DS Stoker. We spoke earlier. Outside the ward. Cleavage... I mean Ryan Harker, the man who nearly drowned.'

'Yes.'

'Listen to me very carefully, and don't repeat this to anyone yet. Not security. Not another member of staff.'

'Go on.'

'I'm working on a serious investigation,' he explains. 'Cleav... I mean Ryan Harker was the victim of an attempted murder. The people who did it believe he's dead. If they find out he isn't—'

'You're frightening me.'

'I know. I'm sorry. But I don't have the luxury of easing you into this. A man could be killed in the next few minutes if we don't act.'

Another pause. Longer this time.

'What exactly are you asking me to do?' Her voice is tremulous.

'Move him. Take him from the room he's in now. Somewhere less visible. A side room. Private suite. Observation. Even the fucking basement. Anywhere that isn't where he's expected to be.'

'That isn't a decision I can make on my own.'

Zac is losing patience fast. 'Amara, we don't have time to fuck around. His life could be in imminent danger. I'll call Scarborough Police the second I hang up. Officers will be there within fifteen minutes, but you need to act now.'

Silence again. He can hear movement—footsteps, voices, the hum of the ward.

'I should alert security,' she says.

'*No!* For Christ's sake, don't call security!' Zac snaps. 'Move him somewhere safe first. *Then* call security. Please, I'm begging you, Amara. Just bloody move him somewhere else right now.'

The line goes dead.

'Shite!' Zac screams, slapping his hand repeatedly against the dashboard in anger.

He stabs at his screen and brings up Scarborough Police, already knowing he might be too late.

# 51

## 10:59 am

The lift pings open.

Squeaky boots step out onto disinfected tiles, the sound briefly too loud in the hush of the ward. No one at the desk. A nurse carries a tray table without urgency. An old man in a dressing gown, pyjamas, and slippers shuffles past, clutching a Zimmer frame, breathing hard, eyes fixed on the floor.

The man with the flowers spots a nurse pushing an empty trolley.

'Excuse me,' he says, falling into step beside her. 'I'm looking for Ryan Harker.'

He lifts the flowers slightly, an unconscious gesture.

The nurse doesn't slow.

'Side room five,' she says. 'Down the corridor. On the left.'

'Thank you. And—he is all right—yes?'

'He's fine. Still sedated.'

He nods, relief washing over his face.

'Is anyone with him?'

She shrugs. 'Not at the moment.'

He hesitates, then adds lightly, as if the thought has only just occurred to him.

'Has there been any... police involvement?'

That makes her stop.

She looks at him now. Really looks.

'Police?' she repeats.

'Only because of the accident,' he adds quickly, smiling. 'In my country, the police, they attend everything.'

Her expression flattens.

'There's nothing like that noted,' she says. 'If you'll excuse me.'

She moves off, her mind already elsewhere.

He watches her go until she turns a corner and disappears from view. Scanning the area, he ambles across to the ward desk and deposits the flowers in an empty vase. Feels inside his jacket for reassurance then turns down the corridor towards side room five.

◆

The room is dimmer than the corridor.

Three beds. Two empty. Curtains drawn back.

The occupied bed is by the window.

A figure lies in it. Face turned away from the door. Still.

The man pauses just inside the doorway.

The only sounds are the soft beep... beep... beep of the cardiac monitor and the faint wheeze of laboured breathing.

He steps forward.

Stops at an empty bed. Lifts a pillow. Light. Clean. Fluffy.

He moves closer to the occupied bed.

Hovers over the patient.

With his free hand, he slips the gun from inside his jacket.

Silencer already attached.

The monitor beats out its indifferent rhythm, counting down the seconds.

*Beep*

*Beep*

*Beep*

Leans in, pillow raised.

Finger tightens on the trigger.

The patient shifts.

His head rolls back to the centre. Eyes flutter—then open.

The assassin freezes.

An old man, at least eighty, stares up at him, unfocused but awake. Confused. Breathing rough.

The gunman hisses softly.

Cocks his head.

Faint at first, the sound of sirens filters in through the open window. More than one. Closing fast.

Curses in a foreign tongue.

Slips the gun back into his jacket. Lets the pillow fall. It hits the floor without a sound.

Turns and leaves the room.

Out in the corridor, the sirens rise and fall, nearer now, spilling into the car park.

As he passes a door, slightly ajar, a woman stands frozen inside—watching.

A nurse.

Their eyes meet for a fraction of a second.

Then... he's gone.

# 52

The incident room smells of coffee and marker pens. As usual, it's stuffy, airless.

Frank takes it in from the doorway—Prisha perched on the edge of a desk, Dinkel already worrying the cap off a pen.

Zac stands at the whiteboard, jacket still on, his usual smart demeanour somewhat bedraggled. He looks wrung out. Wired. The look of a man who's been carrying something heavy all day and is finally allowed to put it down.

Frank nods at him.

'Hell of a day, Zac. Take us through it.'

Zac doesn't waste a word. He turns to the board and writes four headings, stacked, block capitals.

**WEST BEACH**

**BEALE – TRIP ONE**

**BEALE – TRIP TWO**

**HOSPITAL**

He steps back, breathes once, then points to the first line.

'Early this morning I'm down by the bandstand having a quiet coffee. Five minutes' peace before the day really begins, when an ambulance turns up.'

He glances around the room.

'A body's washed up on West Beach. I lend the paramedics a hand, and it turns out the bloke is Cleavage.'

A faint ripple of reaction, but Zac keeps going.

'Now, Cleavage is a keen swimmer. Loves the sea. Always has. My first assumption is simple—day off, early-morning dip, gets into trouble. Unfortunate, possibly tragic, but nothing sinister.'

He shrugs, almost apologetic.

'I follow the ambulance to the hospital. To be honest, I don't think he's going to make it. He's in a bad way. But after an hour—tests, tubes, oxygen, the lot—I'm told he's going to be fine. They've got him sedated, so I don't get a chance to speak to him. At that point, as far as I'm concerned, it's an unlucky accident. As I get back to the car, my phone pings. It's a text from Beale asking me to meet him at his digs urgently.'

Taps at the board.

'So, this is what Beale told me. He goes out on The Whitby Rose, Tuesday evening. First trip. They head for Dogger Bank, drop the nets, bring up a decent haul—haddock, cod. Proper fishing.

'At that point, Beale thinks he's wasted his time. Everything looks kosher. These lads can fish. Most of the crew turn out to be Albanians—four of them. Dritan's running it. His brother Stefan. Two others—Mika and Arben. One important point to note—Stefan has a scar running down his left cheek.

'They start heading back to shore, and Beale and Cleavage turn-in to get a few hours kip. Middle of the night he wakes up, fancies a smoke. Feels the engines drop to idle. He can't find his boots, so he slips on Cleavage's wellies. Cleavage is out cold. Beale goes up on deck. There's another vessel sitting off the starboard side. They do a mid-sea transfer. A wooden box comes across. Inside—handguns. Semi-automatics. Proper kit. Then a man's brought aboard. Small. Asian—Chinese or Vietnamese, possibly. The guy looks terrified. They take him straight into the skipper's cabin behind the wheelhouse. Beale never sees him again.'

'Trafficking?' Prisha asks.

Zac raises an eyebrow. 'Possibly, but not in the traditional sense. I'll come back to that. Now to add to the drama, jump a few hours ahead, early Wednesday morning, and The Whitby Rose is nearing the harbour. The coastguard show up and board them, routine safety inspection. They search the container holding the weapons.'

'And find?' Frank asks.

'Winch parts. Nothing illegal.'

Dinkel lets out a low whistle. 'They'd hidden them?'

'It appears so,' Zac says.

He points at **BEALE – TRIP TWO**.

'Second trip. Hastily arranged. Thursday morning. Beale's below doing odd jobs. He comes on deck just as three of the Albanians are about to throw Cleavage over the side. Beale tries to stop it. Pleads with them, but they point a gun at him. Dritan tells him Cleavage knows too much.

'At this point, Beale is unaware that Cleavage is a police informant. My informant. Next thing, Cleavage is gone. Concrete block tied to his feet. As far as everyone onboard is concerned, that's the end of him.'

'Ruthless bastards,' Prisha says. 'They thought he'd tipped off the coastguard after the first trip?'

'Yes. What other reason could there be?'

'Paranoid bastards,' she mutters.

'That night there's another mid-sea rendezvous. Beale manages to get the name and ID of the transfer ship.'

Zac jots the details down carefully on the board.

**ZEEWOLF – ENI 07741066**

'Two oil drums come across. A hundred gallons each. Marked as diesel. One makes it onboard. As the second one is winched across, a strap snaps. It ends up in the drink. Storm conditions,' Zac says. 'Which matters.'

'Because nobody risks a manoeuvre like that in a storm unless it's for real,' Frank adds. 'This is definitely not a decoy mission.'

'Precisely. At that point, Beale's got what he needs—the name of the transfer vessel—so he decides it's time to return to his cabin. He rounds a corner and runs headlong into the skipper, Francois. Beale thinks he's finished. He's about to go the same way as Cleavage. He feeds Francois some bullshit about feeling seasick. Francois clearly doesn't buy it. Orders Beale to get below—quickly. Beale spends the rest of the night expecting a knock on the door from the Albanians.'

'What happened?' Dinkel asks, mouth agape as if he's listening to a Boy's Own adventure on the radio.

'Nothing,' Zac says.

'Nothing?' Frank repeats.

'Zilch, zip, zero—*nothing*. Returning to Whitby, they put out a Mayday—man overboard. They tell the coastguard one of their men was last seen an hour ago. Suspect a freak wave has taken him. Of course, a full air-and-sea rescue kicks off, but with that missing hour you're talking about a search area the size of a small county. Practically impossible to cover in those conditions.'

Frank nods slowly. 'So when they came into harbour—'

'The MCA—the Maritime and Coastguard Agency—went through the vessel with a fine-toothed comb,' Zac continues. 'Every life ring present, no cut lines, rails secure, logbook consistent, fuel genuinely low. They checked their safety procedures, walked the timeline, and every single crewman was singing from the same hymnbook.'

'Even Beale?' Frank asks.

'Especially Beale—though it near killed him. If he'd deviated from his undercover story, he could've blown the whole operation.'

Frank exhales. 'So... a sad, tragic accident, but ultimately nothing to see here.'

Zac nods in agreement. 'An hour or so passes and things die down. The oil drum is quickly winched onto the quayside. At that point, Dritan gives Beale some clean-up jobs to do below deck. By the time he finishes, and is about to set off back to his digs, the drum had gone. As he's leaving, Dritan pays him very handsomely, and says they won't be setting sail again for at least another week due to the weather conditions. Oh, and one last thing before I move on. Beale and Dritan shared a couple of heart-to-hearts over the two trips.' He hesitates, as if still reconciling himself with the facts. 'It appears, and God only knows how or why, that Dritan has a soft spot for Beale.'

'Beale—*our* Danny Beale?' Frank exclaims, eyes agog, as if there could be a Beale impersonator at large in the community.

'Aye. My sentiments entirely.'

Without looking, Zac points at the last heading—**HOSPITAL.**

'Which brings me to the last revelation of my whirlwind day. Beale has a tendency to witter on, and as I was taking notes, something kept nagging away at me. I'll admit, I was shocked when Beale revealed how Cleavage had nearly died. But I knew he was safe and well—until I realised he wasn't. A man overboard, a body on the beach, the public, the ambulance—how long before it got around town and into the local media and shared on socials?'

Prisha nods. 'And you realised that when Dritan heard the news, he'd put two and two together.'

'Correct.'

'And if you attempt murder, and fail, then the survivor lives to point the finger.'

'Yes. I knew time was against me, so I rang the hospital and asked the nurse I'd spoken to earlier to move Cleavage to a private room, or anywhere away from where he was officially registered to be. Luckily, she did as I asked. I owe her a drink.'

Frank harrumphs. 'And did Dritan send a man over to kill him?'

Zac shrugs. 'No explicit evidence. But a man did turn up claiming to be his stepbrother. Carrying a bunch of flowers. Went to the ward. Found Cleavage wasn't there, then left.'

'CCTV?'

'Yes. But he kept his head down and was wearing a cap. Receptionist said he had a Mediterranean accent. And most tellingly, a scar on his left cheek.'

'Stefan,' Prisha mutters, already deep in thought. 'So what about this Asian guy?'

Zac looks at Frank. 'Remember Silas telling us about how fentanyl precursor is usually sourced from China?'

'Aye.'

'Maybe they also sourced a chemist. Someone to cook it.'

Frank nods. 'Hmm... it's all falling into place. Oil drum, possibly full of powder. A cook. The weapons, and four ruthless bastards. I think we've found our foreign cartel.'

'We need to act, Frank,' Prisha says. 'Operation Blackout needs this—now.'

He rises wearily and gazes out of the window. 'The problem is, after my meeting with Silas the other day, I'm still unsure about him. The man's an enigma. Is he deliberately tight-lipped because he has to be, or is he hiding something? He certainly didn't flinch when I told him about Typhoon's death. It was almost like...' he pauses, searching for the words.

'Like what?'

'Like—he already knew.' He glances at Zac. 'What did Beale say? After all, he's their undercover man with the intel. It's his job to relay the information back to the chain of command.'

Zac cringes. 'Ah, well, here's the rub, Frank. You know Beale. He's usually unequivocal. Calls a spade a spade.'

'I sense a—but—coming.'

'But—he'll wait for your guidance on this one.'

'Bloody wonderful.'

# 53

There's an unusual tension in the incident room. Normally when the pieces of a puzzle begin to slip into place, there's a crackle of excitement. The scent of blood. The hunt.

But not today.

If there is a leak in Operation Blackout, then feeding the intel they've gathered to the Op could be disastrous.

And yet, if they don't relay the information, not only is it a dereliction of duty, but it could have untold consequences.

They can't sit on it indefinitely.

Everyone is aware of the consequences, especially Frank. His gut instinct, right at the start, when he was introduced to Silas Carmody and the NCA operation, was correct—teaming up with other agencies always ends in a shit show.

Zac looks at Dinkel. 'Did you do those calculations I asked you for earlier?'

'Yes.' He walks to the board, pops the cap off a pen, and sketches a neat outline of an oil drum. Numbers follow alongside in a tidy column.

'A standard drum holds two hundred litres.' He taps the next figure. 'If the drum was filled with fentanyl precursor as a loose powder, you'd barely manage fifty kilos because of all the air gaps. But if it was vacuum-sealed and compressed, that changes everything. You get a bulk density much closer to liquid—call it one kilo per litre, give or take.' He finishes the calculation with a quick stroke. 'So a two-hundred-litre drum of precursor, fully compressed, lands at around two hundred kilos of product.'

Frank grunts. 'And that would produce how many fentanyl tablets if cut with filler?'

'Two hundred kilos of precursor, even allowing for lousy yields, gets you roughly a hundred kilos of actual fentanyl,' Dinkel explains. 'Dose that at about a milligram a tablet and you're looking at something in the region of a hundred million street pills. Halve the dose and you double the count.'

Prisha shakes her head, incredulous. 'Even if they flog it dirt cheap—two or three quid a hit—that's two, three hundred million pounds.'

Zac nods. 'And if they hadn't lost the second barrel, double it.'

'This isn't some mid-level outfit dreaming of a villa in Tenerife,' Prisha mutters. 'This is organised crime at the highest level.'

Frank shifts uncomfortably in his chair. 'With numbers like that, you're not just buying fast cars. You're buying power and influence.'

Zac taps the board with the end of the marker. 'And we know the script. Flood the market. Hook the punters. Then crank the price. They can choke the supply whenever they like to inflate the cost. Basic economics.'

'And let's not forget the human cost,' Frank says. 'I'm sure we've all seen the online videos of cities in America, such as Portland, Denver, San Francisco. Upwards of two hundred people dying daily from fentanyl overdoses across the country. It's a scourge.'

Prisha, impatient as ever, presses again. 'You need to make a decision, Frank. At the moment, we're in limbo. We can't let this slide.'

It's times like this he wishes he'd never quit smoking. He pops a mint into his mouth and checks his watch.

'It's been a long day. And as we'll *all* be working tomorrow, I suggest we go home, relax and get a good night's sleep. Act in haste. Repent at leisure. I'll make my decision tomorrow.'

## Saturday Morning – 2:45 am

Prisha tosses and turns. Plumps up her pillow and tries to drift off again. That's half the problem—you should never *try* to sleep. It should arrive unannounced, like a cold-caller selling double glazing.

No use.

Flicks the side light on. Flops from the bed. Heads to the window and lifts the sash fully up. The sea air rushes in, sharp and clean. She leans forward and breathes deeply, head pushed into the night. Streetlamps glow below, orange and soft-edged. The town lies silent. Waiting for a new day.

She knows this feeling.

Something's not right.

If she'd been in at the start, it would have helped. That's the trouble with joining an investigation late. It's similar to arriving at a party late. You feel disconnected, like an intruder. You're handed conclusions without having lived the questions. You see the moves, not the thinking behind them.

'That bloody cold case,' she mutters.

She leaves the window open and pads downstairs to the kitchen. Pours milk into a saucepan and sets it on a low heat. While she waits for it to warm, she flicks through the Whitby Gazette, killing time.

A yawn.

Page after page passes without registering.

Near the back of the paper, her eyes snag on a nondescript item. No photo. A small headline that simply reads: *Council Meeting—Sunday Night*. It's tucked away, almost hiding. Easy to miss.

'Hmm...'

The roil of the milk has her discarding the paper. She makes a mug of hot chocolate, takes it back upstairs, and sits on the edge of the bed, pyjamas creasing at the knees, hands wrapped around the mug.

Sips. Thinks.

'What—what is it?' she murmurs. 'Something—but what?'

Five minutes later, feeling the wave of tiredness landing on her shore, she closes the window, pulls the blinds, clicks off the light and snuggles down.

Better now. Relaxed. A good night's sleep and it will sort itself out. Anyway, Frank is running this one. She trusts his instinct.

Sleep wraps its arms around her.

———◇———

Bounces up in bed.

'Fuck!'

Looks at the clock—3:14 am.

Too late and too early to ring Frank.

Paces back and forth around the tiny bedroom, replaying everything in her head. Prodding and poking at the disparate parts.

Five minutes.

Ten minutes.

*Got it!*

It's not much, but it's something. And maybe there is a plausible explanation. A slip of the tongue would explain it.

But Frank and Zac are too wily for that. They wouldn't make a rookie error.

Is she grasping at straws?

Comes at the oddity from different angles.

Picks it apart.

But always arrives at the same conclusion.

She jots the word down onto a notepad just in case she dies in her sleep. A clue for Frank and Zac. They'll figure it out. Not that she plans on dying in her sleep—but who does?

Sits on the side of the bed feeling relaxed. Sleep will arrive soon enough now.

Leans over to turn off the lamp. Takes one last look at the word.

**COASTGUARD**

Picks the pen up and writes underneath:

**MONEY**

Now she can rest.

# 55

## 6:24 am

Frank is in fine spirits as he climbs the stairs and enters the incident room. He's a little surprised to see Dinkel sitting at his desk, beavering away at his laptop.

'Eh up, lad. What's wrong with thee—did you shit the bed?'

Dinkel lifts his head, face creased in confusion. 'I most certainly did *not* shit the bed, sir.'

'No, what I meant was, how come you're in so early?'

'Oh, I received a call from Prisha at 5:30. She asked me to come in.'

'I see,' Frank replies, slipping from his jacket as Prisha enters from the kitchenette, carrying two steaming mugs.

'Morning, Frank,' she exclaims, also rather chipper. She places a cup down on Dinkel's desk. 'Here you go, Dinks. It's not often you get an inspector making a constable a cuppa. Coffee. Nice and strong. Will help you focus.'

He eyeballs the offering with apprehension. 'Actually, I find that caffeine can make me jittery. I prefer herbal tea. Chamomile in particular.'

'Get it down you, and shut up. You have a lot of work to do.'

He relents. 'Ma'am.'

She turns to Frank. 'So—come to a decision about the intel?'

Frank chuckles. 'Indeed, I have, Prisha. And do you know what? The answer was staring me in the face all the time. I was tossing and turning all night when it popped into my head.'

'It usually does,' she says, reflecting on her own early-morning revelation. 'And what was the answer?'

'Hedley Keegan. He's the reason we got involved at all. He's the intelligence supervisor on Operation Blackout, so I'll pass all our intel onto him. Now, although he didn't say as much, I got the impression that Silas Carmody was on his radar as a possible leak. Simple. Hedley will know what to do. He's an old hand. Then it's up to him who he shares our information with. No doubt he'll keep it from those he doesn't trust—even if it's the head of the Op.'

Prisha grins. 'Nice handball, Frank.'

He laughs. 'Here, catch—hot potato,' he says, miming throwing her something.

'Why didn't you think of that yesterday?'

A shrug. 'That's what happens when you're tired and overloaded. Now, what brings you in so early, and what have you got Dinkel working on?'

'Two things, Frank.' She places her cup down and scribbles on the whiteboard.

Frank stares at the single word—**COASTGUARD**.

'What about the bloody coastguard?' he asks, frowning. He knows that Prisha's leaps of intuition can sometimes solve a case in one fell swoop. And other times, they can cause him an almighty headache.

Before she can explain, the door swings open as Zac ambles in, looking decidedly jaded after the previous day's trials.

'What's all this?' he asks, sipping coffee from a cardboard cup.

'Just in time,' Prisha replies. 'Take a seat. I have an issue.'

'We noticed but didn't like to mention it,' Zac says as he and Frank flop into chairs.

'Ha-ha. Amusing—not. Now pay attention. Zac, according to Danny Beale, why was Cleavage thrown overboard?'

'Because Dritan thought Cleavage had seen the weapons come aboard, and informed the coastguard.'

'Exactly—and it doesn't make sense.'

'Why else would they ditch him over the side? They obviously suspected him of something. They may be ruthless psychopaths, but they don't kill innocent people on a whim.'

'I'll explain. Let's pretend we're Dritan for a moment, and we suspect Cleavage has witnessed the arms drop, and the Asian guy being transferred to the boat on their first trip.'

'Okay.'

'Why didn't they kill Cleavage then?'

Zac and Frank share a look but merely shrug.

Prisha continues. 'Now let's jump into the skin of Cleavage.'

'Do we have to?' Zac groans.

'Be serious. Let's now pretend that Cleavage *did* witness the transfers.'

'But he didn't.'

'Yes. I know he didn't. That's why I said pretend.'

'Sorry.'

'Who would Cleavage have called? Certainly not the coastguard. He knows they're not armed. He'd have called you, and you'd have passed the information on to—'

He cuts her off. 'Border Force. With firearms onboard, they're the only ones equipped to deal with it.'

'Exactly. Now, we don't know much about Dritan, but we can assume he's no fool. And according to Beale, he definitely has seafaring experience.'

'Your point being?'

'He'd be aware that if Cleavage had witnessed the transfer, there's no way he'd have informed the coastguard, knowing they're unarmed.'

'Makes sense,' Frank says. 'So why did they throw him overboard?'

Prisha taps the top of the pen against her palm, her face a puzzle of confusion.

'Yes... that's what's bugging me. All I can suspect is they found out he was a police informant and didn't want to take any chances.'

Zac sighs. 'Well, that was a great big cup of fuck all.'

Frank frowns at him. 'You said you had two things to discuss, Prisha.'

'Ah, yes. Dinkel?'

'Ma'am?'

'How far off are you?'

'Just collating the information now. Another couple of minutes and I'll print it out.'

'Excellent.'

She walks over to her desk with a spring in her step and collects a clutch of papers.

'Did you drop something in her coffee?' Zac whispers to Frank.

'No. But whatever she's on, I want some.'

She returns, brandishing the sheets. 'I've uploaded this information onto the board. But before we get onto that...'

She picks up the pen and writes on the whiteboard the word—**MONEY**.

'What about money?' Frank enquires.

'We've estimated how much money this fentanyl operation could generate if it goes into full swing.'

'Yes. Millions.'

'Possibly hundreds of millions, Frank. And what do you do with that sort of cash? You can't deposit it in a bank—it would set alarm bells ringing. You can't stick it under the mattress.'

'You launder it through legitimate businesses,' Zac says, struggling to keep up.

'Correct. Which brings me to this,' she says, waggling the papers at him. 'Now, Zac, what I'm about to divulge isn't a reflection on you.'

He grimaces. 'When a sentence starts like that, you know you're in for a flogging.'

'Earlier in the week, you did a background check on The Whitby Rose.'

'Aye. All tickety-boo.'

Prisha taps the whiteboard and a screenshot of paperwork appears.

'On the surface, the trawler is exactly what you said it was. French-owned. Properly licensed. Clean paperwork. Nothing to see here. But when you stop looking at the boat and start looking at the company behind it—that's when it gets interesting.

'The French fishing firm isn't really a business. It's a shell company. Minimal turnover. No meaningful assets beyond the vessel. Directors rotate. Funding comes in from accounts that have nothing to do with fishing.'

She pauses.

'When we follow the money trail back far enough, it doesn't lead to France.'

'Then where does it lead?' Frank asks.

'To none other than George Sykes.'

Frank's jaw drops. 'George Sykes—King George of Whitby?'

'Yes. The local businessman. And why would George Sykes go to such an effort to hide his name behind a supposedly legitimate fishing vessel?'

Frank rubs at his chin, pondering. 'Before you go off on any more tangents, Prisha, I'll tell you this—I don't much care for George Sykes. We have history. But he has no police record, and he's the registered owner of three boats locally. One lobster and crabber in Scarborough. A whitefish boat in Hartlepool. Another lobster boat up in Seahouses. He also runs the biggest seafood processing plant in the North of England. And a distribution arm. Makes sense he'd own a few boats.'

'And did you know he also owns amusement arcades?'

Frank frowns. 'Aye. He has one here in Whitby and another in Scarborough. But if you're suggesting George plans to launder millions of quid through a couple of crumby little amusement arcades, then you've taken leave of your senses.'

The rattle of the printer distracts them as Dinkel collects the sheets and hands them to Prisha.

'Not quite,' she says, scanning the paperwork. 'He owns more than two arcades.'

'How many?'

'Thirty-two. Looks like he's been quietly buying them up over the last few years. From as far south as Skegness, right up to the Scottish border. And he's planning to build a casino right here in Whitby. I read about it in the *Gazette* last night... this morning. All it needs is the final council sign-off tomorrow night. A casino and a string of arcades are perfect for laundering large volumes of small, untraceable transactions. No receipts. No oversight. Just cash in, cash out.'

Prisha is feeling just a little bit pleased with herself. 'And that's the final piece slotted into place. He has the men who import, cook, and distribute, plus the muscle. And the businesses to wash the money. And here's another tangent, Frank—what better place to cook drugs than a seafood processing plant. It would mask the smell. It's a beautiful plan. It's perfect... almost.'

As excited chatter breaks out amongst his three officers, Frank deliberates, his mind playing with one unexplained event—why *was* Cleavage thrown overboard?

Frank sticks his hands deep into his overcoat and strolls along the path, the Abbey receding behind him. It's one of those mild autumn mornings where the world feels briefly balanced. A soft breeze lifts off the sea and brushes his face. The sun is out but half-hearted about it, offering warmth only if you stand still long enough. The air smells of grass and salt and damp earth. The sort of morning that invites you to slow down—whether you mean to or not.

He spots Hedley Keegan seated on a bench on the Cleveland Way, gazing out over the cliffs.

Keegan rises and the men shake hands, Frank offering him a jaded smile.

'Sorry for dragging you out so early on a Sunday morning, Hedley.'

Keegan grins. 'Don't apologise. I've been sitting here twenty minutes enjoying the peace and serenity. It's funny how you forget about the simple pleasures in life.' He extends an arm out. 'Shall we walk?'

'Grand idea. I've been cooped up in the office all bloody week.'

They set off together, boots crunching on the gravel, easy in each other's company. For a minute or two, neither feels the need to speak.

Frank finally breaks the silence. 'I think it's my time, Hedley.'

'Retirement?' he replies, half-turning to look at his old friend.

'Aye. I think I'm past my sell-by date.'

Keegan slows slightly, studying him. 'That's a big decision. You've more than earned it, mind. Meera will be over the moon. What will you do with yourself?'

Frank looks out at the sea—flat, grey, deceptively calm. 'Potter about, I suppose. Fix things that don't really need fixing. Meera wants to travel once she finally pulls the pin.'

'You don't sound thrilled.'

'I'm not cut out for travelling. Airports, hotels, stinking hot weather, foreign food and—even worse—foreign beer. No one outside Britain seems to know how to brew a decent pint of bitter, or pour one.'

Keegan laughs. 'I'm inclined to agree with you there.' Then, more gently, 'Has this been coming for a while—or has something tipped you over?'

Frank puffs out his cheeks and exhales. 'Bit of both, if I'm honest.' He hesitates. 'You'll be up to speed on what happened to Typhoon and his three lieutenants?'

Keegan's expression tightens. 'Yes. Nasty business. Any idea who was behind it?'

'Not really. Looks like a rival gang. It happens in that line of work.' Frank shrugs. 'We've got a few lines of enquiry. One key witness.'

Keegan turns his head. 'Who?'

Frank stops walking and turns to face him. 'Where it all began, Hedley. Young Smiler.'

Keegan blinks. 'He's alive?'

'Yes.'

'Thank God for that.'

'We've got him holed up in one of those new apartments down by the river near the road bridge.'

'Whitehall Court?'

'Aye.' Frank nods. 'Seeing what nearly happened to him made me stop and think. I should never have put him in the firing line.'

Keegan winces. 'That one's on me, Frank. Using him to draw you into the operation—'

Frank shakes his head. 'No. That part was sound. Letting him plant the bug was my call. And then there's Cleavage.'

Keegan slows. 'Cleavage—the informant?'

'Do you know another bloke round here who goes by that name?'

'No, but I don't—'

'He's a trawler man. Fifteen years at sea.' Frank keeps walking. 'Picked up work on The Whitby Rose because he knew the coast. They dumped him overboard. Must've suspected him of something. It's a miracle he survived.'

Keegan stops altogether now, brow furrowing. 'You're saying he wasn't feeding you information about the boat?'

'No. He didn't even know we were interested in it.' Frank glances back at him. 'He's in the police safe house near Pickering.'

'Hmm... wise move.'

They walk on in silence for a few steps.

'And lastly,' Frank says, almost as an afterthought, 'Danny Beale.'

Keegan's jaw drops a fraction. 'Beale? Police Scotland?'

'Yes. He was our undercover man on The Whitby Rose.'

Keegan shakes his head slowly as they walk. 'Well, I'll be.'

'So, you see, Hedley—three lives put at risk. I can't pretend that some of those cock-ups weren't my fault.'

Keegan frowns. 'That's not fair on yourself, Frank. Beale's seasoned—he knew exactly what he was walking into. Cleavage was an unfortunate coincidence. And Smiler—well, if memory serves, that was Silas Carmody's idea.'

Frank chuckles softly and pats Keegan's shoulder. 'I know what you're doing. And I appreciate it. But we both know how these things really work.'

Keegan watches him for a moment. 'So that's it then? Your mind's made up?'

'About retirement? Aye, it is.' Frank nods. 'I met Carmody yesterday. Passed on some of what we've learned—what he needs to know. Turns out The Whitby

Rose is a decoy. A bloody good one, mind. But not the real operation. That wraps tonight. But I suppose you're aware of that.'

'Yes. We had a debrief yesterday. Tonight in Hull, a specialist team will take out all the major players.'

'So maybe there wasn't a leak after all.'

Keegan pauses. 'Perhaps. Though in matters like this, you can never be too careful.' He rests a hand briefly on Frank's arm. 'I'm truly sorry, Frank. It was me who dragged you into this mess, and it turns out I was wrong.'

Frank studies him. 'You never did say who you suspected of being the mole. Just someone at the top.'

Keegan looks away, uncomfortable. 'Silas.'

'Thought as much.'

'And what about Dritan and his gang?'

'They've gone to ground. No idea where they are or even if they're still in the country. We'll seize The Whitby Rose tomorrow.'

Hedley raises one eyebrow. 'Tomorrow?'

Frank snorts softly. 'Aye. Border Force has to detain her, harbourmaster has to sign it off, magistrate for a warrant, then forensics. And it's bloody Sunday—half the country's still in bed and the other half's not answering their phones. Have you forgotten the hoops we have to jump through?'

Hedley chuckles. 'Ah yes. The machinations of law—slow, complicated, and impossible to rush.'

Frank watches a large gull glide over the clifftops. 'Shall we head back? I'm feeling peckish. We can grab breakfast in the old town.'

Keegan smiles warmly. 'Another day, Frank. I've a lot on, I'm afraid. I need to be in Leeds before noon.'

'Not to worry.'

'By the way, I'd like to catch up with Danny Beale before I leave town. Have a quick chat about old times and thank him for his work. Can you give me the address where he's staying?'

'Aye. No problem.' Frank pauses and glances at the Abbey bathed in golden light.

'I tell you what, Hedley—it's turning into a smashing day.'

## Sunday Evening - 7:45 pm

Dritan fills the shot glasses with vodka as his men grin, buoyed by the moment.

The liquid catches the bare bulb above the table, clear and hard.

They lift their glasses and clink them together.

'Gëzuar,' Dritan says.

'Gëzuar.'

'Or as they say over here—cheers.'

'Cheers.'

The vodka goes down in one hit, sharp and burning.

Dritan bends, lifts the holdall from the floor, and drops it onto the table. The thud is solid, satisfying. He unzips it.

Cash spills into view—bundles thick with elastic bands. He takes no pleasure in it, but he understands its language. One by one, he tosses a wad to each of them.

'This is the end of phase one,' he says. 'And I am proud of each of you.'

Arben and Mika lift the notes to their faces, inhaling theatrically.

'Ah—the taste of success,' Mika says, grinning.

Stefan simply slips the wad inside his bomber jacket without comment.

Dritan checks his watch, then closes the bag and stands.

'You all know what you must do?'

They nod. No hesitation.

'Good.' His eyes drift to Arben—the cook and killer. 'Remember, I want his heart. Take a plastic bag with you and put it in the freezer.'

Arben grins and nods.

Dritan turns to his brother. For a moment—a solitary second—a crease of sadness crosses his face.

Stefan rises and they embrace.

'I'll miss you, Dritan.'

'And I you, little brother.' Dritan pats his back once. Firm. Final. 'I will be back in three weeks. Until then, you are in charge. You run the operation.'

'Yes. You can rely on me.'

Dritan cups Stefan's cheek briefly with his palm. 'I know I can. Remember—production and supply lines are everything. When I return, I will bring a fresh crew. All Albanian.'

Stefan nods. 'The pill press is already running.'

Dritan zips his jacket and lifts the holdall.

'And Mika, Arben.' He eyeballs them with intensity. 'No mistakes tonight. Clean. Quiet. Efficient.'

They nod again.

'You can trust us,' Mika says. 'But one question.'

'Yes?'

'What if the wife and child are there?'

Dritan purses his lips, considering it with the same casual air he might give to a menu choice.

'Kill the woman,' he says. 'Leave the child.'

'Very well.'

Dritan checks his watch one last time.

'What time do you sail?' Stefan asks.

'Ten o'clock. High tide.' He smiles faintly. 'The smuggler's tide—no? Take care, my friends. Francois and The Whitby Rose are waiting.'

# 58

## 9:32 pm

The moon hangs over the moors, creating shadows and ghosts. A cool breeze stirs the heather, carrying a damp, earthy scent downhill. In the distance, the lights of Pickering glimmer like a scatter of silver coins.

It's quiet.

Very quiet.

Mika lowers the binoculars and rubs grit from his eyes.

The worker's cottage sits at the base of the hill, isolated and squat. An outside security light burns steadily. Inside, a single downstairs lamp throws a yellow square onto the curtains. Now and then, a shadow crosses it—broad-shouldered. The same shape every time.

He scans the verge, the lane, the hedgerows. No parked car. No movement. No sign of police.

He was expecting at least one guard. A car tucked in somewhere. Maybe someone inside. But the figure behind the curtain never changes. Big. Alone.

Maybe the place is too remote.

Maybe they think he's not in imminent danger.

Maybe they've run out of men.

Either way, it makes life simpler.

Mika settles back into the seat and chews a protein bar, jaw working slowly. He washes it down with water and lifts the binoculars again.

The downstairs light fades to black.

A moment later, an upstairs window glows.

Mika watches, breathing steady, until that light goes out too.

He smiles.

*Too easy.*

He waits ten minutes. Long enough for routine to take over. Long enough for Cleavage to settle in and become sleepy.

Out of the car. Collar up. Ski mask down. The pistol sits cold and familiar at the small of his back.

The silence is oppressive.

No dogs. No traffic. Not even the hoot of an owl.

He could kick the door in and be done with it—but Dritan had been clear—quiet, efficient.

He slips over the low stone wall at the rear of the property and pads across damp grass. The back door comes into view.

Another Yale lock.

'Idiots,' he mutters.

He wedges the micro torch between his teeth, the beam bobbing as he works. The pick slides in, metal scratching against metal.

*Click.*

The lock gives without resistance.
The door eases inward.
Mika smiles—and steps inside.

# 59

## 9:35 pm

The small moped rolls into Whitehall Court and stops outside one of the new apartment blocks. The engine cuts. Silence rushes in behind it.

The rider swings off, flips open the delivery box, and takes out the warm pizza. Steam ghosts from the vents, the air briefly rich with yeasty dough and Mediterranean herbs. He crosses to the entrance, raises the visor on his helmet, and presses the buzzer.

A pause is followed by a tentative male voice—Smiler's voice.

'Yes?'

'Pizza delivery, my friend.'

'Pizza?'

'Yes. Pepperoni with olives and fresh basil and oregano.'

'I didn't order a pizza.'

'This is the address I was given.' Stefan rustles the delivery docket. 'Let me check the order.'

Seconds tick by. 'Yes. Definitely the correct address. You are Mr Finnegan—no?'

A laugh crackles through the intercom. 'No, I'm not.'

'Ah.' Another pause, apologetic now. 'Well, the pizza was paid for by a Mr Finnegan and sent to this address.'

Silence.

'Oh. Right. I get it.' A faint smile in the voice. 'Okay. I'll buzz you up. Fourth floor. Turn left out of the lift. Far end of the corridor.'

'Very good, my friend.'

The lock buzzes and the door clicks open.

Stefan pushes through and steps into the lift. Presses four.

As it rises, the cable whining softly, he slips his hand inside his jacket. His fingers settle on the grip of the pistol.

The lift doors part.

Steps out. Turns left.

The corridor smells faintly of paint and cheap carpet cleaner.

Slips the visor down with a soft snap.

Stops at the last door.

Draws a slow breath.

Raps sharply—rat-a-tat-tat.

'Pizza, my friend.'

'All right. Coming.'

## 60

Arben waits opposite the boarding house, traffic sliding past in lazy pulses, headlights occasionally flaring white and forcing him to blink. He smokes patiently, shoulders loose, breath steady.

Across the road, a youngish man staggers along the pavement, cheerfully off-balance, a cardboard tray of chips clutched in one hand. Vinegar rides the air. The man stops at the gate, fumbles in his pockets.

Arben drops his cigarette and steps off the kerb. Hood up. Eyes down.

The man finds his keys, pushes through the gate, and climbs the six steps to the front door. Arben slips in behind him, silent as a shadow.

Key in the lock. The door opens.

The man turns. 'Oi—do you live here?'

'Of course,' Arben says mildly. 'I take flat on third floor yesterday. Not bad place—no?'

The man sways, squints at him, shrugs. 'Oh. Fair enough, then.'

Arben is already past him, climbing the stairs.

First floor.

Second.

Third.

The air thickens with stale smoke and damp carpet. Old cooking fat. Cheap aftershave.

He sidles along the hallway until he reaches number thirteen.

Knocks hard.

Waits.

Knocks again.

'Alright, alright—keep yer fucking wig on.'

A gruff Glaswegian voice.

Coughing. Shuffling.

'Who is it?'

'Maintenance,' Arben calls. 'Sorry to bother you, my friend. Electrical issue. Need to check fuse board.'

'There's nowt wrong with my fucking fuse board. Now piss off.'

'My apologies, sir. Landlord's orders. Checking all flats. Fire risk. It is urgent.'

A pause.

'For fuck's sake. And on a Sunday night. I was just about to watch a re-run of Songs of fucking Praise.' More coughing. 'Give me a moment. I need to put some keks on.'

Arben draws the pistol, the suppressor already fitted. Two-handed grip. He aims at the centre of the door, chest height.

Footsteps approach. Close now.

The handle shifts.

Arben squeezes the trigger.

The bullets punch through the wood, muffled. Six rounds in quick succession, still enough left in the magazine to put a few more through his head. The smell of burnt propellant fills the narrow hall.

Silence.

Then a heavy thump.

Satisfied, Arben steps back, lifts his heel, and drives it hard beneath the handle. The frame splinters. The door creaks open.

He moves inside, pistol raised, the other hand already sliding the filleting knife from its sheath.

*Bring me his heart.*

The carpet is grimy. Floral. Empty.

No body.

A blink of confusion.

'Armed police! Drop the weapons now!'

The shout slams into him from all sides.

Arben twitches.

The world explodes.

Four sharp impacts hammer into his chest. He's airborne for a moment, then the floor rushes up. Blood floods his mouth.

Danny Beale steps out of the bathroom, cigarette hanging from the corner of his mouth.

Saunters over and looks down at the lifeless body.

'Fucking amateur,' he sneers.

He glances at the four armed officers in the room.

'Right, lads, I'll let you clean this mess up. I've got a boat to catch. You know what they say—time and tide wait for no man.'

# 61

## 9:43 pm

Frank taps a finger constantly against the edge of his desk.

The office is dim, the lights low, the rest of the station long gone quiet.

Prisha sits forward in her chair, hands clasped, eyes fixed on nothing in particular.

Zac leans back, arms folded, watching Frank more than the room.

They exchange a glance.

No one speaks.

Frank's phone vibrates on the desk.

He reaches for it, hesitates, then slips on his spectacles and reads the message. A long breath leaves him. A dispirited shake of the head and a resigned sigh.

Zac breaks first. 'What?'

Frank lowers the phone. 'That was the last one.'

'And?'

'Same as the other two—dead.'

A moment of reflection before Prisha jumps to her feet.

Purpose snaps back into her voice. 'Okay. Then let's move.'

Frank pushes himself up from the desk, the effort visible, the night not done with him yet.

'Aye. Let's wrap this up tonight.'

# 62

## 9:53 pm

The council chamber smells faintly of polish and stale air, the kind of room that doesn't often see night meetings. Heavy curtains are drawn tight across the tall windows. The lighting is low—functional rather than welcoming.

George Sykes stands at the head of the table, jacket off, sleeves rolled, palms resting on the polished wood like he owns it.

Around the table sit twelve councillors. Some weary. Some alert. A few are already convinced. Others, wavering.

'Let me be absolutely clear,' Sykes says, his voice smooth, confident. 'This project is ready to go. Contractors are lined up. Local firms. Local labour. But they won't wait indefinitely.'

A murmur circles the table.

'If we delay again,' he continues, 'those contractors walk, which means I have to get new quotes and estimates, which inevitably pushes the budget up. I'm not prepared to go through that process yet again. This is a once-in-a-generation opportunity for Whitby. Don't let it slip through your fingers because of procrastination.'

Ever the manipulator, he throws in a theatrical pause.

'A high-end casino,' he continues, 'not some tacky slot-machine barn. This is discreet. Exclusive. High rollers. People who spend big money—on hotels, restaurants, taxis. This town thrives or it withers. That's the choice.'

A councillor clears his throat. 'There are concerns about—'

'Which I've addressed,' Sykes cuts in, not sharp, but firm. 'Planning, security, community impact. All covered. This isn't rushed. It's overdue.'

A few nods. One woman frowns but says nothing.

Sykes smiles again, softer now. 'I'll also give you my word that five per cent of annual profits will be donated to charitable causes in Whitby. Youth services. Regeneration projects. Heritage.'

He lifts his hands slightly. 'Not to curry favour. But simply because I'm a Whitby man through and through and the town deserves to benefit.'

Silence.

The chair leans in to speak quietly with the councillor beside him. Heads bend together. Low voices. A brief, tense conference.

At the back of the chamber, a door opens.

No one notices.

The chair straightens. 'Right,' he says. 'We'll proceed to the vote.'

The councillors nod, some more enthusiastically than others.

King George knows he's got this one in the bag.

'Before we do,' the chair adds, 'I'm required to ask whether any members of the public present—'

George Sykes interjects with a sneer. 'Anyone present? There's no one bloody present. Get on with it.'

The chair won't be bullied into short-circuiting protocol. '—whether any members of the public present wish to raise any objections.'

Prisha steps forward out of the shadows, flanked by two uniformed officers.

'Yes,' she says clearly. 'I do.'

Heads turn. Squints in the low light. Sykes blinks, irritation flickering across his face as he tries to place her.

'And who the bloody hell are you?' he demands.

Prisha stops a few feet from the table. The uniforms fan out behind her as she pulls out her warrant card.

'Detective Inspector Prisha Kumar,' she says. 'North Yorkshire Police.'

A ripple runs round the chamber. Chairs scrape. Someone swears under their breath.

Sykes straightens. 'This is highly irregular. I'll have your badge for—'

Prisha cuts him off, calm, precise. 'George Sykes, I am arresting you on suspicion of conspiracy to import and supply Class A controlled drugs, possession of an article for use in the manufacture of Class A controlled drugs, and conspiracy to pervert the course of justice.'

'Bloody nonsense!' he thunders.

She continues, voice steady. 'You do not have to say anything. But it may harm your defence if you do not mention when questioned something which you later rely on in court. Anything you do say may be given in evidence.'

For a moment, Sykes says nothing. His eyes dart around the table, searching for something—someone.

There is nothing as the councillors shrink away.

Prisha nods to the officers. 'Cuff him.'

As they step in, the chamber erupts—questions, protests, disbelief.

'This is an outrage. I'm on personal terms with the chief constable. I demand to see my lawyer,' he bellows.

'All in good time, Mr Sykes.'

As King George is led away, Prisha leans in close to him and whispers in his ear.

'I have a message from Frank. He says you can stick that nightwatchman job up your arse. His words, not mine.'

# 63

## 9:55 pm

Dritan wakes before the alarm, the way he always does when things matter. The boat engines are already running. For a few seconds he lies on the bunk, eyes open, letting his surroundings settle around him.

He's feeling good, calm, and in control.

Checks his watch. Five minutes to sailing. High tide. Exactly as planned.

He swings his legs out of the bunk and pulls on his jacket, movements unhurried. There's nothing left to do tonight. The danger has already been outsourced. What remains is transit—metal and water and distance.

In the galley, Francois is waiting. A mug sits on the table, steam lifting faintly.

'Coffee.'

Dritan takes it, nods. Strong. Bitter. The sort of coffee men drink when they expect to be awake a long time.

'Weather?'

Francois shrugs. 'Calm enough. We should have a clear run.'

'And the transfer?'

'Usual spot. Whale Cemetery. Quiet.' He pauses. 'A patrol boat will take you onto Oudeschild on the Dutch coast. From there—car to Tirana.'

'How long?'

Francois gives his familiar Gallic shrug. 'Six hours to the transfer. Four more to the Netherlands.'

Dritan smiles. 'Excellent. I'll arrive in time for breakfast.'

Francois opens a locker and takes out a pistol, offers it grip first.

'You shouldn't need it,' he says. 'But just in case.'

Dritan accepts it, slips it inside his jacket.

He opens the holdall and pulls out a thick roll of notes and hands it over.

'This is just the beginning,' Dritan says, bearing a wide, toothy grin. 'There's plenty more on the horizon.' He slaps Francois on the shoulder. 'You have done well, my friend.'

Francois pockets the cash. No smile. Just business.

'I'll cast off,' he says, turning for the steps.

Dritan watches him go. Something, he's not sure what, tickles at the outer edges of his thoughts.

He calls after him. 'I'll join you in a minute, Francois. I just need to make a few calls.'

Stares around the galley. The silence feels morbid. This is where they ate, laughed, shared stories. But tonight it feels like a mausoleum.

Taking a seat, he checks his messages—blank.

Calls Stefan. It rings out.

Tries Mika. Voicemail.

Arben. Nothing.

'Hmm...'

Slugs down the rest of the coffee, the caffeine hit beginning to buzz.

He tries again, irritation creeping in. Phones die. Men forget to charge them. It happens.

Glances at the time on his mobile—10:02 pm.

He waits. Counts silently. The boat should be moving by now.

The unnamed thought circles again.

He climbs the stairs and steps out onto the deck.

Whitby glows along the harbour edge—streetlights smeared across black water, a few figures still wandering the promenade, laughter drifting across from the old town to the east. The smell of fish and chips from the restaurants and takeaways. A quiet night, but normal, nothing untoward.

He takes out his phone again and sends the same message to all three.

A single character.

?

As he turns, his gaze falls onto the quayside.

The ropes are still fast around the mooring bollards.

His jaw tightens as unease creeps through his veins.

He walks quickly along the starboard side and enters the wheelhouse.

Francois stands at the controls, side-on, hands resting lightly on the helm, as if waiting.

'Why haven't you cast off?' Dritan barks. 'We're already running late.'

Francois doesn't answer straight away. When he turns, his expression is calm, almost apologetic.

'Because we're not going anywhere,' he says. 'At least—I'm not.'

Confusion and anger collide.

'What the fuck are you talking about?' Dritan snaps.

A fresh gust rushes in as the door opens behind him.

Spins around, already reaching for the pistol.

Blinks as if witnessing a ghost.

'You... but this cannot be. You should be—'

'Dead?' says Beale.

Dritan throws a hurried look at Francois before returning his gaze.

'Danny,' he murmurs, thoughts choking him. Moves forward and places the barrel against Beale's forehead. 'Where is Arben?'

Beale croaks a laugh. 'Now—he *is* fucking dead. Along with Mika and your brother. They were given the chance to drop their weapons and surrender, but that was never going to happen. Dick swingers to the last.'

'Stefan, dead?'

'Aye. As dead as the proverbial fucking dodo.'

Dritan swallows hard, throttling back the emotion.

'Now you die and I'll see you in hell.'

Pulls the trigger.

A toothless click.

Repeats, again and again, ever more frantically.

Beale smiles. 'You're right, Dritan. I will see you in hell. It's a lottery as to who'll arrive there first. But if it's me, I'll make sure the fire's well stoked.'

'Drop the gun, Dritan. It's over,' Francois says, resignedly.

Dritan stares at him. 'Not you as well?'

'Oui.'

'How long?'

'Long enough.'

The door clanks open again as Zac enters, warrant card in hand.

Beale gently takes the unloaded pistol from Dritan's grip and sticks it in his jacket as Zac reads out the caution.

Dritan stares into Beale's eyes. 'Tell me one thing—Stefan—was it quick?'

He nods. 'Aye. He wouldnae have felt a thing. Sorry for your loss.'

Zac cuffs him and spins him around.

Dritan shoots Beale one last look. 'For a time there, Danny, I believed in you. I gave you a chance.'

'True. But you believed in a lie. I don't feel particularly good about myself, but as you said, sometimes good men have to do bad things.'

# 64

## 10:08 pm

Frank sits in his car at the edge of the car park. Sneaton Castle looms above him, all stone and soft uplighting—moneyed, discreet, comfortable with a touch of class.

His phone rests face-up on the passenger seat.

He waits.

The screen lights.

A message from Prisha.

*One down.*

He exhales long and slow, then opens the door and steps out into the night.

---

Inside, the reception area is hushed. Muted chatter from the handful of diners in the main hall. Frank performs a quick sweep of the room but cannot see his man.

A young woman behind the desk offers him a polite, apologetic smile.

'I'm sorry, sir—we've stopped serving dinner for tonight.'

He smiles. 'I'm not here to eat. I'm meeting a friend for a glass of wine, if that's okay?'

She nods. 'Of course, sir. Your friend's name?' she asks, head poised over the reservations ledger.

Frank leans in, glances, spots the name.

'Mr Carmody—Silas Carmody.'

'Ah—yes,' she says. 'He's through there.' She gestures to a door on the right. 'Dining room two. Sitting alone.'

Frank thanks her and heads towards the dining area.

Phone pings.

Checks the message from Zac.

*Two down.*

Enters the second room, which is smaller. Quieter. Low lamps. Crisp linen. Only one table is occupied.

A lone man sits there, jacket on the back of his chair, a half-finished bottle of red between him and an untouched second glass. He checks his watch. Then his phone. Irritation flickers—just briefly, like he's waiting for someone.

Frank crosses the room without hurry.

Another ping. A text from Dinkel.

Frank allows himself a whisper of a smile.

*Game, set, and match.*

'Mind if I join you?' Frank asks the solitary diner.

The man looks up.

The smile he starts with dies halfway.

'Frank,' he says, recovering quickly. 'Of course. Please take a seat.' He gestures to the empty chair, lifts the bottle. 'Just finished eating. I'm indulging myself with a bottle of red, which is excellent, by the way. Care for a drop?'

'Aye, why not,' Frank replies. 'Just a small one.'

He pours. The wine glugs softly, comforting.

They sit. Drink. Watch each other over the rims of their glasses.

Frank sets his down first.

'Thought you had things to do today,' Frank says mildly.

The smile tightens. 'Plans change.'

'They do,' Frank agrees.

A pause.

'By the way, George is running late,' Frank says.

The man frowns, lifts his glass, takes a measured sip.

'George? Sorry, I'm not sure who you mean.'

'George Sykes.'

'Can't say the name rings a bell.'

Frank leans back and sighs, swilling the wine around his glass.

'It's over, Hedley—or should I call you Silas? We arrested George Sykes and Dritan moments ago.'

Hedley Keegan absorbs the news with a small, resigned smile.

'Ah,' he says. 'The best laid plans and all that, eh?' He takes another sip. 'Yes, using Carmody's name for the reservation was a bit of ego. Apologies. So, when did you...'

'When did I suspect?'

'Yes.'

'I'd like to take the credit, but I can't. You know Prisha, of course.'

'Yes. DI Kumar. The rising star. She's a blessing, Frank. One in a million. Moulded in your own image.'

'I wish.'

'So, what was it that gave the game away?'

'Cleavage. It was Prisha who raised the question yesterday. The coastguard intercept. Beale assumed he was killed because he'd tipped off the coastguard. But it wasn't.'

Hedley listens, expression unreadable.

Frank continues. 'Which led me to the only possible conclusion.'

'Which was?'

'Cleavage *wasn't* thrown overboard because of the coastguard intercept. It was because he was a police informant. And only three people were initially privy to that information. Me. Zac. And you. You must've heard his name mentioned at some point in your discussions with George or Dritan—and panicked. It must have come as quite a shock to find out a police informant was part of the crew. You weren't sure what he'd seen or what he knew. But you couldn't take a risk, so disposed of him.'

Hedley nods slowly. 'Congratulations, Frank. You're on the money as usual.'

Frank slumps forward, feeling tired, not elated.

'Why, Hedley—why?'

He chuckles softly. 'Thirty years in the force. Not a lot to show for it.'

'Money?'

'Yes. And why not? We can't stop the flood of drugs. We can't even get a grip on what we produce ourselves. If you can't beat them—join them. Call it my retirement nest egg.'

Frank shakes his head. 'You're no different from Smiler. But he's a naive twenty-two-year-old street dealer with dreams of the high life. You do realise seven men are dead because of this?'

'Seven? You mean four—Typhoon and his men. Street scum.'

'Street scum with mothers, fathers, brothers, and sisters. They *were* loved by somebody. And I do mean seven. Three of Dritan's men died tonight trying to assassinate—'

'Cleavage, Smiler, and Beale. Nice game you played up on the clifftops this morning. Seems such a long time ago now.' He shrugs nonchalantly. 'There's always fallout. And don't pretend you wouldn't have been tempted if the opportunity had come your way.'

'No,' Frank says quietly. 'I wouldn't. Why would I want to spend the rest of my life looking over my shoulder? Life's hard enough. Nothing beats a good night's sleep.'

Hedley smiles. 'Reassuring to hear there are still some honest coppers left.' A frown crosses his face. 'And all that stuff about retirement, was that all part of the ruse?'

'I'm afraid so. Thought it would lull you into a false sense of security—the dispirited, jaded, beaten copper. Truth is, it's the job that makes me jump out of bed on a morning. Keeps me young.'

'Well, your ruse worked. You should try amateur dramatics when you finally do retire.'

Frank sighs. 'This breaks my bloody heart in two, Hedley. It really does. But I have to do it.'

'Of course you do. Without reading the caution, it wouldn't even make it to court.' Hedley glances at the bottle. 'Do you mind? Would be a shame to leave such an exquisite Shiraz unfinished. Cost a small fortune. And I doubt I'll have the chance to enjoy another glass for a while.'

'Be my guest.'

Hedley pours the last of the wine, drains it, savouring the final mouthful.

Frank slips the cuffs from his jacket.

'Hedley Keegan, I am arresting you on suspicion of conspiracy to import controlled drugs *and* misconduct in public office. You do not have to say...'

Frank's words trail off in Hedley's mind as he gazes out of the window at lights shimmering from a distant container ship.

# 65

## Monday Morning – 9 am

To her credit, Superintendent Anne Banks has remained silent throughout. However, her demeanour doesn't fill Frank with the joys of Christmas. Halloween, possibly, but definitely not Christmas.

Her cheeks have taken on the hue of boiled beef, and if she keeps blinking so rapidly, she's in danger of losing all her eyelashes. And to irritate him further, she's sitting in *his* chair, in *his* office.

It's the small things that get under his skin.

Frank glances up at Silas Carmody, then continues his summary of events from the previous day.

'And Constable Dinkel led the raid on the seafood depot belonging to George Sykes, with armed response, of course. No casualties. Behind the main depot were a couple of purpose-built sheds. One contained a pill press and a hundred kilos of fentanyl precursor, along with various drug-making paraphernalia. In the other shed was a very scared Chinese gentleman named Chen Hao. We're still waiting on an interpreter to get his full account, but from what we could ascertain, he was brought over on the pretext of making vitamin pills. Something about working for a year, and then Dritan would bring Chen's family across. We'll know more later. So, you see, ma'am, all in all a rather successful conclusion to the operation.'

He decides to end on a high rather than waffle on.

Banks stares at him, then leans back in *his* chair and cradles her hands. She's a petite lady, but her gaze could drop a rampaging bull elephant from fifty yards.

The silence lingers like a bad smell as Silas Carmody, unaccustomed to the double act, shifts uncomfortably.

Finally, she speaks. 'Frank, we've worked together for longer than I care to remember, and it's only now that I've realised something.'

'Oh, yes?' Frank enquires.

'We are on different ends of the spectrum.'

'Ma'am?'

'We had one man decapitated. One burnt alive in his car. Another shot through the head, and one garroted in the backstreets of Hull. Oh, and an attempted drowning of an innocent civilian. Then last night, our armed officers shot dead three assassins.'

'Your point being?'

Her anger is a slow boiling pot of water. 'On what planet... no, let me rephrase that. In *which* universe could that result be construed as *rather successful?*'

Frank fidgets. 'Ahem, well...'

'I haven't finished!' she snaps.

'Sorry.'

'Not only that, but when did we start putting members of the public at risk?'

'I don't follow.'

'Cleavage, Smiler.'

Frank grimaces. 'Ah, I see. Maybe I didn't explain myself well enough. Cleavage was not in danger. He was never at the safe house in Pickering. I simply told Keegan that to smoke him out. I knew he was aware of the safe house and its location. And as for Smiler, well, yes, it's true he was used in the operation last night but in a limited and entirely safe capacity.'

'Please explain.'

'We had him in the targeted apartment merely to answer the intercom for the pizza delivery man. Once Smiler had relayed instructions and buzzed him through the main entrance, Smiler was escorted by an armed officer to the unoccupied apartment next door. So, he was never in danger.'

Banks taps her pen on the desk. 'And Sergeant Beale?'

'It's Constable Beale, ma'am. And he isn't a member of the public. We needed him to be in the flat at the boarding house. He has a rather unique voice, and as Dritan's gang had spent time with him, we needed to be authentic.'

'Authentic?'

Frank reflects. 'Possibly the wrong choice of word. What I was trying to allude to is that Beale has a peculiar cadence to his vocal range and annunciation as well as certain... let's say, off-the-cuff colourful phrases he employs.'

'He's a foul-mouthed ticking time-bomb with a screw loose.'

'If you say so, ma'am. But he gets the job done. Beale had to be in that room to convince the third assailant he was the real deal and it wasn't a set up.'

Carmody finally intervenes. 'Anne, we need to look at the bigger picture. As unfortunate as it is, none of the dead men were choir boys. We always anticipated there'd be fallout from this operation. We just hoped and prayed that none of those casualties were our own. Down to due diligence, careful planning, incisive intel, and some excellent intuitive detective work by Frank and his small team, Operation Blackout turned out better than any of us ever envisaged. No corners were cut, all protocols and risk assessments were adhered to, and the health and safety of our team was always paramount.'

*Carmody is good at this,* Frank thinks. *He's ticking all her boxes. She goes into a hot flush on hearing words like risk assessment, protocols, health and safety, and due diligence. If he'd mentioned KPIs, I think she may have experienced a mini-orgasm.*

'And we met and surpassed all our KPIs,' Carmody adds, right on cue.

Banks reddens and bites down on her lip, eyes closed. She goes off the boil and onto a simmer.

'And what about the skipper, the French national, Francois?' she eventually asks.

Carmody smiles. 'He was one of ours. A petty criminal who our associates in Europe recruited—at a hefty price.'

Banks is surprised. 'Then Beale's undercover actions on the boat were superfluous.'

'Not at all. When you do a deal with the devil, you're never entirely sure whether the devil will keep his side of the bargain.'

She snorts. 'When you refer to the devil, are you alluding to Beale or Francois?'

Carmody chuckles. 'Ha-ha, most amusing, Anne. Anyway, I was unaware of Beale's actions on The Whitby Rose. He was acting off his own volition. As you inferred earlier—he is a maverick.'

'That's one word for him,' she mutters. Composing herself, she rises. 'There'll have to be an internal inquiry.'

Frank groans. 'Of course there will. God forbid we should have a moment of respite, and pat ourselves on the back for a job well done. Having thwarted a cut-throat gang, captured their leader and prevented millions of fentanyl pills from hitting the streets, we wouldn't want praise. Not to mention arresting a corrupt businessman and outing a mole within our own ranks.'

She glares at him. 'Was that an attempt at sarcasm, Frank?'

'It wasn't an attempt, ma'am.'

'I don't appreciate humour in times like this. It's serious business.'

Carmody comes to the rescue again. 'I was on a conference call with the home secretary and the chief constable earlier, Anne.'

'And?'

'Let's just say, to use the common parlance, the home secretary was cock-a-hoop. A real feather in his cap.'

'What did he have to bloody do with it?' Frank grumbles under his breath, which luckily goes unheard.

'And if the home secretary is happy,' Carmody continues, 'then the chief constable is happy.'

Banks sniffs. 'Hmm... home secretaries come and go with alarming regularity these days.'

Collecting her handbag, she heads for the door, stops, and spins around.

'You know, Frank, if I were a conspiracy theorist, I'd say you deliberately set those three men up, knowing full well they wouldn't relinquish their weapons.'

Frank stares at her coldly.

'Only a deluded crackpot with no understanding of the harsh brutalities of the real world would think such a thing, ma'am. And I know you're not that.'

They hold each other's gaze for a few seconds.

Banks is the first to blink.

'I want a full, detailed report of your part in this operation by close of business on Wednesday, Frank. Keep me posted on any updates. Good morning, gentlemen.'

The door slams behind her and both men let the air settle for a while.

Carmody smirks. 'Sheesh! Has she ever cracked a smile?'

Frank contemplates the question. 'Yes. Once. In 1998. Although, I had a sneaking suspicion it could have been trapped wind.'

----◆----

Frank escorts Silas Carmody out of the station, then returns to the incident room. He glances around at his team; Prisha, Zac, Dinkel. A sense of pride washes over him. They all had their part to play. Whatever weak links they have individually, they pick up the slack as a team, and that's why it's called teamwork. The whole is greater than the sum of its parts.

'They're not a bad bunch,' he murmurs to himself.

He claps his hands together to grab their attention. 'Right, you sorry looking lot, finish your paperwork by midday. Then it's knock-off time, and a well earned celebratory drink or five at the White House. The drinks are on Zac!'

There's a chorus of cheers as he heads back to his office with a spring in his step.

# 66

## Two Days Later: Wednesday 11:34 am

He stops beneath the post and looks up at the name bolted to it. Fumbles a scrunched-up piece of paper from his pocket. Checks the street name, then checks it again.

He's not good at remembering names. A major inconvenience in his line of work.

Glances at the cascading line of homes. A crescent of inter-war ex-council houses, tucked behind the Abbey.

Ambles along the pavement with a slightly bow-legged gait, a large box wrapped in brown paper tucked under his arm—awkward, and distinctly conspicuous.

Sights the number on the house. Semi-detached, sitting awkwardly as the road bends.

Hesitates, opens the garden gate and walks the path to the front door.

Second thoughts crowd in. He's not cut out for this. He swallows hard.

*Come on. Steel yourself. In and out. Get it over and done with.*

Knocks on the door.

It's weak. Weak as piss.

Clears his throat and knocks again, this time a lot harder. Maybe too hard.

'Christ, they'll think it's a fucking police raid. Nothing like being discreet.'

Cringes and looks over his shoulder. The street is quiet.

Voices from within. Male, female, a small boy's irritating squawk.

The door cracks open and a woman peers out at him.

Early thirties. Not unattractive, if she wasn't metaphorically sucking a lemon. Her scowl could curdle milk.

'Yes?'

'Ahem... I'm here to see Cleavage.'

If she was sucking a lemon before, she's now onto grapefruit pith, washed down with battery acid.

'I hate that name. You mean Ryan?'

'Sorry. Yes. Ryan.'

Her eyes narrow behind the slit of the door. 'And who's asking?'

'Oh, just an old seafaring buddy.'

The door slams shut in his face.

He's not sure whether to stay or go.

Raised voices. Then the door is slung open.

Cleavage appears, sporting his predictable gormless grin.

'Danny!' he yells, before clamping him in a bear hug that nearly squeezes the life out of him. 'Come in, come in. It's great to see you.'

Beale is overwhelmed by the reception—and not in a good way.

He's ushered into a tidy, tastefully decorated living room which smells unnaturally fresh and clean. Not a hint of tobacco smoke, much to his annoyance.

Through the double sliding doors, the Abbey looms in clear view, beyond a glass conservatory and a neat, grassed lawn scattered with young boy's toys—a football, a bucket and spade, a gleaming red pedal car.

Cleavage turns to his wife, beaming. 'Raquel, let me introduce you to Danny—or should I say Detective Constable Beale. He was the undercover cop on the boat.'

Raquel offers Beale a half-hearted smile. 'Hello,' she says, without much enthusiasm.

Beale shifts under her frosty reception—not that he can blame her.

'Pleased to meet you, Raquel.'

'Zac explained everything,' Cleavage continues, patting Beale warmly on the shoulder. 'I tell you what, Danny, you certainly had me fooled.' He lets out a belly laugh, as if it's all been a grand adventure. 'If you ever tire of police work, there's a life for you on the boats. Six months with me and I'll soon knock you into shape. You've got real promise.'

'Aye, I'll bear that in mind.' *Fuck me, he's dumber than he looks*, Beale thinks.

Cleavage cups his hand to the side of his mouth and bellows, 'Fergus, come downstairs. There's someone I want you to meet!'

A clatter of tiny feet rattles down the stairs and a young boy appears.

Beale and the boy stare at each other in mild shock.

The boy breaks the silence first. 'You're ugly.'

Cleavage guffaws.

Raquel is mortified.

'Fergus, that's so rude,' she snaps. 'Apologise. Now.'

*Pot, kettle, black,* Beale thinks. *If I had a misshapen watermelon head like yours, I'd never leave the fucking house.*

He smiles benevolently at the child and rubs his head, a little roughly.

'Oh, the wee little scamp,' he says, forcing a chuckle. He glances at Cleavage and Raquel. 'Out of the mouths of babes, eh?'

Raquel doesn't smile. 'Fergus, I've asked you to apologise. If you don't, you'll be sent to your room for thirty minutes—and there'll be no *Peppa Pig* tonight.'

*Fuck me rigid,* Beale thinks. *When I was a lad, I'd have got the belt—buckle side first—if I'd said that to a stranger.*

Fergus squints up at his father. 'What's his name?'

'Danny.'

Fergus reluctantly offers an apology. 'Sorry, Danny.'

'Ah, no problem, son.' Beale remembers the box tucked under his arm. 'Oh—almost forgot. This is for you. Your da told me it was your birthday soon.'

Fergus jumps up and down. 'It was yesterday. I'm a big boy now. Four.'

Beale hands him the box and Fergus rips the paper off in about five seconds flat—roughly half the time it took Beale to wrap it.

The boy stares at the box, eyes wide with excitement. 'A train set!'

He sets it carefully on the floor, then barrels straight into Beale, flinging his arms around him, head landing uncomfortably low around his genital region.

Beale stiffens—in the back.

*Careful*, he thinks. *Be very fucking careful. You're on thin ice. I can't claim I'm part of the priesthood.*

He can already see the headline:

## DISGRACED EX-COP IN TOY-TIME SCANDAL WITH FOUR YEAR OLD

He knows how the baying mob love nothing more than an unsavoury paedophile witch-hunt.

Unsuccessfully, he tries to prise the boy away. Glances at Cleavage for help, but the addle-pated ape is oblivious to the compromising situation.

Thankfully, Raquel is more attuned. She steps in and lifts Fergus off him, casting Beale a look that suggests she's already run the same mental risk assessment as he did.

'Go and play with your train set,' she says.

Fergus scoops up the box and scurries into the conservatory, happy as a sandboy.

'It's great to see you, Danny,' Cleavage says. 'You must stay and have some lunch with us.'

Beale holds up a hand in protest. 'No, I couldn't possibly. I just called round to see how you were doing. You've had a hell of a time. How are you feeling?'

'Right as rain. And I'm serious,' he says, turning to his wife. 'Aren't I, Raquel? Danny must stay and eat. We've a lot to catch up on.'

'Of course,' she says, already heading for the kitchen. 'I'll put the kettle on. We'll start with a cuppa.'

This is *exactly* what Beale feared.

He's meticulously mapped out his last day in Whitby. If he'd been this assiduous in his police work, he could have been a Chief Superintendent by now.

A quick chat with Cleavage and a toy for the brat. Then into town for a Thai massage with a happy ending. After that, a long afternoon session on the lash. A big fish and chip supper—mushy peas, curry sauce, bread and butter. Afterwards, a quiet little watering hole. Five, maybe six, whiskies. Bed. Attempt a wank. Abort wank. Sleep.

Perfect.

Life doesn't get any better.

Tomorrow morning, eight o'clock, the train back to Glasgow.

And not a moment too soon. He's had a bellyful of England—and the English.

'No, honestly. It was just a quick catch up. You need your space,' he says, turning to leave.

Cleavage is crestfallen. 'Oh. Right. Well... I suppose I'll see you later then?'

Beale hovers at the door as an unfamiliar feeling creeps in—a sensation he doesn't much care for.

There were *two* reasons he visited Cleavage.

One selfish. One unselfish.

Guilt at not rushing to his aid as he was about to be thrown overboard.

That one still haunts him.

And the second—he thought, for the first time in his life—he'd try being nice. Pleasant. Sociable. Decent.

He turns, against his better judgement, and faces Cleavage—the good man, the family man, the... alright man.

'Hey, here's a thought,' he says. 'How'd you fancy a couple of pints in town and a counter lunch? Nothing heavy. Just you and me. We can have a wee chat about life.'

Cleavage beams like he's won the European lottery. 'Magic!'

Beale narrows his eyes. 'You mean that?'

'Of course. You're my pal. We're buddies, right? I'll just check with the missus. Back in a mo.'

As he disappears into the kitchen, the unwelcome feeling returns to Beale.

Someone else actually likes him.

Fuck knows why.

Cleavage is back in a few seconds. 'Got a leave pass. I'm not to get hammered, though.'

Beale is astonished at the very suggestion. 'Not on *my* watch, sunshine. My number one rule—drink in moderation.'

---

As they head down the path together, Cleavage launches into his miraculous salvation at sea.

'Do you know where I think they went wrong, Danny?'

'No. But I have an uncanny feeling you're about to tell me in mind-numbing fucking detail.'

'I reckon they tied the weight around my boots with a clove hitch. What they should've used was a constrictor knot. Basic ropework. Let me explain how a constrictor knot works—'

Beale flinches, dips his hand in his pocket, and pulls out his smokes.

*Oh, for fuck's sake. What have I let myself in for?*

Sparks up. Remembers the pact he made with himself a few days ago.

Try—just try—to be a better man.

An *alright* man.

# CONTINUE THE FINNEGAN JOURNEY

**Thank you for reading!**
I hope you enjoyed this DCI Finnegan Yorkshire crime thriller.

**COMING SOON!**
The next Finnegan book (13), **LOCK KEEPER** is now on pre-order on my Amazon series page.
Pre-order here
Or scan the QR code below. and scroll down.

# BEYOND THE LAST PAGE

You'll always find the complete DCI Finnegan Reading Order — here on my website. Link or scan below.
**elynorthcrimefiction.com/series-order**
Or head straight to my Amazon series page:
**View the DCI Finnegan Series on Amazon**
Join my reader group for the free Prequel – **Aqua Phobia**
**One Last Favour**
If you enjoyed this story, a quick review or rating on Amazon or Goodreads helps more than you know. If you're reading on a Kindle, Amazon should show you the rating page below.
**NOTE:** Paperbacks are available to order from all good bookshops and libraries through **IngramSpark**.
If there are any issues, please ask the staff to contact me directly at: **ely@elynorthcrimefiction.com**

# Also By Ely North

## DCI Finnegan Series

Book 1: Black Nab

Book 2: Jawbone Walk

Book 3: Vertigo Alley

Book 4: Whitby Toll

Book 5: House Arrest

Book 6: Gothic Fog

Book 7: Happy Camp

Book 8: Harbour Secrets

Book 9: Murder Mystery

Book 10: Wicker Girl

Book 11: Crucifix Knot

Book 12: Whale Cemetery

Book 13: Lock Keeper

Prequel: Aqua Phobia (available free by joining Ely North Newsletter)

All books are available on Amazon in ebook, paperback, and some in audio. Paperbacks can be ordered from all good bookshops, distributed by IngramSpark.

www.ingramcontent.com/pod-product-compliance
Lightning Source LLC
Chambersburg PA
CBHW010420170726
48283CB00011B/2981